ONE OF OURS

ONE OF OURS

A
JOE ERICKSON
MYSTERY

LYNN-STEVEN JOHANSON

LEVEL
BEST BOOKS

Praise for One of Ours

"A cold case and the murder of a police captain combine to propel this fast-paced, engaging police procedural novel! Fans of Michael Connelly and Ed McBain will find much to love here!"—Richard Helms, Shamus Award-winning author of *A Kind and Savage Place*

"When Detective Joe Erickson's police captain is executed in cold blood, the trail leads to corruption at the highest level of Chicago politics. Johanson has knocked it out of the park again."—Susan Van Kirk, author of the Art Center Mysteries and the Endurance Mysteries

Chapter One

Detective Joe Erickson walked through the parking lot to his black Camaro, preparing for his daily drive to work. He clicked his key fob, and the driver's door unlocked. Sliding into the leather seat, he inserted the key in the ignition, and after buckling his seatbelt, he turned the key expecting the car to start. Instead, the car exploded in a huge ball of flame, sending shards of shrapnel, body parts, and a cloud of blood blasting high against the morning sky.

Jolted violently awake, Joe sat up in bed with a cry that awakened Destiny, his partner, who was sleeping beside him.

"Joe, what is it?" she gasped.

"Oh, god! That one was vivid," he said, trying to catch his breath.

"A nightmare?"

"Yeah."

Placing her arm around his lean body, she asked, "Want to tell me about it?"

After a moment, he gathered his thoughts. "I...was sitting inside the Camaro, and when I turned the key, it blew up...body parts were flying all over the place...including my own."

"Eww!"

"Yeah."

"That's horrible. You haven't had one of those nightmares for a long time now."

"I know. I thought maybe I was past getting those...Damnit!"

"It's only one. Almost getting blown up by that bomber was a traumatic

1

event. I don't think it would be surprising for you to have a bad reaction at some point, given your PTSD."

"Yeah."

"Maybe you should bring it up with Dr. Lemke during your next session."

"Mm. I will."

Destiny glanced over at the alarm clock, seeing it was set to go off in fifteen minutes. "You want to lie in bed for a while longer, or do you want to get up?"

"If I can cuddle with you, I could go for a little longer," he said with a wry smile.

"You got it."

* * *

Joe was getting pretty tired of using Uber rides to take him back and forth to his job. Working out of Chicago's Area 3 Detective Division, he and his fellow detectives are responsible for investigating crimes in the 1st, 12th, 18th, 19th, 20th, and 24th Police Districts, those located on the North Side, primarily along the lakefront.

Reluctant to buy a replacement for his Camaro, he was still concerned the Scalise organized crime family would try to kill him again since he busted Vincent Scalise for human trafficking and solicitation of murder for bombing his car. He figured if no one made another attempt to take him out in the next few months, then it would be safe to get a new set of wheels. And since he and Destiny had purchased a house with a garage, his car would not be as vulnerable as his Camaro was sitting in an open parking lot in front of his former apartment building.

What started as a typical morning at Area 3 quickly turned strange. Dropping off his lunch at the refrigerator, Joe's cell phone rang. It was Captain Vincenzo. Vincenzo, Joe's former lieutenant, had been promoted to the rank of Captain six months ago, and he was now working as the Detective Commander out of Area 5.

"Good morning, Captain," said Joe.

"Come on over to my office," said Vincenzo. "I need to talk to you about something."

"What's going on?"

"I'll explain when you get here."

Vincenzo never sought Joe out like this. Even when he was lieutenant. If he wanted to talk to him, it usually involved a case, and that almost always included Joe's partner, Sam Renaldo. He ran his fingers through his dark hair and thought for a moment. He had the feeling this was something more personal.

When Joe arrived at Vincenzo's new office at Area 5, Vincenzo gestured to the chair in front of his desk for Joe to sit. Rather than move to his chair, Vincenzo uncharacteristically sat on the corner of his desk.

"So, what's up, Captain?" asked Joe.

As usual, Vincenzo got straight to the point. "I'm going to retire at the end of this year. I've put in my papers, so as of December thirty-first, I'm done."

Taken aback by Vincenzo's announcement, all Joe could say was, "I…guess congratulations are in order, huh?"

"I guess."

"But you were just promoted to Captain."

"I know. But I've been thinking. I'm fifty-two, and I've got thirty years in this year. I figured it's time to start enjoying myself. But before I turn in my star, there's a cold case I'm determined to solve. It's one I worked ten years ago with Nate Smith. We never did solve it, and it went cold."

"I think every cop winds up with at least one of those."

"You may be right," agreed Vincenzo as he moved around his desk and sat down. "Nate and I used to talk about it now and then. But when he died, I just let it go. I'd look at it now and then, but…Then, when I started thinking about retirement, it started bugging me, and I've been working on it on my own time for the last year."

"Okay. But what's that got to do with me?"

"I've been making some progress. And if I get what I'm looking for, it has the potential to blow the case wide open. If that happens, I want you and Sam to take it because it's a crime Nate and I investigated. It happened within Area 3. You're the best damned detective I had, and when you sink your teeth into something, you're a lot like me. You won't let go."

"I'll take it on, Captain. You know me."

"Yeah, I do. And I appreciate it. But it's going to be tricky because it involves important people, people with money and power."

"After the Fielding case last year, I think Sam and I can deal with those types."

"I know you can."

"Any idea when you might get what you're after?"

"Depends. I'll let you know." He paused and slid his chair back. "Oh—and keep my retirement decision to yourself, will ya? No one else around here knows yet. And I want to keep it that way for a while longer."

"Gotcha." Joe could read Vincenzo and knew he was finished. "Get outta here time, right?"

"Yeah," Vincenzo smiled. "Get outta here."

Back at Area 3, Joe sat down at his desk. He could not believe Vincenzo was retiring. But if he had thirty years on the force, he would be looking at retiring, too. The lieutenant Joe had worked under for nearly all his time as a homicide detective was Vincenzo, and he succeeded in earning Joe's respect. And while Vincenzo could be a hard ass sometimes, he was a good guy to have your back. Joe knew Vincenzo liked him, but he didn't always agree with Joe's unorthodox methods. However, he was always willing to overlook a few things since Joe had the best closure rate of any of his detectives. Joe was trying to get used to their new lieutenant, and from what he had experienced so far, he was not fond of her, personally or professionally.

He logged into his computer, and moments later, his partner, Sam Renaldo, walked in with two cups of Starbucks coffee. He set one down on Joe's desk.

"Good morning," said Sam.

"Good morning."

Sam and Joe had been partners for over three years. The two men were polar opposites. Joe Erickson was forty-two and ruggedly handsome with intense dark brown eyes. At six foot tall, he was lean, like a distance runner. Sam Renaldo was forty-eight, five-foot-ten, a little paunchy, and had a

Fu Manchu mustache than could use some enhancement. While Joe was intuitive and creative in his assessment of things, Sam diagnosed things by facts and figures. They made a good team.

"When are you and Destiny going to invite me to see your new digs?" asked Sam.

"You'll have to ask her. She's busy working with a decorator friend of hers, so I'm just staying out of her way. I'll let you know when she's finished redecorating."

"I drove past. Nice house."

"Yeah. It is. Beats my old apartment by a long shot. Thanks for the coffee. What's the occasion?"

"Thanks for writing up the report on the Cramer case."

"No problem."

Sam sauntered over to his desk, and Joe pulled up the final report he was writing on the Cramer case, the drowning death of a six-year-old boy with severe autism. What appeared to be an accident at first turned out to be a suspected homicide based on the autopsy report and the large life insurance policy, taken out by his father six months prior to the child's death. It was enough to bring the father in for questioning. When Joe and Sam interrogated Jerold Cramer, he eventually broke down and confessed to holding his son's head underwater in the bathtub until he drowned because he could no longer deal with the child's behavioral issues.

All homicides are bad. But the murder of a child is especially heinous. Joe hoped Cramer would do the right thing and plead guilty so he would not have to testify in a court case.

Chapter Two

Sal Vincenzo left his condo on North Kenmore Avenue and drove to meet with a source outside an elementary school on North Campbell Avenue in the Ravenwood Gardens neighborhood. He had worked for weeks in an attempt to locate this person, and he was hoping she would be the key to finding a piece of evidence that would open up the case. Until now, there was no hard evidence, only rumors.

Pulling up in front of the tree-lined school, he parked and waited for his source to arrive. At eleven o'clock at night on a weekday, there was very little traffic since the neighborhood around the school was comprised of residential apartment buildings. No wonder the person wanted to meet here. It was quiet, and there were very few people out and about.

Five minutes later, Vincenzo saw a car pull in behind his and shut off its lights. He looked in the rearview mirror, and from the streetlight, he recognized the vehicle by the description he was given. Getting out of his car, he looked around and saw no one. A woman emerged from her car and stood behind the door apparently sizing him up. *She looks a little wary*, he thought. He shut the door to his Challenger, and they both walked toward the sidewalk. As he began to turn toward her, he felt the impact of a bullet hit his chest, and his legs collapsed under him. Instinctively, his hand reached for his gun, but as soon as he hit the ground, Captain Vincenzo, the former decorated homicide lieutenant for Area 3, was dead.

When she heard the shot and saw Vincenzo go down, the woman jumped back in her car, pulled away from the scene, and sped down the street. At the same time, firecrackers went off from behind the school, adding to the sound of the gunshot.

Vincenzo's lifeless body lay on the sidewalk next to his car until 11:25 p.m. when an officer on patrol came upon his car, saw the body, and stopped to investigate. Confirming Vincenzo was dead and seeing what looked like a gunshot wound, Officer Sanchez requested detectives and the medical examiner.

Since it happened in the 19th District, a district covered by Area 3, Joe and Sam were notified because they were the detectives on call that night. Joe had a squad car checked out since he was on call, and he arrived first, being it was close to where he lived in the Lincoln Square neighborhood.

Getting out of his car, Joe held up his ID and identified himself to Officer Sanchez, the patrol officer. "What do we have?" he asked.

"Male victim. Gunshot wound to the chest."

Joe started to walk toward the body when Sanchez got his attention. "Detective."

"Yeah."

"He's one of ours."

"One of ours?" asked Joe, stopping in his tracks. "Who?"

"He had his ID on him. Captain Salvatore Vincenzo."

It was a gut punch that left Joe speechless. For a few moments, he couldn't move, couldn't breathe. Glancing over at the car, he recognized the Charger as the car Vincenzo drove. Then he looked over at the body near the sidewalk.

"You know him?" asked Sanchez.

"He was...my lieutenant. Homicide, Area 3."

"Sorry."

"Yeah. He's a captain now. Detective-Commander, Area 5."

"Detective-Commander?" repeated Sanchez, shocked that such an upper-level police official would be the victim. "Jesus."

Joe gloved up and worked up the courage to walk over to the body. He was hoping it was somehow a mistake. But it was Vincenzo. And he was dead. His eyes and mouth were open, and a trickle of blood ran down the corner of his lower lip. Joe kneeled down, reached over, and closed Vincenzo's eyes. Here lay what was left of the man that chewed his ass for screwing up, who

7

stood by him when he had his nervous breakdown, looked the other way when he chose unorthodox ways of investigating, and always said, "Get outta here," when he was done talking to him in his office.

The wound in his chest looked to be a direct hit to the heart. He wondered if Vincenzo even knew what happened to him, if he was meeting with his killer, and if he had left any clues behind about why he was here tonight.

Before getting up, Joe made the sign of the cross and said, "May perpetual light shine upon you, Sal Vincenzo." As he looked at Vincenzo's face, tears began to well up in his eyes, but he choked them back. He could not get emotionally involved. As he stood, he saw Sam pull up just as the ME arrived. He walked over to Sam to deliver the bad news. Sam could see by the look on Joe's face that something was seriously wrong.

"What is it, Joe? You look terrible."

"Bad news, Sam. It's Vincenzo. He's dead. Shot in the chest."

"Omigod," responded Sam in a whisper.

"From the looks of things, I doubt he knew what hit him."

Sam gloved up and walked over to see the body.

Joe looked at the ME's van and saw Kendra Solitsky get out. Seeing him, she walked over. Of all the MEs Joe worked with, Kendra was the one he preferred. She was as good as they come, and she had helped Joe out on a lot of cases, especially when she was the one who performed the autopsies.

"Good evening. What do you have for me tonight?" she asked in her usual sardonic tone.

"Our...our former lieutenant. Sal Vincenzo," replied Joe.

Silence. "Omigod. You're not kidding, are you?" she said, taking in Joe's mournful expression. "I'm so sorry."

"Yeah. Shot in the chest."

"Okay. Let me get ready, and I'll let you know more later." She went to the van and began suiting up. After doing a preliminary examination, she called in the Evidence Techs to process the scene.

Joe called the Duty Sergeant at Area 5 with the bad news and asked him to alert the proper authorities within the department. He gave the sergeant Vincenzo's home address and told him to send over an officer to seal his condo.

The crime scene was cordoned off, and an hour later, the Evidence Techs were doing their job. A few gawkers had begun to stop and look. Uniforms kept them back and sent them on their way unless they lived nearby. Joe and Sam wanted to speak with neighbors to find out if they saw or heard anything.

After midnight Joe and Sam interviewed three neighbors who had come out of their homes to see what the flashing lights were all about. When asked if they had heard a gunshot, two of them stated they heard firecrackers go off shortly after eleven o'clock, but neither of them said they heard a gunshot.

"Firecrackers?" asked Sam. "As in one or two or what?"

"A whole bunch of them," said Molly Belasco, who lived across the street. "It was like somebody lit off a whole pack of 'em."

"That's what it sounded like to me, too," said James Frohman, another neighbor. "Kids, probably."

After the interviews, Sam asked Joe, "You suppose the firecrackers were used to disguise the gunshot?"

"That would be a clever way to cover it up. Blame the noise on kids goofing around so as not to attract attention to the gunshot. Let's look for the remains of some firecrackers around here."

Joe and Sam began searching around the school building for remnants of spent firecrackers. In the back, by one of the dumpsters, Sam's flashlight revealed what they were looking for.

"Joe! Over here."

Sam's flashlight revealed a package of firecrackers that had been set off. Most of them had exploded while a few were duds.

"I'll let the Evidence Techs know, and one of them can bag these," said Joe. "Maybe they can get a print or DNA off one that didn't go off."

"Something else," added Sam. "Take a look at the vantage point from this dumpster. It's a perfect line of sight to where Vincenzo was shot."

"You thinking it could have been a rifle shot?" asked Joe.

"If it was one guy, it makes sense. Shoot Vincenzo, set off the firecrackers. Then get the hell out of Dodge."

Maybe the techs can get some GSR off this dumpster if the shooter used it to steady the gun."

"Worth a try."

Joe called over Jerry Bristow, who was busy processing the scene, and told him about what he and Sam had found. Bristow began processing the area around the dumpster. That left Art Casey to continue with the primary scene.

Kendra had completed her work and was waiting for Casey and Bristow to release the body. She motioned Joe over.

"What can you tell me, Kendra?" asked Joe.

"It looks like he was killed within an hour of when we got here, so that places time of death sometime around eleven o'clock."

"The patrol officer discovered his body at 11:25."

"Sounds right. Now, the bullet entered the center of the sternum, right where the heart's located. There's no exit wound, so the slug should still be in there. I'll be able to retrieve it during the autopsy tomorrow. You, uh…sure you want to be there for this one?"

Joe knew it was going to be tough, but he said, "Yeah. I need to be."

"Okay, I'll text you the time."

"Any idea on the caliber?"

"The entrance wound was small. Could be a rifle. But I could be wrong. I've been wrong before. We'll see."

School officials announced that school would be starting an hour late, and by 7:00 a.m., the ME was removing Vincenzo's body, and the Evidence Technicians were packing up their gear and getting ready to head out.

Uniformed officers from the 19th District would start canvassing door to door to determine if any of the neighbors saw or heard anything thing related to the shooting. In the meantime, Joe drove to Area 3. The drive was grim, and the day was not going to get any better. They had to contact the US Army so they could relay the sad news to Vincenzo's younger son. And they had to find the address of Vincenzo's older son, who is an attorney somewhere in Virginia. Worse yet, Joe would have to attend the autopsy of the man he had grown to know so well. Some days really suck.

Chapter Three

Sam, an Army veteran, took responsibility for going through Army channels to inform Captain Mark Vincenzo that his father had died. Having done this previously in a case involving next of kin serving in the military, he knew the proper procedures.

Joe remembered Vincenzo saying his oldest son lived in Chesapeake, Virginia. He confirmed the address on the internet, called the Chesapeake City Police Department. After explaining the situation, they agreed to make the notification. He filled out the requested document and listed his cell phone number so Steve could contact him. No doubt, he would want to know details.

Joe knew Vincenzo had long been divorced from his wife, Gloria, who succumbed to a brain tumor several years ago. As far as any of them knew, he was not involved with anyone, but he was guarded about his personal life, so they could not be sure if that was the case. It appeared there was no one to notify other than his two sons.

Sam and Joe were running on strong coffee and adrenalin since neither of them had slept the night before. Detectives working at Area 3 were eager to get any information they could about what happened to their former lieutenant, and Joe and Sam were providing them what little information they could. Michelle Cardona was so distraught, she had to go home.

Detectives from property crimes, narcotics, and other areas offered their condolences, but it was still business as usual. Crime doesn't stop when a police officer is killed, and neither do investigations. Joe noticed all the lieutenants were conversing among themselves, and they entered the conference room with the Area 3 Detective-Commander when he arrived.

Half an hour later, Lieutenant Briggs walked up to Joe and said, "You and Renaldo, my office. Now."

That rubbed Joe the wrong way. Even so, he tapped Sam on the shoulder and said, "Briggs wants to see us right away."

Her door was open, and they walked inside.

"Close the door," she said. She didn't ask them to sit. "As you know, Captain Vincenzo was killed in the 19th District, so it's within our area of investigation. In spite of his role at Area 5, they cannot investigate. The Detective Commander informed us that the Deputy Superintendent believes the investigation should be our responsibility, even though he used to be a lieutenant here. The commander specified the two of you to head the investigation."

For some reason, Briggs did not look pleased, so Joe asked, "Is there a problem with that, Lieutenant?"

"What makes you say that, Detective?" snapped Briggs.

"You don't seem too pleased, if I may say so."

"It's nothing. You're dismissed."

Leaving Briggs' office, Sam remarked, "I wonder what set her off today."

"Maybe she got her ass chewed by the Commander."

"Or maybe she didn't want us to lead the investigation and got 'rebuked.'"

"That would do it."

You want to check out Vincenzo's home?"

"Yeah," replied Joe. "I don't dare sit down for long. I have to keep moving."

"You and me both."

Sam drove them to Vincenzo's condo on North Kenmore Avenue. Joe called ahead and spoke to the manager, and he was expecting them when they got there. He did not know about Vincenzo's death and had not seen the tape sealing Vincenzo's door.

Entering the vestibule of the condo, Joe and Sam were buzzed in by a man in his late fifties. Presenting their IDs, they introduced themselves.

"I'm Merlin Fitzgerald, the condominium manager," the tall, thin man said, shaking their hands. They told him about Vincenzo's death, and he was saddened to hear the news.

"This business about Mr. Vincenzo. Terrible. Just terrible."

"It is," said Joe. "Did you see him often?"

"No. Only at homeowner association meetings. He wasn't one to contact me with complaints or problems."

"And those meetings are how often?" asked Sam.

"Once a month. He always attended."

"I see," said Joe. "Well, as part of our investigation, we need to see his condo. So, you'll need to let us in."

Fitzgerald balked at the idea. "Well, I don't know if I should open—"

"We're the police, Mr. Fitzgerald. Captain Vincenzo was murdered. We need to see if he left any information in his home that could lead us to his killer."

"Now, we can take you to our office and have the Detective Commander explain it to you," said Sam. "But he's not in a very good mood today. You can understand why."

Fitzgerald thought for a few moments and asked, "Can I see your identification again?"

Joe and Sam showed him their IDs, and Fitzgerald put on his reading glasses and read both of them carefully. Then he looked up and said, "All right. But I'm not going to allow you to remove anything."

"If we find anything important, we'll call in Evidence Technicians, and they'll process his condo. It could take all day," said Sam.

"You mean like CSI?"

"Exactly."

Fitzgerald took them down the hall to Vincenzo's condo. Joe and Sam gloved up, and then Joe slit the yellow tape from the door with his pocketknife. Fitzgerald pressed keys on the door's keypad and let them in.

"I'll wait out here until you're done." Sam looked at Joe and rolled his eyes, then shut the door.

The condo was a spacious, open-concept space with gray walls and a wooden floor replete with comfortable furniture and masculine furnishings. A seventy-two-inch television was in a prominent position on the wall opposite the couch. Sports magazines lay on the coffee table.

They surveyed the kitchen: the sink was empty, and there was only an empty pot sitting on the stove. The granite countertops had been wiped clean.

"Vincenzo was a neat housekeeper," remarked Sam.

"He was," said Joe. "Either that or his maid service recently cleaned the place."

"Maybe. But by the look of his office, he was no slob."

Sam opened the refrigerator and saw neatly stacked containers of leftover food. The freezer revealed frozen ingredients any cook would use to prepare meals—meat, fish, and frozen vegetables. "Looks like he did his own cooking."

"Anything suspicious?"

"He drank light beer."

"That's suspicious as hell. Better bag it," said Joe facetiously. "Let's check the bedrooms."

Sam opened the door to the master bedroom, and it was as neat as a pin. But when Joe opened the door to the guest bedroom, he could not believe his eyes.

"Sam! You gotta see this."

The guest bedroom served as an office rather than a bedroom. A desk and a file cabinet were positioned on one wall. And an adjacent wall was filled with photos, Post-it notes in various colors, photocopies, tacks with colored yarn connecting one tack to another, and typed forms pinned to the wall. Cardboard boxes with file folders were piled against another wall.

Sam stepped into the room behind Joe. "What the hell…."

"He told me he was working a cold case," said Joe.

"I guess he was. Look at all this!"

"He called me into his office and told me he wanted to solve it before he retired. Said he thought he was making progress."

"Retire?"

"Yeah. He told me he was retiring at the end of the year."

"I never heard anything about that."

"No one did. He didn't want it to get out. Asked me to keep it to myself."

"And he never got to enjoy it. What a rook."

Joe and Sam walked over to the wall and began looking at all the photos, notes, and yarn connections.

"Can you make sense out of all this?" asked Sam.

"It's going to take a while to decipher everything," replied Joe. Then he stepped to Vincenzo's desk and began looking at the items on it. It contained the usual stuff an office desk would have, except one thing—a computer. There was a cord running to a printer, but no computer.

"Hey, Sam. Did you see a laptop in the living room or the bedroom?"

"No. Not one here?"

"No."

"Let me check again. I wasn't looking for a laptop when I went through those rooms. I might have missed it." Sam left, leaving Joe to continue checking the room.

Seeing a daily planner on the desk, Joe opened it to yesterday's date and saw an entry that read, "Meet PT 11 pm." *11:00 p.m. was when he was at the school,* Joe thought. *Who is PT? And could PT be his killer?* He left the planner open to that page so Sam could see it.

Joe began checking the closet and file drawers. After finding nothing of value, he went back to Vincenzo's desk and began opening drawers looking for flash drives. He didn't find any. There weren't any to be found on top of his desk anywhere, either. Strange. Nothing to back up his computer files?

Sam came back into the room and said, "I didn't see a laptop anywhere. You suppose he took it to his office?"

"We'll have to check, but I didn't see one when I was going through his Rolodex.

"Maybe he stuck it in a drawer."

"Maybe. You know what's strange? I don't see any flash drives, either. There's nothing here to backup any files on his computer."

"Nothing?"

"It's like someone wiped the place clean."

"Maybe Vincenzo had a hiding place in case someone burgled the place," said Sam. "Maybe he keeps it on him. In his pocket or on a keychain."

"That's possible, I suppose."

Joe pointed to the planner open on the desk. "Take a look at yesterday's date."

Sam looked at the entry and then back at Joe. "He was meeting someone last night. Any idea who PT might be?"

"Not off the top of my head. At least we have something to go on."

As Joe bagged the daily planner, he said, "We need to check his effects. Let's give the kitchen a once-over before we leave."

Joe pulled out his phone and snapped several photos of the wall and boxes of files prior to leaving the room.

The two detectives searched Vincenzo's kitchen. They didn't find his laptop or hidden flash drives in any of the drawers, cupboards, or refrigerator.

Joe received a text from Kendra that read, "Autopsy 1:00."

"Hey, Sam," said Joe. "It's past eleven-thirty. I just got a text from Kendra saying the autopsy starts at one. I need to get back to the office."

"Okay. Why don't I search Vincenzo's office for his laptop and any flash drives he might have taken there."

"Yeah. You might check his personal effects, too.

"Will do."

"You'd better hide that daily planner in your coat, or Merlin will muscle it away from you," said Joe.

Sam chuckled. "He might try."

Chapter Four

Joe skipped lunch and grabbed a double-shot cappuccino at Starbucks before heading to the Medical Examiner's Office on West Harrison Street. He walked into the back of the imposing light tan building where all the county's dead are taken and autopsied when a death is suspected to be a homicide, suicide, accident, or from sudden unexpected natural causes. With thirteen medical examiners on staff, and a county of 5.2 million residents, the M.E.'s office teems with activity.

After donning scrubs, he entered the autopsy room where Kendra and her assistant, Kenny Miller, were finalizing their preparations.

Kenny was arranging the M.E.'s tools of the trade next to the autopsy table where the body was laid out. But it wasn't just any body. Despite working with him closely, the man was always Lieutenant Vincenzo, never Sal. Joe didn't like how casual things had become in the police force, especially with the younger detectives who called superior officers by their first names. If he saw the duty sergeant off-duty, he was Rodney, but on-duty, Rodney was always Sergeant Brown. In Joe's eyes, they deserved the respect of their office.

As Joe looked at the covered body, he thought, *This is real, and it's going to happen.* He always had the ability to compartmentalize things, and that was a good way to put unpleasantries out of mind. And he had learned to detach himself and think of an autopsy as nothing more than a scientific procedure. Today would test those abilities.

When the sheet was pulled back, it suddenly became quite real. *This is why they use the term "remains,"* Joe thought. It was Vincenzo, or at least what remained of him. Then he detached himself and became an observer.

The procedure lasted two hours. At times, Joe had to look away or down at the floor, but he stuck it out. He told himself that is what Vincenzo would have wanted him to do. And out of respect for him, that is what he did.

Joe learned that Vincenzo was relatively healthy for someone his age. The bullet Kendra retrieved from his body was a 7 mm slug fired from a rifle. It would go to ballistics to determine if it could provide any additional information. The bullet had passed through Vincenzo's heart before lodging in his spine. Given the damage it did to his heart muscle, Kendra stated death was most likely instantaneous.

As with other autopsies, Joe didn't stick around for the tissue dissection. He walked out, ditched his scrubs, and headed for the nearest restroom. After splashing water on his face, he leaned over the sink a few moments as he gathered his thoughts. Today was a day he hoped he would never have to repeat. Seeing someone you know autopsied is pretty tough. After drying his face, he drove the seven miles back to Area 3, curious to know if Sam had found anything.

On his way to find Sam, Joe bumped into Michelle Cardona's partner, Rick Murphy.

"Rick," acknowledged Joe.

"Got a second?" asked Murphy.

"Yeah."

"You're lead on Vincenzo's case, right?"

"Uh-huh."

"Michelle is taking this pretty hard."

"Yeah. We all are."

"Well, she just fell apart when she heard."

"That's not like her. She's as tough as any guy here."

"Yeah, but you need to know something. She and Vincenzo had a little thing going on."

"Really." Joe was surprised to hear that, especially since he was a superior officer, even though she was no longer under his command.

"So far as I know, it hadn't been going on long. I don't think anybody else knows about it except me."

"And you know this how?"

"Not that long ago, she started acting different. Happier, like. So, I figured she had a romance going on, see. So, one Saturday night when we were both off-duty, I tailed her."

"You surveilled your partner?"

"I was curious, that's all. I sure as hell wasn't going to bring it up and discuss it with her."

"And..."

"She went to Vincenzo's condo."

"You sure she wasn't seeing someone else in his building?"

"No. Instead of buzzing her in, he met her at the door and kissed her after he opened it. And it wasn't just a peck. I'd say that was pretty solid evidence, wouldn't you?"

"Yeah, that would cinch it for me."

"Anyway, I thought you should know. Don't know what you can do with it. But she might know something that could help."

"Yeah. You never know. Thanks, Rick."

Murphy walked away and left Joe standing there pondering this new information. *Why would Vincenzo, who was such a "by the book man," set himself up for a potential conduct violation? If he was planning on retiring in six months, then maybe he figured it didn't matter. He wasn't her supervisor any longer.*

Joe would have to approach Cardona at some point, but he was going to let it go for a while until he felt the time was right. But for now, he needed to find Sam. Glancing at his watch, it was only half an hour until he would be done for the day. *Please, God. No calls tonight.*

Sam was practically a zombie at his desk, awake but not altogether there.

"Hey," said Joe, jolting Sam back into reality. Sam chuckled at his miserable, zombie-like state.

"Oh, god. I should never have sat down. I'm shot."

"So am I. We can go home in a few minutes. What did you find out?"

"There's no laptop or flash drives in Vincenzo's office, and there's no flash drive with his personal effects."

"Great. That means he either gave it to someone or it's been stolen."

"Who would he have given it to?"

"As much as I hate to, I'm going to ask Cardona about it tomorrow."

"Why her?"

"Because I just found out that she and Vincenzo were more than just Chicago's finest."

The news perked up Sam, who straightened in his chair. "No shit? Vincenzo and Cardona?"

"Keep it to yourself."

"Of course. No wonder she went home so upset."

Joe sighed, "I hope we don't get called out tonight. I have to sleep."

"No problem. Sergeant Brown got people to cover for us, given the circumstances."

"Good for him." Joe pulled out his cell phone and began scrolling to find a number to call.

"Calling for a ride?"

"Yeah."

"Well, don't. I'll give you a lift. Your new digs aren't that far out of my way."

"Anyone ever tell you you're a good man, Sam?"

"All the time, man. All the time."

When Joe got home, Destiny greeted him at the door. Her energy levels were three times what his were, and he was curious what she was so excited about.

"Come here. I want to show you something," she said, leading him into the living room. "Now, sit here and have a look."

Joe sat on the couch with Destiny beside him. Displayed on the coffee table were color chips neatly arranged with fabric swatches. He looked them over and then looked back at her.

"You'll have to explain these to me."

"You know I've been working with Lindsey, my friend, and designer who decorated my apartment. And this is what we've come up with for the living room." She pointed as she described the items. "This is the fabric for the drapes. And this is the color for the walls. And these are the accent colors."

"Ah," was all Joe could manage in his exhausted state.

"So, what do you think?"

"You know what? I haven't had any sleep or hardly anything to eat in over thirty-six hours, so I'm in no condition to give my opinion about anything. Right now, my mind is a muddled mess."

Destiny was clearly disappointed, and Joe could read it in her face.

"Sorry." He leaned over and kissed her. "Tell you what, let me sleep for an hour, and then I'll have a look, okay?"

"That's fine. I should've realized you'd be overwhelmed with Vincenzo's death."

"I am, but we've made some progress already. I'm anxious to talk with you about that, too."

"Great."

"Anything for a starving boy to snack on before his nap?"

Chapter Five

Joe woke up to his alarm after napping for an hour. He needed more sleep but knew if he slept more, he would never fall asleep this evening. After showering, he walked into the kitchen and was greeted by the table set and the aroma of meat cooking.

"You're cooking meat?" he asked.

She opened the oven door and removed a bacon-wrapped filet mignon from the broiler. "Medium rare, just the way you like it. After your ordeal over the last thirty-six hours, I figured you deserved something special. Sit down."

She placed the filet on his plate, and from the second oven, she removed a tray. She spread tahini sauce on a plate, placed the roasted Brussels sprouts on top, and sprinkled them with roasted sesame seeds. She laid the plate on the table, then poured them both a glass of Cabernet.

From the refrigerator, she removed a chickpea, avocado, and feta salad for herself. "You must have had a terrible time," she said, sitting down. "How are you doing?"

"Better now that I've had a nap and a shower. The steak is terrific. Thanks."

"I meant dealing with Vincenzo's death."

Joe put down his fork and picked up his wine glass. "It was probably the most personally disturbing case I've ever had to deal with. And the autopsy...But I kept telling myself that Vincenzo would have wanted me to be there. I kept hearing his voice in my mind. 'You have to do this, Erickson.' That's how I got through it."

"Literally?"

"No," chuckled Joe. "I'm not psychic."

Destiny knew him well enough to know she should leave it alone and not pursue it any further. She changed the subject, and during their meal, she talked about the design concept for the living room decor and how its traditional style would work better with the house's architecture than the contemporary style of her apartment's furniture. It took his mind off the darkness of his day, and her excitement picked up his spirits.

When they had finished dinner, they adjourned to the living room, where they looked over the color chips and fabric swatches. Joe liked the colors Destiny and her designer friend, Lindsey, had chosen. After that discussion ended, Joe brought up the case again. He had come to rely on Destiny's perspective and the knowledge she had gained from her days at the FBI.

"Vincenzo called me into his office and told me he was investigating a cold case from ten years ago. He was looking for a key piece of evidence, and if he found it, he wanted Sam and me to take over the investigation. You wouldn't believe what we found in his second bedroom."

"What do you mean?"

"You remember that series we watched on Netflix where the offender had this room with the walls covered with articles and pictures of the woman he obsessed over?"

"Yeah."

"Well, that's what one of Vincenzo's bedroom walls looked like—covered with pictures, notes, strings going from one thing to another. He had every aspect of his investigation laid out on that wall. Let me show you."

Joe pulled out his phone and showed Destiny the photo he had taken of Vincenzo's bedroom office wall.

"Oh, my," said Destiny. "You weren't kidding."

"I'm going to have to figure all that out."

"So, you think he was killed because of what he was doing?"

"Yeah. He had a meeting noted in his daily planner with someone he called 'PT' on the night he was killed. No idea who that was."

"You have access to his computer?"

"Can't find it. It's nowhere to be found. And something else—there are no flash drives anywhere, either."

"That's weird. You think someone stole his laptop?"

"That would be my guess."

"You think it could have been in his car?"

"Maybe."

"Does his place have video surveillance?"

"That's what Sam and I are going to look into tomorrow. But it didn't look as though his condo lock was tampered with."

"What kind of lock does he have?"

"It's one of those keypad types."

"Hackers can gain access to those codes if the building doesn't have a good security system. Did you know that?"

"No."

"You need to have someone check into the condo's security system if you think someone got into his place."

"We will. Call me old fashioned, but I like a deadbolt lock with a key."

"You are old fashioned," said Destiny with a grin.

"Thanks."

"But that's not a bad thing. I wouldn't want a keyless entry system on this house."

At that moment, Joe's phone rang. He looked at the number, saw the Virginia area code, and assumed it was from Steve Vincenzo.

Answering it, he said, "Joe Erickson."

"This is Steve Vincenzo," came a voice that Joe found unnerving. He sounded just like his late father.

"Hello, Steve. I was expecting your call. My sincerest condolences about your father."

"Thank you…I'd like to know what happened," he said in a business-like tone. "The police here didn't give me any details other than the fact Dad was killed while investigating a case."

Joe gave him basic information about his father's homicide, told him the investigation into his death is ongoing, and that he is lead detective on the case.

"My wife and sons and I will be flying out tomorrow and should be arriving at O'Hare in the late afternoon. We'll be staying at the Hyatt Regency downtown."

"Call me when you get settled. I'll meet with you when it's convenient. What about your brother?"

"He's on his way back from Germany. I've reserved a room for him at the Hyatt, too. I'm not sure yet when he'll get in."

"You have my number and my email address. Feel free to call or get in touch via email or text if you like."

"Thank you, Detective Erickson. I look forward to meeting you." Steve ended the call, and Joe sat staring at his phone.

"What is it?" asked Destiny.

"A little unsettling." He looked up at Destiny. "Sounded just like his dad." Joe sat staring at his phone when Destiny broke the silence.

"You can't take this so personally, you lose perspective, Joe. If you feel too close or too emotionally connected, maybe you should let someone else take over the investigation."

"No. I can do it. It's just a matter of getting past the initial shock of it, just like everyone else. Sam and I are up to it."

"Good," she said, putting her arm around him. "I know you and Sam are best equipped to unravel a tough case."

"He'll be a hard man to replace, you know?" Joe picked up his wine glass and finished the last swallow.

"They'll find someone."

"They will. But I wouldn't want to be the one who has to fill his shoes."

Destiny could feel Joe's breathing was easy and regular. He seemed relaxed. Looking up at him, she said, "You want to go into the bedroom and watch TV?"

"May as well. I can't think of a better sedative than that."

Chapter Six

At 5:00 a.m., Joe slipped out of bed and was jogging less than ten minutes later, thinking about everything that needed to be done, categorizing each thing in his mind. Clearly, he and Sam needed to split up some aspects of the investigation.

At the office, Joe met with Sam.

"I think we need to follow up on any possible surveillance video at Vincenzo's condo," said Joe. "We need to know if anyone got in there after he left for his meeting that night."

"Okay. I'll call the building manager and find out about security cameras," said Sam.

"And see if they have a digital record of times his door was accessed. If they have a good security system, it should tell us that."

"Will do."

"While you're doing that, I'm going to check on Michelle Cardona. See if she's in today."

Joe checked with the duty sergeant and found that Cardona had taken several vacation days. He decided to call her, hoping she would answer.

"Hello, Joe," she said in a voice that was uncharacteristically soft.

"Hi, Michelle. I don't know if you know it or not, but Sam and I caught the case." He paused. "I know about you and Vincenzo. How are you doing?"

Silence. A breath. Then she said, "Not very well."

"None of us are doing very well, to be honest."

"How did you find out?"

"Doesn't matter. Only Sam and I know, and it's no one else's business, so…I'm calling because I need to know something, and I'm wondering if you could give me a few minutes."

"Okay."

"Do you happen to have Captain Vincenzo's personal computer?"

"No, I don't. Why?"

"It wasn't at his place, and there weren't any flash drives in his home office, either."

"That's odd. I assume you checked his office at work."

"Yeah. Did he ever talk to you about the cold case he was working on?"

"Cold case? No, he never mentioned anything about a cold case to me."

"What about retiring? Did he ever mention anything about that?"

Cardona hesitated. "Well, yeah. He did. He was going to retire at the end of the year. That's why he wasn't concerned about our relationship. Normally, he was by the book and wouldn't allow that to happen."

"I know," said Joe.

"But he'd been without a partner for a long time, and he only had nine months to go before it didn't matter anymore. I asked him about it, and he said, 'as long as it doesn't come up, it won't matter.' We kept it quiet, didn't go out so we'd be seen in public."

"So, he bent the rules. Hey, I'm not going to come down on anyone who bends the rules occasionally. You know me."

"Yeah," said an amused Cardona. "I've heard about you."

"I take it you never saw his second bedroom, then? The one he was using for an office?" asked Joe.

"No."

"So, he never showed it to you?"

"No."

"But you said you saw his computer and flash drives. Where would that have been?"

"On the coffee table. In his living room."

"Ah. Did he ever mention anything about an old case that he and Nate Smith worked on?"

"No. We didn't talk about work much when we were together. He was looking forward to the future," she said. "His grandkids, hunting, fishing, spending time together...." Her voice beginning to tremble.

Joe had all the information he needed from her and didn't want to press her for any more. He thought it best to move on.

"Thanks, Michelle. I appreciate your time. You know when you're coming back to work?"

"Next week. I took a week's vacation. I think I need to get back to work, get my mind off things, you know? Sitting at home isn't helping me any."

"If you want to come over to our place, you're welcome. Come for dinner. Getting out of the house might do you good."

"Thanks for the offer, Joe. I'll keep it in mind."

His call to Cardona didn't yield much, but at least he knew she did not have Vincenzo's laptop. It was time to check if there could be any surveillance video of the entrance to Vincenzo's condo.

A few minutes later, Sam told Joe he had contacted Merlin Fitzgerald, the condominium's manager. He said the condo had a security system for the entire building that included keypad codes and video surveillance. Sam told Fitzgerald to expect them at the condo shortly.

Fitzgerald met Joe and Sam as he had previously. He did not seem pleased to see them, and Joe wondered why. Fitzgerald escorted them to his office to discuss the security system and to view video surveillance.

"Can you tell me how your security system works?" asked Sam.

"Each condominium owner creates a five-digit code for their door lock, and that code is stored in a database in this office. Each owner is also issued a key which unlocks the door in case of an electrical outage."

"So, you have access to both the codes and an extra key. Would that be correct?"

"Yes, as manager, I'm the only other person, besides my assistant, who has access to that database and the key storage."

"Is your assistant here?"

"He's been on vacation for the past ten days. He should be back later today."

"I see."

"Is there a digital record of each time-of-day owners access the doors to their condos?" asked Joe.

"No," said Fitzgerald. "I'm afraid our system isn't that sophisticated."

"If I was an owner and I wanted to change the code to my front door, what would I have to do?"

"You would have to contact me with your new code, and I would then input that new code into the system."

"So, I couldn't get into the system with a password and change it myself?"

"No. That's not possible."

"Is your security system connected to an online umbrella system that manages the security for multiple condominiums?" asked Sam.

"No, our system is self-contained," explained Fitzgerald. "That's how the security company set it up."

"So, it's not connected to the internet at all?" asked Joe.

"Well, it's connected to the security company that set it up. If there's ever a problem, we can contact them so they can provide maintenance or troubleshoot our system."

"So, it's theoretically possible for someone, who knows what he's doing, to hack your system and gain access to your door codes," suggested Joe.

"I should hope not. I would like to think the security firm that set this up would have safeguards against that, wouldn't you think?"

"One would think," replied Sam. "How about checking the video surveillance for Captain Vincenzo's front door."

Joe gave Fitzgerald the date and the time parameters they were interested in. Fitzgerald entered the information into his computer, and the screen appeared, showing Vincenzo's front door. At 10:38 p.m., it showed Vincenzo leaving his condo for the 11:00 p.m. rendezvous at the elementary school. As they continued to watch, Joe asked Fitzgerald if he could fast-forward the video to 11:00 p.m. He did, and nothing showed on the video between 10:38 and 11:00.

At 11:08 p.m., an individual wearing gloves, a hat, glasses, and a standard white medical mask over his nose and mouth punched in the code on Vincenzo's door lock and entered his condo. At 11:14, the same individual left Vincenzo's condo carrying what looked like a laptop computer. The individual was in and out in six minutes.

Joe looked at Fitzgerald and said, "Appears someone got the code to Vincenzo's door."

"I…I don't know what to say," said Fitzgerald. "He must have gotten the code from Mr. Vincenzo."

"Highly unlikely," said Joe.

"I think it might be best for one of our cybercrimes people to check your system to see if you've been hacked," suggested Sam.

"I don't know if that's something—"

"You want your other owners to get robbed, too?"

"No. No, of course not. We can't have something like this going on here."

"We'll need this footage," said Joe.

"Certainly."

"I'm going to need to get into Captain Vincenzo's condo to conduct a search and to try to make sense of his office wall," said Joe.

"His office wall? I don't understand."

"Why don't you open his door, and we'll show you," said Sam.

Fitzgerald, who was shaken by the fact someone broke into one of his owner's condos, agreed to open Vincenzo's door. Joe and Sam gloved up, and Sam handed Fitzgerald a pair of gloves and asked him to put them on before they entered. Joe took him to Vincenzo's office and opened the door.

"You see that wall?" asked Joe, gesturing to the maze of pictures, notes, printouts, and strings of yarn.

"Oh my gosh," gasped Fitzgerald.

"I'm going to have to decipher all that. Captain Vincenzo was investigating a ten-year-old cold case, and this wall contains all the evidence and leads he was working on."

Fitzgerald was still staring open-mouthed when Joe asked, "I'm going to need a phone number where I can reach you anytime I need to get in here to work."

Fitzgerald gave Joe his cell phone number and said he could reach him at any time of day or night. His somewhat sour attitude had changed over the course of their visit, probably because he was worried about building security as well as his job.

"I assume you will not share this with anyone," Joe warned.

"Absolutely not," replied Fitzgerald. "Do you think your cybercrimes people could prevent this from happening again?"

"If someone did hack your system, I think one of our people can suggest something," said Sam.

"Do you know when this will be?"

"You'll get a phone call, and they'll set up a time."

Joe noticed Fitzgerald fidgeting like a little kid needing to go to the toilet. "You can go if you want. We're going to stay and complete a search of the premises."

"Okay, thanks."

"And one more thing. In case someone decides to come back to destroy the evidence on this wall, I want you to change the code on Vincenzo's door lock every day. Got that?"

"Yes, I can do that."

"Good. You can go," said Joe, and Fitzgerald left.

Joe looked at Sam. "We didn't do a very thorough search the other day. I think we'd better do a more extensive one today."

"Yeah. Where do you want to start?"

"Why don't you take the bathroom, and I'll take the closets."

"Why don't you take the bathroom, and I'll take the closets."

"You have a problem with bathrooms?"

"Sometimes."

"Okay. I have no problem taking the bathrooms."

Joe walked to the master bathroom and began by looking in the storage cabinet. Since there was a mirror rather than a medicine cabinet, Vincenzo's personal items were housed in there. He was a neat person, and everything was easily found and examined. No laptop and nothing hidden in any boxes or containers.

Under the sink, there was nothing hidden or suspicious either. Joe was about to leave when he thought of one more thing. He stepped to the toilet and lifted up the top of the tank. Lo and hold, there was a flash drive inside a sealed zip-top bag suspended from the backside of the tank.

"HEY, SAM!" he yelled. "COME TAKE A LOOK AT THIS!"

Sam entered the bathroom and saw the flash drive. "Well, I'll be damned! Clever place to hide a flash drive."

"Find anything in the closet?" asked Joe.

"Clothes, shoes. Nothing in the pockets so far. You want to help me go through his drawers?"

"Sure."

After finding nothing in the bedroom closet, dresser drawers, and main bathroom, they moved on to the kitchen. Following a thorough search of every cupboard, drawer, open box, and spice container, they found no laptop stashed away and no additional flash drives.

They searched the living room, the coat closet, vents, and every nook and cranny in the condo. Convinced they had found the only hidden piece of evidence left by Vincenzo, they stepped out into the hall.

"You think we should call in a forensic team?" asked Sam.

"By the looks of the video, the thief was wearing a hat, medical mask, gloves, and long-sleeved shirt. And he spent a total of six minutes in there. Besides that, we've already contaminated the scene. I don't know what a forensics team could get, do you?"

"Yeah. Waste of time."

When they returned to Area 3 in the late afternoon, Joe made a copy of the flash drive before entering the original into evidence. Then he made a call and spoke with Craig Redmond, the head of the cybercrimes division, and explained what the surveillance video showed. Joe told him he suspected a hack of the condo's security system. Redmond agreed to investigate and would put one of his people on it first thing tomorrow. Joe thanked him and gave him Fitzgerald's contact information.

A glance at the clock told Joe it was Miller time.

Chapter Seven

J oe's Uber ride dropped him at home, but Destiny was not there. A note
on the kitchen island told him she had gone to the grocery store. After
getting his laptop from the living room, he sat down on a stool at the
island.

Removing the copy of Vincenzo's flash drive from his pocket, he inserted
it in his laptop and began reading files. What he discovered were the
details about the cold case Vincenzo was trying to solve. It involved Robert
Wallingford, who witnessed a businessman named Carson Byrne kill a
blackmailer named Troy Winslow. Vincenzo interviewed Wallingford, a
friend of Winslow, when he came forward as a witness to the murder. Based
on Wallingford's eyewitness account, Vincenzo arrested Byrne, who was
subsequently charged with first-degree murder. Byrne was brought to trial,
and the day before Wallingford was scheduled to testify, he was found shot to
death at his residence. As a result, the DA's case fell apart, and Byrne walked.
Wallingford's homicide remained unsolved, and the case is still open.

Because Carson Byrne is now a city alderman, Joe realized what Vincenzo
meant when he told him the case would be tricky. It not only involved people
with money and power, but also with political pull. *Great*, thought Joe. *Tricky
doesn't even begin to describe this case.*

Joe grabbed a spiral notebook and began making notes as he scrolled
through Vincenzo's files. He would need to print these pages from the flash
drive later so he could continue to study them. After reading through much
of Vincenzo's findings, he had not seen any indication regarding the nature
of the blackmail. What did Winslow have on Byrne that would lead Byrne

to kill him? And if Wallingford was a friend of Winslow, did he know? Was he in on the blackmail scheme? Was he waiting for Winslow when Byrne killed him? Was that why he was in a position to witness the murder?

Joe continued reading when Destiny returned from the grocery store.

"I could use your help," she said as she put down several bags on the counter. "There are more bags in the car."

"Sure," said Joe, getting up to help her.

Once the groceries were brought in and put away, Destiny noticed Joe's open laptop.

"Working from home?"

"I found a flash drive Vincenzo had hidden in his bathroom. I made a copy before turning in the original. I'm going through it now."

"You did what?"

"I know, I know. It wasn't protocol, but I needed to know what was on it now."

"Any good stuff?"

"Yeah. It's all about the cold case he was working on. Very detailed. I'm going through it, and once I'm done, I plan to go back to his condo and compare what I've learned with what he posted on his wall."

"So…Are you going to tell me about it, or do I have to ply you with wine?"

Joe closed his laptop and teased, "A glass of wine might loosen my tongue."

Destiny chuckled. "I thought as much." She opened a new bottle of Cabernet Sauvignon and poured two glasses.

"It's a new Cabernet I bought."

Joe rose from his stool and took the glass from her. After he took a sip, she watched for his reaction.

"Very nice. I think this deserves full disclosure."

"You'd make a terrible spy. Spill your guts over one glass of wine."

"Call me 'Loose-lips.'"

They moved to the living room and kicked back on the couch. Joe told Destiny what he knew about Vincenzo's cold case so far, and she became concerned.

"Carson Byrne is a powerful man, Joe. If he knows you've reopened the

Wallingford murder case, there's no telling what he might do. Things could get dangerous."

"Wallingford was a friend of Winslow. If Wallingford was in cahoots with Winslow in blackmailing Byrne, what were they blackmailing him about? What did they have on him? That's what I want to find out."

"Whatever it was, it was bad enough to kill for. And that was before he became a powerful politician. Now that he's connected, he wouldn't hesitate to kill again if he thought this information could become public. It must be pretty bad."

"That's why it's going to be crucial for Sam and me to play this close to the vest. The fewer people that know, the better."

"Where do you start on something like this?"

"I haven't gone all the way through Vincenzo's files on the flash drive yet. After I do, then I'll have to spend time deciphering his wall. There may be more there than what's on the flash drive. That could take days. I have to get all this down on paper, so it's clear in my mind."

"Someone found out Vincenzo was getting close to something, and he had to be stopped," noted Destiny. "Pretty audacious move assassinating a police captain."

"He must have spoken to someone who alerted Byrne he was investigating the Wallingford case, and Byrne got scared. Otherwise, how would he have found out?"

"I wonder if Vincenzo kept any of the information from his flash drive on his laptop. If he was crafty and anticipated a possible theft of his computer, he may have kept everything on the flash drive he was hiding. It may not have been a backup at all."

"So, you're saying they may not have gotten any of his files by stealing his laptop?" asked Joe.

"It's possible. You know him better than I do. Does it sound like something he might do?"

"He wouldn't leave anything to chance, that's for sure. He would've had a contingency plan for everything." At that moment, Joe thought of something. "Shit!"

"What is it?"

"Whoever stole Vincenzo's computer saw his wall. If there were no files on his computer and no files on flash drives, that leaves all that information on his wall. I'd better warn Fitzgerald."

"Who's Fitzgerald?" asked Destiny.

"Vincenzo's condo manager. He's the only one who can unlock Vincenzo's door."

Joe pulled out his phone and called Merlin Fitzgerald's number. There was no answer. He tried his other number, the day or night number he was given. No answer there, either. Suddenly, Joe got worried.

"This isn't good. I need to get to Vincenzo's condo right away."

"Let's go," said Destiny. "I'll drive you."

After pocketing the flash drive, they drove to Vincenzo's condo on North Kenmore Avenue. Joe got out and pushed Fitzgerald's button. There was no response. So, he pushed more buttons until someone answered. After explaining he was a police detective concerned about Mr. Fitzgerald's welfare, he was buzzed in. Destiny followed him down the hall, and they were met by Ira Goldstein, who had buzzed him in. They went to Fitzgerald's office door and got no response.

"Let me call his assistant, Dennis Coben," said Goldstein. "He can let you in."

Ten minutes later, a paunchy man in his late thirties arrived and said he was Dennis Coben.

Joe told him he had concerns about Fitzgerald's welfare since he was unable to contact him via the phone number he was given. Coben opened the door to Fitzgerald's office, and Joe and Destiny went in. On the floor, they found Fitzgerald, bloodied and unconscious but still alive. His hands and feet were bound with an extension cord. He was breathing, but his breaths were shallow. While Destiny tended to Fitzgerald, Joe called in an assault and requested an ambulance. Then he went outside to Coben and Goldstein.

"Fitzgerald's apparently been the victim of an assault. He's unconscious. I've alerted the police and called for an ambulance."

"Omigod," said Goldstein.

"Mr. Goldstein, maybe you could wait at the door and let the police and medical personnel in," Joe suggested.

"Of course," Goldstein replied and left.

"Mr. Coben, can you open Captain Vincenzo's door? I need to see if his place has been tampered with." He handed Coben a pair of gloves before entering the office. After checking the database for the code to Vincenzo's door lock, he walked down the hall, punched in the code, and opened Vincenzo's door.

Joe walked into the second bedroom and saw that the wall with all of the information was now blank. No pins, no yarn, no Post-it notes. Nothing on the wall or on the floor but some empty boxes. Wiped clean."

"God dammit!" growled Joe. He returned to Fitzgerald's office and kneeled next to Destiny, who was tending to Fitzgerald.

"How is he?"

"Breathing. Someone really worked him over."

"Poor guy. He must have been forced to give up the code to Vincenzo's door. His office wall has been wiped clean."

"Oh, no."

"Oh, yeah. Nothing left. Not even a pin."

"Wow. Hopefully, he'll be able to identify his assailant."

"Yeah."

Joe left and spoke to Dennis Coben, who was waiting by the door.

"We're going to need video surveillance of both Vincenzo's door and this door. I'm pretty sure the same person or persons who assaulted Mr. Fitzgerald forced him to give them the code to Vincenzo's door."

"I'll get that for you once things have quieted down," said Coben.

"We'll have a forensics team here to collect evidence in here and in Vincenzo's condo. It's going to take a while before they finish."

"Is Merlin going to be okay?"

"We don't know. Someone worked him over pretty good."

"Oh, man. To think it could have been me."

"What do you mean?"

"Merlin was scheduled to go on vacation. I would have been in there if they'd come next week."

"Count your lucky stars."

A few minutes later, a uniformed officer from the 20th District showed up, and Joe explained what had happened and why he was there. The 20th was one of the districts covered by Area 3, so Joe called and requested Evidence Technicians.

When the EMTs arrived, they assessed Fitzgerald, administered an IV, loaded him onto a gurney, and transported him to the hospital.

Joe called Sam to let him know what had transpired. He was appalled.

"What the hell is going on, Joe?"

"Someone is desperate to destroy all the evidence Vincenzo accumulated in his investigation."

"What did Vincenzo have that the police didn't have already?"

"I haven't completely gone through the flash drive information yet. I hope everything on the wall is on the flash drive."

"Let's hope. I think Vincenzo was meticulous enough to keep his information current, don't you?" asked Sam.

"There's no way to tell now. I guess we'll have to trust his attention to detail. You'd better get over here. I've called for Evidence Techs to check both Vincenzo's condo and Fitzgerald's office, and we need to interview the other owners to see if they saw anything."

"Be there in twenty."

Destiny said, "You don't need me here, but I could make myself useful, monitoring Fitzgerald's condition at the hospital."

"That would be great. You know where they took him?"

"I asked, and they said Methodist.

"Okay, let me know his condition. If they give you a hard time, call me and let me talk with them."

Destiny left, and Joe continued managing the scene. Another uniformed officer arrived, and Joe told him to keep the area around Fitzgerald's door clear of other condo owners wanting to know what was happening. Fitzgerald's office and the area around it had to be preserved so further contamination could be minimized.

Sam got there just before the Evidence Techs showed up. Joe was speaking with the owner of a condo across from Fitzgerald's office door. When Joe saw Sam, he dismissed the woman, and she opened her door and went inside.

"She see anything?" asked Sam.

"No. Didn't see or hear a thing. She was working at her computer and didn't hear any noise coming from Fitzgerald's office. Said these places are full of soundproofing."

Joe looked over Sam's shoulder and saw Jerry Bristow and Art Casey, two Evidence Techs Joe had worked with on many occasions, walking toward them carrying their equipment.

"Hello, boys," said Bristow. "What do we have here?"

"A two-fer," said Joe. "A theft from Captain Vincenzo's condo and an assault that happened here."

Art looked at Bristow and asked, "What do you want to do, process them together or split up?"

"Let's split up, if it's okay with you," said Bristow.

"Makes no difference to me," said Art. "You want the theft or the assault?"

"I'll take the assault."

"Okay. I guess that means you get the blood this time."

Joe explained about the theft of Vincenzo's laptop and the cleansing of everything from his makeshift office.

"We haven't pulled up the video surveillance yet, but it's my guess at least one person went in and packed up everything in that room and carted it off. It would have been a lot of paper, pins in the wall, Post-it notes, yarn. Now everything's gone."

"Okay. Where is it?"

"I'll show you," replied Joe, and he called to Coben. "You need to open Vincenzo's door for Mr. Casey."

"Mm. Mr. Casey," mused Art. "I like that."

"Never tell me you don't get any respect, Art. I've never believed what they say about you."

Art snorted something Joe couldn't make out. Once Vincenzo's door was opened, Art suited up and went in to begin work, concentrating on the second bedroom.

Joe felt good about Art conducting the search in Vincenzo's condo. Art went out of his way to help to him during the David Eugene Burton serial killer investigation, and Joe knew how thorough he was. If anyone could turn up some evidence, Art would be the guy.

While the Evidence Technicians were doing their jobs, Joe and Sam began knocking on doors. After ringing the bell on a second-floor unit, a man answered.

Joe showed his ID and said, "Detective Joe Erickson, Chicago PD. We're here investigating the homicide of one of the residents in this complex. We'd like to ask you a few questions."

"All right." And he slid the chain off his door and opened it for them.

"This is Sam Renaldo, my partner."

"And you are?" asked Sam.

"Kenneth Saroyan," the white-haired man replied. He led them into the main room which was dominated by a Steinway grand piano. "Make yourselves comfortable," he said, pointing to a couch.

"You said you're investigating a homicide? May I ask who it was?"

"A police captain who lived on the first floor. Sal Vincenzo," said Joe.

"Oh, no...."

"You knew him?" asked Sam.

"Not well. I just knew him through our owners' meetings. What happened?"

"That's what we're trying to find out," said Joe. "So, you know all the owners when you see them?"

"I do."

"Did you see anyone who was not an owner in the lower hall or hanging around the past several days?"

"No. Now, wait...I did see someone with our building manager."

"When was that?" asked Sam.

"Earlier today."

"Can you describe him?"

"He was wearing a mask. You know, one of those white medical masks."

"Besides that."

"Well, he was about my height, so I guess, six foot tall, but thicker built, maybe two-hundred pounds, dark hair…and dark eyes. He was wearing sunglasses, but I saw his eyes from the side. I remember those eyes because he looked me over. Made me feel uncomfortable."

"What was he wearing?" asked Joe.

"Oh, uh…one of those Greek fisherman caps, what looked to be a t-shirt and jeans. And he was wearing one of those nylon windbreakers. Dark blue, I think."

"How old, could you tell?"

"Middle-age. He had a few gray hairs on the sides that the cap and mask didn't cover."

Anything else you can remember?"

"He had ugly hands."

"Ugly hands? Can you be more specific?"

"I'm a professional musician, piano, organ, anything with a keyboard. And I notice people's hands and fingers. It's weird, I know. It's like a dentist noticing people's teeth, I suppose. But…."

"Can you describe them?" asked Joe.

"They were gnarly, like a boxer's hands. Or someone who lifts weights. You know what I mean?"

"Yeah, I know what you mean," said Sam. "Kinda swollen with popping veins?"

"Precisely. And he bit his nails."

"You're pretty observant," complimented Joe.

"He unnerved me, so I paid attention to him."

"We think this man may have been responsible for an attack on Mr. Fitzgerald earlier today."

"Omigod," Saroyan gasped. "Is Merlin going to be all right?"

"We don't know yet. He's been taken to the hospital, and I haven't been informed of his condition."

"That's horrible," said Saroyan, shaking his head. "Poor Merlin."

"Your description's been helpful," said Sam. "Thanks for your time."

Joe and Sam rose from the couch, and Saroyan followed them to the door. "Am I in any kind of danger since I saw him, and he saw me?"

"He's not interested in you," said Joe. "He only wanted the codes to Vincenzo's door so he could steal items from his condo. I doubt he'll be back."

"Besides," said Sam, "We probably have him on the building's video surveillance. I think you're okay."

Back out in the hall, Joe and Sam went knocking on the remaining two doors but got no information from the residents. They walked back down to Fitzgerald's office. Jerry Bristow was finishing up and getting out of his Tyvek coveralls. Three hours had passed since he and Art had arrived on the scene, and he seemed ready to pack it in.

"Got what you need, Jerry?" asked Joe.

"The office wasn't that big, but I was able to collect a lot of material. They weren't very good housekeepers, so there's going to be a lot of junk to go through. A lot of fingerprints, too. We'll see."

"Thanks, Jerry. Can we go in now?"

"Yeah. Guess I'd better go see if Art needs any help."

Bristow picked up his equipment and made his way to the van to deposit the evidence. After checking with Art, he dressed in a new suit of Tyvek gear and entered Vincenzo's condo with his equipment.

Dennis Coben brought up the surveillance video Joe wanted. It showed the man described by Kenneth Saroyan walking with Merlin Fitzgerald down the hall to his office. They went inside and closed the door. Less than ten minutes later, the man emerged from the office, and surveillance showed him at Vincenzo's door, entering the code and going inside.

Fifteen minutes later, the man came out of Vincenzo's condo carrying a large garbage bag. He left the building and walked down the street, where exterior surveillance lost him.

"We'll need this video for evidence," said Joe.

"Sure," said Coben. "No problem."

An hour later, Art Casey and Jerry Bristow completed work in Vincenzo's condo. Joe and Sam were waiting.

"It's all yours," said Bristow as he began removing his protective clothing.

"He was a good housekeeper," said Art. "Not like some who never vacuum or dust for months at a time."

"Many prints?" asked Joe.

"No," replied Bristow. "Didn't look like he had many guests. He live alone?"

"Yeah," said Sam. "Was seeing someone, but she lived elsewhere."

"So, you know who she is?"

"Yeah."

"Since he's one of ours, this'll get priority," said Art.

Joe called Destiny at the hospital to get an update on Merlin Fitzgerald. It rang and eventually went to voicemail. Joe got worried.

"I think we need to check on Fitzgerald at the hospital."

"Destiny with him?"

"Yeah, but she's not picking up."

"Let's go."

Chapter Eight

Sam drove Joe to Methodist Hospital, where the EMTs transported Merlin Fitzgerald. Joe called Destiny again from the car, and this time she answered. She told them to meet her inside the North Paulina Street entrance but didn't mention anything about Fitzgerald's condition. A few minutes later, Sam parked in front of the entrance, and they both went inside. Destiny was there waiting for them.

"What's going on?" asked Joe.

"He's in surgery," replied Destiny. "They started giving me a hard time about privacy and not being a relative, so I pulled out my old FBI ID. Good thing they didn't look closely." Joe smiled at her clever act of deception.

"You could get in trouble for that," said Joe.

"She didn't even look at my name."

"Is he going to make it?" asked Sam.

"Abdominal hemorrhaging is their main concern."

"Great," said Joe. "I'd better go up and give them my number so they can contact me about his condition. You shouldn't be pretending to be an FBI agent any longer."

Joe left to speak with hospital personnel. Ten minutes later, he was back, but Sam was no longer there.

"Sam decided to go. No need for him to wait around. It's getting late, and he didn't figure he needed to hang around any longer."

"Yeah. You didn't answer my phone call earlier."

"I couldn't. I was trying to talk with the emergency room doctor, and he wasn't being very cooperative."

"So, that's when you went FBI on him?"

"Uh-huh. Then I had to deal with the head nurse on the surgical floor. After that, I wasn't in any mood to return your call. Sorry."

"The head nurse was nicer to me. She's going to call me when Fitzgerald is out of surgery."

"Of course. You're a man."

"Must be my charm."

"Well, you're full of it. Charm, that is."

Once at home, Joe poured himself a healthy glass of Pinot Noir and sat down at the kitchen island.

"How about we order something?" suggested Destiny.

"Sounds good to me. I'll let you choose. Whatever you decide is good with me."

"Wow. You're easy to please."

"Well, when you're starving, almost anything will do." Joe opened his laptop, which he had left sitting on the island. He was going to read more of Vincenzo's notes, but before he could enter his password, Destiny closed it.

"Hey."

"No, you don't. You've put in enough time today. It'll still be there tomorrow. Now, go into the living room and relax."

She was right. He needed to let go of work and kick back tonight. "Yes, dear."

"Don't you start that," she teasingly warned.

Joe chuckled. He carried his glass into the living room and sat down on the couch. In the background, he heard her making a call to a restaurant. The remote was handy, so he turned on the television and began watching Headline News. A few minutes later, Destiny sat down next to him.

"So, what did you order for us?"

"Italian. Farfalle Aglio Olio for me, and Farfalle with Shrimp and Arrabiata sauce for you."

"Oo, so I'm living dangerously tonight, huh?"

"This place uses whole wheat pasta, and they make a healthier version of the standard Arriabiata sauce. I doubt you'll be able to tell the difference between theirs and the version made with heavy cream."

"My coronary arteries thank you," said Joe as he leaned over and kissed her.

"You see, I take good care of you."

Joe's phone rang. He listened to the caller and occasionally responded with "uh-huh" and "I see." Finally, he thanked the caller and breathed a sigh of relief as he put down his phone.

"Well?" asked Destiny.

Looking at her, he said, "Fitzgerald's out of surgery. He's in the ICU. It was touch and go. They had to remove his spleen. For now, he's critical but stable. They'll know more tomorrow."

Destiny was about to speak when Joe's phone rang again. He recognized the Virginia phone number. Looking at Destiny, he said, "Sorry. I have to take this. It's Steve Vincenzo."

"Detective Erickson, I just wanted to call and let you know that my brother got in this morning. We've spent most of the day making funeral arrangements."

"I understand," said Joe.

"Is there a time when it would be convenient for you to meet with us tomorrow?"

"Sure. How's your morning schedule?"

"It's open."

"Let's say ten-thirty at your hotel?"

"Sounds good. We'll meet you in the lobby area."

The call ended, and Joe looked at Destiny, saying, "A lawyer and an army captain. Should be interesting."

"In what way?"

"To see if they're friendly or hostile. It could go either way."

Destiny put her arm around Joe. "I'm sure you and Sam will put Vincenzo's sons at ease and give them assurances you're working on solving his murder."

"We will." Joe clicked the mute feature on the remote. "I just don't know what to expect. Steve has been very business-like on the phone. I've never met or seen either one of them. Vincenzo always kept his private life and his work separate. That went for his cold case, too."

"You know what he was investigating, and you have his notes. That's a lot to go on, Joe. Someone has a lot to lose if they have to resort to killing a police captain to stop him from probing into this murder."

"If they thought it would stop the investigation, they're sadly mistaken. I won't rest until I find out who's responsible and who pulled the trigger."

"Out of curiosity, how many copies of his flash drive are there?" asked Destiny.

"I have one," said Joe, "and Sam has one. And there's the original, of course."

"You might consider making one more as a backup. One you can keep at home just in case the worst happens."

"The worst?"

"Someone influential finds out and doesn't want you having copies."

"Ah, I see what you mean. I'll do that."

"If you need me to access any of my FBI contacts, you only have to ask. I'll help any way I can, you know that."

"I appreciate it. You've always been a great help." He reached down and picked up his glass of wine. "I think I want to turn in early tonight."

"I think I'll join you. But first…."

"Food!"

"But I probably can't sleep on a full stomach."

"Who said anything about sleep?"

Chapter Nine

Arriving ten minutes early the next morning, Joe and Sam entered the lobby of the Hyatt Regency Hotel on East Wacker Drive. Joe phoned Steve Vincenzo, who told Joe that he and his brother were already in the lobby at a table behind the bar area. He said they could recognize him by his blue-and-white-striped golf shirt.

Joe and Sam walked toward the bar and saw the brothers. Joe gave a wave, and Steve and Mark stood to greet them. Both men resembled their father in size and facial features. After exchanging handshakes and making introductions, they sat down.

Mark was the first to speak, and he got straight to the point. "What exactly happened to Dad? No one has told us anything about the circumstances."

Joe could sense the frustration in his voice, so he started from the beginning. "Captain Vincenzo approached me regarding how he was investigating a cold case on his own time, and how he was getting close to some answers. At that point, he wanted to hand off the investigation to me and my partner. On the night of the shooting, he was meeting someone he referred to as "PT" in his daily planner. Apparently, they had agreed to meet in front of an elementary school. That was where he was shot and killed."

"Do you know who this 'PT' is?" asked Steve.

"Not yet," said Sam. "It would have been helpful if your father hadn't used code for who he was meeting, but we're working on who that was."

"Could that person have been the killer?" asked Mark.

"It's not probable as I see it," said Joe. "I think the person may have been used to lure your father there so a sniper could shoot him."

"A sniper?" asked Mark.

"He was killed by a round from a rifle, not a handgun. We think someone was waiting behind the school with a rifle, and when your dad got out of the car to meet with 'PT,' the shooter fired the fatal round."

"So, in other words, he was set up," said Steve.

"It looks that way," agreed Sam.

"Right now, we're reviewing and working off his notes on this cold case from ten years ago. Someone was getting very nervous about your dad digging into an old unsolved murder," said Joe. "You don't eliminate a police captain unless you have a lot to lose."

"And we're picking up where your father left off," said Sam. "Did he ever talk with either of you about this cold case or any old cases he was working on?"

"No," said Mark looking at Steve.

"Not with me," concurred Steve. "He wasn't in the habit of sharing his work with us. Not when we were kids and not as adults."

"Your dad was a pretty private guy. Do you know who his friends were?" asked Joe.

"Well, he and Nate Smith were pretty tight. They were partners for a long time. But Nate's gone now," said Mark.

"There's Nick Esposito," said Steve. "They used to go pheasant hunting downstate."

"Yeah. He was a detective but had to retire after he got shot up by a gang member," said Mark. "Lost an eye."

"He still around?" asked Sam.

"As far as I know," said Steve. "He'll probably show up at Dad's funeral. Wears an eyepatch."

"Do you know if they were still close?"

"I assume so," said Mark. "He mentioned him to me a couple of months ago when I was talking to him on the phone. Said they were planning to do some deep-sea fishing in the Bahamas when he retired."

Steve shook his head slowly. "Yeah. He was looking forward to a lot of things. Spending time with my two boys, going to Italy to see where granddad came from, going to the Vatican." He took a deep breath and let it out. "All those dreams, gone in a split second."

"I hope you find out who's responsible, detectives," said Mark. "We're not out for vengeance. We want justice for our dad."

"So do we," said Sam.

"Your dad meant a lot to me," said Joe. "I won't quit until I've found those responsible and put them behind bars. That's a promise."

There was a pause, and after a moment, Sam asked, "You have any other questions?"

Steve looked at Mark and then back to Joe. "One. Can we get into Dad's place? I was told it wasn't accessible because the police had it sealed."

"I'll look into it for you," said Joe. "I don't think it needs to be sealed any longer. It's been gone over by Evidence Technicians, and we've searched it for his laptop and any other evidence that might be pertinent to our investigation."

"You said you made funeral arrangements," said Sam. "Do you know when and where yet?"

"Day after tomorrow at Saint Ida Catholic Church. Ten o'clock," said Mark.

"There'll be a large police delegation which will include those he worked with at Areas 3 and 5," said Joe. "We'll both be there."

"We appreciate that," said Steve, rising from his chair, signaling their meeting was over. "Thank you for giving us the details about Dad."

Joe, Sam, and Mark got up as well. "I'll let you know later today about your dad's condo. How much longer do you plan to be in Chicago?"

"I have to get back two days after the funeral," said Mark. "I'm needed for maneuvers. I work in a sensitive area, and my presence is required."

"We'll be here for a week," said Steve. "I need to take care of things, and while we're here, we're going to show the boys around the city. Treat them to a baseball game, the zoo, things they'll enjoy."

"How old are they?" asked Sam.

"Eight and ten."

"It's a shame the captain didn't get to spend more time with them. He would've enjoyed that, I'm sure."

"Yeah. They're taking it pretty hard. They always loved seeing him."

After parting company, Joe and Sam drove back to Area 3. Joe needed to get Vincenzo's condo opened up for his sons, and he wanted to find address information for Nick Esposito in case he didn't attend the funeral.

As soon as they returned, they were called into the office of Lieutenant Briggs again. Joe and Sam didn't quite understand why she would need to speak with them so soon.

Walking past the three sergeants in the outer office, Sam knocked on her door, and Briggs, a tall, masculine woman about forty-five, said, "Come in. I was hoping I'd see you again today. Sit down." She walked behind her desk and sat.

"What can we do for you?" asked Joe.

"I want to apologize," Briggs said. "After the meeting with the Commander, I was in no mood to see anyone. I should have waited to speak with you."

Okay," Joe said.

"I want you to keep me apprised of your investigation. This is a priority, so if there's anything you need, I want you to let me know. The brass wants results."

"Understood," said Joe.

"We'll do that," replied Sam.

"Where does it stand right now?" she asked.

Joe and Sam explained Vincenzo's cold case investigation, the burglary of his condo, video surveillance, and the discovery of his flash drive. He didn't mention anything about having copies of the flash drive.

"It would help if you could lighten our load so we could concentrate more of our attention on this case," said Joe.

"I'd like to do that," replied Briggs, "but we're down a team at the moment. Hernandez is out with back surgery, and Fiedler was just promoted to lieutenant. So, you'll have to deal with it for the time being."

Joe had never had many interactions with Briggs since she came in from Area 1 to take Vincenzo's place as Homicide Lieutenant. And based on the meetings he'd had with her, he didn't like her. "Deal with it." She sure as hell didn't win any points with him today. He didn't care for her tone, and he didn't appreciate supervisors looking over his shoulder.

Walking back to their desks, Sam said, "You didn't mention we had copies of Vincenzo's flash drive."

"For good reason," replied Joe. "I don't trust people. Besides, I don't want her getting all pissy about us having unofficial copies of evidence."

"Good thinking," said Sam. "I've printed out all the information on the flash drive, so I have hard copy to look over."

"I'm going to do that, too," added Joe. "It's good to have hard copy back up, just in case."

Joe sat down at his computer, inserted his flash drive, and began printing its contents. It took a lot of time since Vincenzo had his evidence categorized into chapters, and Joe had to send each chapter separately to the printer.

After running through half a ream of paper, the contents of Vincenzo's flash drive were printed. Joe gathered several file folders and separated the contents according to chapters. Vincenzo was very thorough in his analysis of evidence, and it would take Joe some time to put his case together.

Joe made calls to the forensics lab and spoke to Art Casey.

"Captain Vincenzo's sons would like to have access to their father's condo. Do you have any objections to releasing the scene to them?"

"We have what we need," said Art. "I don't foresee any reason why we'd need to check the place again."

"You have any preliminary findings?"

"You'll know when we send the report."

"Thanks, Art."

Typical Art. He never gave you anything beforehand unless it was something so bizarre he couldn't contain his enthusiasm about it.

Joe made two calls, the first to the 20th District to notify them they could remove the seal on Vincenzo's condo.

His second call was to Steve Vincenzo to tell him his father's condo would be available to them. He suggested waiting a day for the police to unseal it, to let the assistant condo manager know, and to give him his phone number if he needed verification.

Chapter Ten

The next day, the homicide detectives at Area 3 received information about Vincenzo's funeral and were excused from duty to attend. In the case of department members slain in the line of duty, police officers from around the city and beyond honored their fallen comrade at the funeral. Joe knew it would be a tough day for himself and many of the other Area 3 detectives who worked under Lieutenant Vincenzo. He wondered how Michelle Cardona was going to hold up.

By mid-morning, the forensics team had retrieved all surveillance video from his condo and began processing it. They were running it through facial recognition programs, but given how much of the suspect's face was covered, identification is going to be difficult. They were hoping the Evidence Techs could provide some leads.

Joe called the hospital to check on Merlin Fitzgerald's condition and spoke to the head nurse, Denise Thomas.

"He's still in the ICU, detective. His vital signs improved somewhat during the night, but his condition is still critical."

"Is he awake?" asked Joe.

"No, sir. He's still unconscious."

"Is that a bad thing?"

"Not necessarily. He was in surgery quite a while. We're hoping he'll wake up sometime later today."

"So, it's still a matter of wait and see, then?"

"It is. Why don't I call you when his condition changes."

"That would be great. I'd appreciate that."

Frustrated, Joe returned to his hard copy of Vincenzo's notes. Joe found that Carson Byrne graduated from Northwestern University and began a floor covering business that became very successful, and his stores expanded throughout the city. The business made him millions, which allowed him to donate large amounts to charities championed by powerful politicians. He later became active in politics himself, eventually being elected as a city alderman.

According to Vincenzo's notes, Byrne was politically ambitious and had his eyes on becoming mayor at some point. However, when he was arrested for the murder of Troy Winslow, his reputation became tainted, and his ultimate aspirations were squelched. But with his court case dismissed, he used his charisma and a lot of his own money to overcome negative publicity and win his race for city alderman.

When Vincenzo and Nate Smith interviewed Robert Wallingford, he stated he had evidence that would not only prove Carson Byrne killed Winslow, but also bring him down because he knew what Winslow was using to blackmail Byrne. He refused to say what that was but said he had a copy of what Winslow was using. At the time, Vincenzo and Smith were more interested in a murder conviction than the blackmail evidence. They did not pursue that angle aggressively since Wallingford told them it would be part of his testimony. With Wallingford, Smith, and Vincenzo dead, the blackmail evidence was now key to Wallingford's murder.

That's what Vincenzo was after, thought Joe. *Whatever that blackmail evidence was, it was bad enough to kill both Wallingford and Vincenzo to keep them quiet. It must still exist.*

Joe walked over to Sam's desk. He was so engaged that he didn't see Joe approach.

"Hey," said Joe, startling Sam out of Vincenzo's notes.

"Oh! Guess I was really focused. Didn't know you were there," he chuckled.

"You're lucky I'm a good guy."

"Yeah. What's up?"

"I was thinking. We should probably ask Lieutenant Briggs to requisition someone to print out the contents of Vincenzo's flash drive, so we have official copies. She might frown on us making our own copies and having printouts without going through channels. You know what I mean?"

"Yeah. Good to avoid questions like, 'Where did you get that?,'" said Sam.

"Okay. I'll send her an email requesting two hard copies of everything on the flash drive," said Joe. "Then it'll be official."

An hour later, Briggs sent Joe a return email stating she would honor his request. Half an hour after that, she called Joe and Sam into her office. She did not offer them a chair.

"I requested the flash drive you entered into evidence, and there's nothing on it."

Joe's skin tingled. "What do you mean there's nothing on it?"

"I mean, it's blank."

"That can't be," said Sam. "We—"

Joe cut him off. "Why would Captain Vincenzo be hiding a flash drive with nothing on it?"

"I have no idea," said Briggs. "I checked with Sergeant Oatman, myself. He's the one who logged it in and locked it up."

"That's right. I saw him do it."

"Then, today, when he brought it up, I gave it to Sergeant Means to print out the contents, and it was blank. Like a new one."

"You know, of course, that was the primary evidence in the murder of Captain Vincenzo, don't you?" asked Joe, his anger simmering beneath the surface.

"I'm aware of that, Detective Erickson," said Briggs.

"Don't you think it's a little strange that a burglar removed all of Vincenzo's hard files, and now someone has removed all the remaining evidence he'd accumulated?" asked Sam.

"Sounds like a coverup to me, and now it involves this office," added Joe.

"Coverup," said Briggs. "You've got to be kidding. Where do you get off suggesting something like that? You have a lot of nerve, Detective Erickson!"

Joe and Sam turned and left Briggs's office, furious that someone had tampered with evidence.

"Someone switched flash drives," said Joe.

"Ya think?" replied Sam. "Something stinks around here."

They decided to visit Sergeant Bill Oatman, who logged in the original flash drive to see what he had to say.

"I figured you'd stop by," said Oatman. "You saw me log it in, and I locked it up right over there."

"You still have it?" asked Joe.

"Yeah."

"Can I take a look?"

"Sure," replied Oatman, and he went over, unlocked the door, and brought over the bagged flash drive.

Joe slid out the USB plug. Looking at it carefully, he looked back at Oatman and said, "This doesn't have my mark on it."

"What?" asked Sam.

"I put a small dot on the USB plug with my Sharpie before I bagged it. You wouldn't notice it if you weren't looking for it. This one doesn't have a dot."

"You're shitting me," said Oatman. "This was never out of the sealed bag. If the bag was tampered with, I would have noticed."

Sam looked at Joe. "Briggs."

"It wouldn't have been Means, that's for sure," said Joe. He looked at Oatman, who was visibly upset. "Keep this to yourself, Sergeant. Something stinks around here, so you need to keep it quiet."

"No one will hear about this from me. Don't worry."

"Thanks, Bill," said Sam. "We'll keep you informed."

They left Oatman and returned to the floor. As they walked toward their desks, Sam asked, "All this hard copy and our flash drives—you think we should even have these things at work?"

"Not anymore. I think it's best we keep this stuff at home."

"Yeah, and let's not plug those flash drives into our work computers."

"Exactly. We have to keep our knowledge of Vincenzo's information from Briggs and whoever else might be dirty around here."

Around lunchtime, Joe kept an eye out for Sergeant Means. He saw him walking toward the conference room and made a beeline to intercept him.

"Hey, Sergeant," Joe said, grabbing a coffee cup.

"How you doin', Joe?" replied Means.

"Can I talk with you about something?"

"I guess."

Joe stopped talking when a young gel-haired detective walked in and popped a pod in the Keurig. "Outside?"

Means gave Joe a look and then realized what it was about. "Yeah, sure."

The two men walked outside into the parking lot.

"This is about that flash drive, isn't it?" asked Means.

"Yeah. When Briggs gave you the flash drive, did you see her remove it from the plastic evidence bag?"

"No. She carried it over to my desk with the evidence bag, but I didn't actually see her open the bag and remove it."

Joe nodded. "What I thought."

"What's going on?"

"Can you keep this to yourself?"

"You mean, can you trust me? Hell yes."

"The flash drives got switched. The one you got didn't have my mark on it. It wasn't the one that I entered into evidence."

"Jesus H. Christ!"

"All the evidence Vincenzo had put together about the cold case he was investigating is now gone. Someone's dirty around here. Only you, Oatman, Sam, and I know about it so it's important no one else gets wind of it."

"You got it. You know who it is?"

"I've got my suspicions but no evidence. But we're working on it."

"Well, if I can help…."

"Thanks, Sergeant."

At mid-afternoon, Joe's phone rang. It was Denise Thomas, the nurse from the hospital.

"Do you have good news for me?" asked Joe.

"I do, sir. Mr. Fitzgerald is awake. We'll be moving him out of the ICU and into a single room later this afternoon. If things continue to go well, the doctor may allow you to see him for a short period tomorrow."

"Thank you for the phone call. We appreciate you assisting the police."

"No problem."

The news of Fitzgerald's condition raised Joe's low spirits. Tomorrow he and Sam would travel to Methodist Hospital, hoping Fitzgerald could provide them with a description of his assailant, the man who also burglarized Vincenzo's condo.

Chapter Eleven

aptain Vincenzo's funeral was typical of the honors paid to fallen police officers in Chicago. Hundreds of officers in dress uniforms were gathering, and police cars from all over the state and beyond lined the streets. Monitors were set up so the overflow crowds could watch the service from outside the church.

Joe and Destiny arrived early at Saint Ida Catholic Church, where Captain Vincenzo attended Mass. Like other officers, Joe wore his full-dress uniform and came to offer condolences to Mark and Steve Vincenzo and his family, who had gathered prior to the service. The family was speaking with six police captains who Joe assumed were pallbearers. After a few moments, he approached the family.

"Once again, my condolences," said Joe, shaking hands with Mark and then Steve. He introduced Destiny.

"Thanks for getting Dad's condo opened up for us," said Mark. "We appreciate that."

"That's the least I could do."

"This is my wife, Sarah, and my sons, Sal and Tony," said Steve. Turning to Sarah, "This is Detective Joe Erickson, who I told you about."

Joe and Destiny shook hands with each of them. Sarah, a tall, attractive brunette, responded, "It's nice you came, Detective, Ms. Alexander."

"Your father-in-law was a special man. I'll miss him."

Joe stepped over to Sal and Tony. "Your Grandpa was one of the best policemen there was. Everyone thought so. It's an honor to meet you." Then he shook their hands.

When Joe stepped back, he saw a tear running down Sarah's cheek. "Thank you. That was nice of you."

Captain Vincenzo's body was clothed in his full-dress uniform. But it wasn't the man Joe had known for so long. It was simply what was left of him. The real Vincenzo, the one who said, "Get outta here" when he was done with his office visits, the one who would chew him out when he screwed up or wanted something outside the box, was long gone. Who knows? Maybe he would meet Vincenzo again someday when his own time came.

He heard a sniff and looked at Destiny, who was dabbing at tears. "I hate funerals," she said.

"I know. Especially ones like this." Joe put his arm around her. "Let's go sit down."

They turned and walked down the aisle and found a place in a pew near the back. Neither of them spoke. They sat quietly and watched as police officer after police officer, along with city dignitaries, entered the church and sat down. They listened to the organ play. Sam entered, spotted Joe and Destiny, and sat beside them.

Joe had been brought up Catholic due to his mother's faith and had attended funeral Masses in the past, and this one was no different other than a little more pomp and a lot more people. The church was packed with mourners and dignitaries, including the mayor and former mayor. The police commissioner spoke, as did the leader of Chicago's Roman Catholic Archdiocese. Steve read his father's obituary and held up remarkably well until the last couple of sentences. Mark, in his army dress uniform, read a poem and got through it fine.

Outside the Neo-Gothic church building, hundreds of police officers in dress uniforms from all over the state and beyond, some from as far away as South Dakota, were on hand to pay their respects to Captain Salvatore Giovanni Vincenzo. They all stood at attention when his flag-draped casket was carried out of the church to the hearse. Cruiser after cruiser followed the hearse to St. Boniface Catholic Cemetery in a final gesture of farewell to one of their own.

As mourners began filing out of the church, Joe spotted a man in a dress uniform sporting an eyepatch and hoped it was Vincenzo's pal, Nick Esposito. Joe kept his eye on the man and worked his way closer to his location. Once the hearse had pulled out and the man began walking away, Joe walked closer and said, "Nick? Nick Esposito?"

The man stopped, turned, and said, "Yeah?"

"Joe Erickson. I'm a detective with Area 3. I'm investigating Captain Vincenzo's death. His son, Steve, told me you were one of the captain's close friends. Is that correct?"

"Uh-huh."

"I was wondering if there's a time when we could get together and talk."

"I suppose."

"I'm sorry to approach you at a time like this, but being a police sergeant, you know how important it is for us to—"

"You don't have to spell it out," Esposito interrupted. "I worked homicide for fourteen years until this happened," he said, pointing to his eyepatch.

"Ended your career?" asked Joe.

"Gang member's bullet. That piece of shit may have ended my career, but Sal ended his life. For that, I'll always be grateful."

"Sounds like you can provide me with a lot of information."

Esposito nodded. "Well, I'm free tomorrow if you are."

They decided to meet in the late afternoon at a bar and grill on West Peterson Avenue near Esposito's home in the West Ridge neighborhood.

Walking back to Destiny and Sam, Joe explained who the guy was and why it was so important he speak with him.

"So, you set up a meeting already?" asked Sam.

"I did."

Sam turned to Destiny. "Is he this efficient at home?"

"I plead the fifth."

Joe smiled. "Let's go home. I need to get into my regular duds. Sam and I need to go to Methodist Hospital and see if Merlin Fitzgerald can tell us anything helpful."

"Meet you at the hospital at 1:30," said Sam. "Gonna need some time for lunch."

"That goes without saying." Sam got cranky if he missed lunch.

* * *

Joe and Sam checked in with Denise Thomas, the head nurse, who contacted Fitzgerald's doctor. About five minutes later, Dr. Viraj Khatri, greeted them.

"You are here to see Mr. Fitzgerald?"

"If it's possible," said Joe.

"Come with me. Mr. Fitzgerald is awake, but his condition is still serious, so I can only allow you five minutes."

Dr. Khatri led them inside Fitzgerald's room, where a large male nurse stood next to Fitzgerald about to administer an injection.

"Who are you?" Dr. Khatri asked loudly.

The masked nurse threw the syringe at the doctor and pushed Sam aside as he bounded toward the door. Joe grabbed him, and he delivered a hard punch to Joe's ribs. Joe didn't let go and sank his fingers into his neck as he grabbed for his collar. The man managed to open the door and slam it hard on Joe's arm, loosening his grip. He slipped away and ran down the hall, shoving carts into the aisle and causing Joe and Sam to lose ground as they chased him. He opened the door to the stairs and bounded down the steps. Joe and Sam followed hot on his heels. At the bottom of the stairs, the man turned, pulled a small handgun, and fired. Joe had begun to dodge right when he saw the gun. He felt the bullet whiz past his left ear and then heard Sam let out a yell. He turned and saw Sam's expression. He'd been hit.

"Go," yelled Sam, his hand reaching for his upper arm. "I'm okay."

Joe ran after the man, but it was too late. He was already half a block down the street when Joe saw him getting into a car and a driver speeding him away. He couldn't see well enough to get a reading on the license plate.

"Dammit!" yelled Joe, and he ran back into the building to check on Sam.

Sitting on the steps, Sam had removed his jacket and was pressing a handkerchief against his arm just below his shoulder.

"How bad is it?" Joe asked.

Sam removed his handkerchief so Joe could see. "Just a graze. It still burns like hell. I take it you either killed him, or he got away."

"Funny. He had a car with a driver waiting for him. Sped off before I could get a plate number."

"Ten to one it was stolen, anyway."

Joe called in the shooting. Sam walked to the Emergency Room, and before the uniforms showed up, Joe went to check on Fitzgerald. Dr. Khatri and a nurse were at Fitzgerald's bedside checking his vitals.

When Joe walked in, Dr. Khatri turned and said, "He's all right."

"Thank God for that." Spying the syringe on the floor, he said, "Make sure no one touches that syringe. We'll need to examine it for evidence."

"Of course," said the nurse.

"I'll need to put off my questioning of Mr. Fitzgerald. Maybe later this afternoon when things quiet down?"

"That will be fine. Just have the nurse page me," said Dr. Khatri.

Joe went down to the exit door and waited for the uniformed officers to arrive. It wasn't long. Evidence Technicians were on the scene half an hour later. They recovered the .38 caliber slug that grazed Sam's shoulder and bagged the syringe from Fitzgerald's room.

Sam was back on the scene of the shooting thirty minutes later with a gauze wrap around his arm and Tylenol tablets in his pocket.

"How's Fitzgerald?" he asked.

"Fine. It's a good thing we went in there when we did. A minute later, and he might be dead."

"Wish I could say my jacket was fine," said Sam, pointing to the hole in the arm. "I just bought this three weeks ago."

"You can always replace the jacket. We can't replace you."

"Nice of you to say so."

Since the offender was wearing gloves, there was no chance for fingerprints. Joe walked up to Evidence Tech Big John Gustafson, who was processing the scene.

"John, you need to do a scraping of my fingernails. While trying to apprehend the offender, I scratched his neck with my right hand. We may have his DNA here."

"Come with me," said Big John. "If there's DNA under your nails, I'll get it."

Joe sat in a chair while Big John scraped and clipped the fingernails on both of Joe's hands. Big John wanted to do both hands, thinking Joe may have inadvertently picked up DNA on his other hand during the altercation.

Once Big John had finished with him, Joe requested a twenty-four-hour police guard outside Fitzgerald's hospital room.

When they were no longer needed for the investigation by the 20th District officers, Joe and Sam went up to interview Merlin Fitzgerald. All he could tell them about his assailant was that he was taller than him, larger than him, had dark hair, and "creepy eyes like Peter Lorre." Well, with apologies to the late actor who appeared in classic movies in the '30s and '40s, the description fit the man with the syringe in the hospital room, too. Fitzgerald was asleep before the altercation, so he could not confirm it was the same man, but Joe recognized the eyes. It made him wonder why the offender didn't kill Fitzgerald in the condo office when he had the chance and why someone wanted him dead, given how little he knew. Something didn't add up.

As they came out of Fitzgerald's room, two women approached the door. The uniformed officer stopped them and asked them for identification.

"I don't understand," asked the thin, gray-haired woman. "I'm his wife. I was told I could see him. This is my sister." The sister looked similar but was taller and had dark red hair.

Joe stepped in to explain. "Excuse me," he said, identifying himself. "There was an attempt on Merlin Fitzgerald's life earlier, and all visitors are being limited to immediate family as long as they can show proper identification."

"Somebody tried to kill Merlin?" the wife gasped as her sister stood open-mouthed.

"That's right. So, you'll need to prove that you're his wife. It's for his own protection."

Once their identification was confirmed, the officer escorted them inside the room. Joe and Sam stuck around outside. When the women came out, Joe and Sam questioned them to see if Fitzgerald may have confided something. They provided no additional information.

"Creepy eyes. Not a helluva lot to go on," said Sam.

"My gut's telling me Fitzgerald knows something. Why else would someone come into his room and try to kill him?"

An idea popped into Sam's head. "Wait a minute. Maybe he wasn't trying to kill him."

"What do you mean?"

"Maybe the syringe was a threat. What if he was trying to extract information?"

"Then the contents of the syringe should tell the tale, right?"

"Maybe we can lean on Fitzgerald once he's out of the hospital."

"Yeah. Let's get out of here."

When Joe got home, he recounted his experience at the hospital to Destiny, except for the part where the bullet came within a couple inches of his head. No need upsetting her by relating that particular detail.

Chapter Twelve

During his morning jog, it occurred to him that he should speak with the prosecutor in the murder case against Carson Byrne. The prosecutor at the time could have some information that would be helpful in their investigation. Granted, ten years had passed, but Joe hoped that the prosecuting attorney was still working in the Office of the State's Attorney.

Sam sent Joe an email saying he was taking he day off. He had a doctor's appointment to have yesterday's bullet wound dressed.

At mid-morning, Joe made a call to the Cook County Office of the State's Attorney. Explaining to the secretary he wanted to speak with someone who could look up information on an archived case, his call was transferred.

"Good morning. Andrea Butterworth speaking."

"Andrea, this is Detective Joe Erickson. I need someone to look up some information for me."

"What is it you need to know?"

"It involves the prosecution of Carson Byrne for the murder of Troy Winslow ten years ago. I believe it may have had something to do with the case I'm working on. I need to know who the prosecuting attorney was."

"You said ten years ago?"

"Yeah."

"Hm. That's going take some time."

"How much time are we talking about? Do you want me to stay on the line or what?"

"No, it could take me a few minutes. Why don't I call you back?"

"Okay."

"Joe Erickson," said Andrea, repeating his name a second time. "You wouldn't happen to be the detective that solved the serial killer case some time ago, would you?"

Joe was taken aback by this. While he received publicity and a commendation for arresting serial killer David Eugene Burton, he didn't think anyone would associate his name with the case two years later.

"That would be me. How did you know that?"

"I'm a friend of Kirsten Welch. Her sister, Kylie was one of the victims."

"I remember her all too well. Small world. How's she doing?"

"Good. She still goes to therapy, but she's getting along okay."

Joe was glad to hear this since Kirsten was knocked unconscious by Burton when she came home to find him still in her apartment after he killed her sister. "Please tell her I wish her well."

"I will." She took his number. "I should have that information for you in an hour or so."

The David Eugene Burton case would probably haunt Joe for the rest of his life. Tracking down Burton almost destroyed him, but he proved he was resilient enough to overcome the acute stress disorder that resulted from his obsessive search for Burton. Now, he was back on the job and firing on all cylinders. The only residual effect was an occasional nightmare. All of which reminded him that he had a session scheduled with his shrink, Dr. Lemke, that afternoon. Over time, she had cut his appointments from weekly to monthly. Joe was hoping she would eventually cut him loose altogether in the near future.

Half an hour later, Andrea returned his call. "I found what you were looking for."

"That was fast," said Joe.

"Well, my colleague agreed to take my phone calls while I looked up the information for you."

"I appreciate that."

"The prosecuting attorney in the case was none other than our present State's Attorney, Casey Wolff."

"Well, that's good news. I was hoping the person was still employed with the office."

"She sure is. Nothing like getting the head honcho."

This news was both good and bad from Joe's point of view. On the positive side, she was still there, but on the negative side, access to her could be difficult. He would need to contact her office and see how agreeable she would be to an interview. He had never met her and didn't know what she was like personally or professionally. Since it was a few minutes past noon and not a good time to call, he went to the refrigerator to get his lunch and to the coffee pot for a cup of coffee.

Michelle Cardona strolled into the room. Joe was surprised to see her, thinking that she would take a few more days off. When she saw him, she gave him a nod and walked over.

"Hey, Joe." Her attitude a good deal softer than it usually was.

"Hi Michelle," said Joe, calling her by her first name rather than her last like he usually did. "I didn't expect to see you back so soon."

"Need to work. Know anything yet?"

"Not a lot. Following up on what the captain was looking into. We think that's the key to everything."

"You know you can count on me if you need an extra person or another eye."

"I know. Say, I need to talk with you about something, but not here. Like a public place, okay?"

She gave Joe an odd look and said, "O—kay."

"I'll get back with you."

Joe left to go eat lunch at his desk. He knew he could make Cardona aware of the departmental corruption and trusted she would keep it to herself. Besides, he could use another ally inside the department if he needed one.

After eating his arugula salad, Joe looked through his notes and came across Vincenzo's reference to "PT" again, the person he was meeting with on the night he was killed. The identity of that person was still bugging him as he prepared to leave for his meeting with Dr. Lemke.

During his session, Joe described the nightmare he had about getting blown up in his Camaro. It was the first nightmare he had experienced in quite some time, and it disturbed him.

"I sat up in bed yelling," said Joe. "It scared the hell out of Destiny."

"This actually happened to your car, didn't it?" asked Dr. Lemke.

"Yeah. If I hadn't noticed the fingermarks on the rocker panel, I would've been blown up. Just like in the dream."

"You told me you caught the bomber, right?"

"Yeah. And the guy who paid him to do it."

"I see. Have you been under more stress, or have you experienced a traumatic event recently?"

"You've probably heard about Captain Vincenzo's death, right?"

"I have."

"He was my former commanding officer. So, for that reason, it's traumatic. And I'm lead investigator on his case. But that happened after the dream."

"Mm. How are you sleeping?"

"Reasonably well. I'm getting six to seven hours a night. And I'm jogging every morning, eating well. I'm in good shape."

"Are you having any adverse reactions to loud noises?"

"No."

"What about work? Are you bringing it home or leaving it at the office?"

"I've had to work some from home. Not a lot. Destiny gets on my case if I do."

"Good for her. You need to make a clean break once you leave work. It's not good for you to take work home with you."

"I know that. But there's some reading I can't do at work."

"Why is that?"

"I really can't go into that."

"Why not?"

"It's confidential."

"So is this session. You know everything you say to me is strictly private. Doctor-patient confidentiality?"

Joe did not want to reveal any specifics, so he kept his answer general. "Let's just say it involves suspected police corruption. That's all I can say because I don't have enough evidence to point fingers yet."

"So…this is on top of investigating Captain Vincenzo's death?"

"Well, you could say they're intertwined. But it's not like I work for hours and hours at home. But there are certain things I can't bring to work."

Joe noticed Dr. Lemke didn't write any of that down. Instead, she chose to change the subject. "How long has it been between your last nightmare and this one?"

"I don't know. Several months, I guess."

The questions and answers went on for the rest of their session, with Dr. Lemke probing in an attempt to get to the source of Joe's issue. At the end of the session, she voiced her observation.

"If these nightmares continue, I want you to make another appointment. Your PTSD could be worsening because of the bombing. A delayed reaction isn't uncommon in situations like this. I've seen that before. Now, I'd be concerned if they continue. Of course, this could simply be a blip in your recovery. In that case, I don't think it's anything to worry about. Only time will tell."

Joe left his session with mixed feelings. He hoped Dr. Lemke was right in saying his nightmare could be an isolated incident. As he sat in his car, he pulled out his phone and called the number for the Office of the State's Attorney. The person answering the phone transferred him to a representative in Casey Wolff's office. With further explanations, Joe was able to get an appointment with Ms. Wolff the day after tomorrow. He stressed that Ms. Wolff should be informed that the subject of the meeting would involve the Carson Byrne murder case she tried ten years ago.

Chapter Thirteen

A few minutes after 4:00 p.m., Joe walked to a one-story brick building on West Peterson Avenue, a bar where he was scheduled to meet with Nick Esposito. Joe spotted Esposito playing a game of eight-ball on one of the bar's two pool tables. Not wanting to interfere, he ordered a bottle of Heineken dark from the hefty bartender.

After Esposito sank three striped balls, he saw Joe standing at the bar watching. He nodded and continued playing until he put away the eight-ball and won the game. Collecting a twenty-dollar bill from his disgruntled young opponent, he unscrewed his cue, placed it in its case, and walked over to Joe.

"Easy money?" asked Joe.

"It was," smiled Esposito. "He thought this one-eyed old guy would be an easy mark."

"You do this often?"

"Only when these young numbnuts want to play for money."

Joe chuckled as Esposito stepped to the bar and ordered a George Dickel on the rocks. "The best Tennessee whiskey there is. They carry it just for me."

When the bartender brought his drink, Joe followed him to the farthest table, where he sat down.

"So, you're investigating Sal's murder?"

"Yeah."

"Well, I hope you nail the son-of-a-bitch."

"So do I. Since you're one of his best friends…."

71

"I was."

"Is there anything you could tell me about what he may have said? You know, about what he was doing? What he may have been working on?"

After savoring his drink, Esposito said, "Sal was working on that Carson Byrne case again."

"Again?" asked Joe.

"Yeah, again. Every so often, he would pull it out and review it, but nothing would come of it. He'd get frustrated and bury it again. I don't know how many times he'd done that. It was like an obsession."

"Anything different this time?"

"This was his last shot at it. He was going to retire and said he had only one last chance to find the proof. He told me he wanted to blow it wide open before he left the force."

"Was he looking for something in particular? Like another witness or…."

"He told me he suspected Wallingford's killer was a cop."

"A cop?!"

"That's what he said."

"Did he mention a name?"

"Not to me."

"I didn't find anything like that in his notes."

"He may not have put it in his notes if he just suspected it. I mean, suspecting someone doesn't mean jack shit without some kind of corroboration."

"What could he have based that on? He must have gotten it from somewhere. But it may explain a lot."

"What do you mean?"

"Just thinking out loud. Did he mention anything about Troy Winslow or Robert Wallingford?"

"The two murder victims in the Carson Byrne case? Yeah. Everybody knows Byrne killed Winslow, and Wallingford witnessed it. And then Wallingford got knocked off before he could testify. "

"I wonder what evidence Captain Vincenzo was looking for the night he was killed," said Joe. "He was supposed to be meeting with someone he identified as "PT" in his planner. That ring any bells?"

Esposito downed the rest of his bourbon, held up his glass. The bartender acknowledged with a nod.

Esposito thought out loud, "PT. PT." He looked at Joe and said, "Damned if I know. I don't know anyone with those initials. Sorry."

"Is there anything else you can think of that the captain may have said that sticks in your mind?" Joe was hoping for the smallest tidbit of information he did not already have.

Esposito thought for a minute, and then his eyes brightened. "There's one thing, and it may not mean anything. But he said he thought there's damning evidence that would ruin Byrne if it ever got out."

"Ruin Byrne? Not convict him?"

"No. 'Ruin Byrne.' Those were his words. 'Ruin Byrne.'"

"Hm. I wonder if that was at the heart of the blackmail scheme."

"Coulda been. I dunno. But if Sal could tie Byrne to having Wallingford killed, it would definitely ruin the hell out of him," chuckled Esposito.

"Yeah." *What did Byrne do that was so serious it could ruin his reputation and be worth killing people to keep it secret?*

Buzz walked up and set Esposito's drink on the table.

"Another Heineken?" Buzz asked Joe.

"I'm good," said Joe, handing him a ten-dollar bill. "Keep it."

"Thanks," said Esposito. "You're a good man."

As Joe took another drink of his Heineken, a gray-haired man in his fifties walked up to the table. "Is this a private party, or can I join you?"

"Sit down," said Esposito. "Meet Joe Erickson. This is a buddy of mine, Will Caruso." After exchanging handshakes, Esposito explained, "Will's retired from the twenty-third. Joe works out of Area 3. He's investigating Sal's murder."

"Oh, yeah?" said Caruso. "Any leads?"

"A few. It's still pretty early. You knew the captain, too?"

"Not really. I mean, we'd met a few times, but I can't really say I knew him. Not like Nick here."

Joe took the last swallow of his beer, put the empty bottle on the table, and slid his chair back. "Thanks for your time, Nick. I need to get moving."

"Stick around. Don't let me spoil the party," said Caruso.

"It's not you. I have a dinner date, so I need to get home."

"She good lookin'?"

"As a matter of fact, she is. Take care, fellas."

As Joe left the bar, he felt good about his meeting with Esposito. He learned two important things. Captain Vincenzo believed a cop was responsible for killing Robert Wallingford, and there was some kind of damning evidence against Carson Byrne. Whether it was the blackmail information, he didn't know. But he guessed PT, whoever he is, knows something about it.

Joe returned his squad car to Area 3 and took an Uber home. Destiny was pulling her Mercedes into the garage as Joe got out of the car. He entered the kitchen at the same time Destiny opened the door from the garage.

"Hi," said Destiny, clad in her workout clothes. "We timed this just right, didn't we?"

"Yeah. How was your workout?"

"Getting back into shape is hard. But I'm getting there. Are you still cooking tonight?"

"Planning on it."

Since Destiny would occasionally eat fish, Joe made a mixed green salad followed by pan-seared sea bass with lemon caper butter over a bed of garlic cauliflower mash. He had prepared it one other time, and Destiny loved it. She loved it again.

When they adjourned to the living room, Destiny asked, "Did you make any progress on the case today?"

"Some."

"Well, are you going to tell me or leave me hanging, Mr. Detective?"

Joe laughed. "Okay. Vincenzo's close friend, Nick Esposito, told me Vincenzo was looking for what he called 'damning evidence' on Carson Byrne. Said it was enough to 'ruin him.' That was the term he used. 'Ruin.' I don't know if it was at the center of the blackmail scheme or if it was something different."

Destiny thought for a second and said, "Ruin implies a professional loss of fortune or career."

"That's what I thought."

"What do you know about Byrne?"

"He's rich, politically ambitious, slick, never married, appears to be a player. But he keeps a low profile and isn't seen in public much."

"Let's brainstorm this. What negative things, if they got out, could ruin a person in the public's eye?"

"He's found to be a murderer," said Joe.

"Or a thief, or an embezzler," replied Destiny.

"A pervert."

"Human trafficker, drug trafficker."

"Abusive, assaults women."

"Tax evader, bribe taker."

They stopped and looked at one another. "Anyone of those things could be used against him by an opponent in an election, and he could lose his seat as an alderman," said Destiny.

"And most could land him in prison."

"Murder, embezzling, trafficking, tax evasion. Those things could not only ruin him politically but ruin his business interests if he was arrested."

"And motivate an ambitious person like Byrne to kill his blackmailer or anyone else who could threaten to expose him. Now, I just have to figure out what kind of damning evidence is out there."

"Shouldn't be that hard," said Destiny with a twinkle.

"Oh, yeah. Piece of cake."

Chapter Fourteen

On Thursday, Joe drove to the West Washington Street address of the building housing the Office of the Cook County State's Attorney. Arriving fifteen minutes early for his eleven o'clock meeting, he took the elevator to Suite 3200, Casey Wolff's office. He was greeted by a young woman in a dark blue business suit.

"Good morning. I'm Detective Joe Erickson. I have an appointment with the State's Attorney at eleven o'clock."

"Yes. Good morning, Detective," she said. "I'm Jada Robinson, Ms. Wolff's administrative assistant. Nice to meet you."

They shook hands, and Robinson said, "If you'll have a seat, Ms. Wolff's expecting you. She'll see you in a few minutes."

"Thank you."

Joe checked his phone for messages and began replying to one from Sam. In the middle of his reply, the door to Wolff's office opened.

"Detective Erickson?" asked the woman.

Rising from his chair, Joe said, "Yes."

"I'm Casey Wolff."

"Thank you for seeing me. I'm a little early for our meeting."

"Early is fine. Why don't you come in."

"Sit down, detective," she said, pointing to a chair in front of her desk. She walked around her desk and sat in a large leather chair. "So, I'm told you're investigating the Carson Byrne murder case."

"I am."

"Why are you interested in a ten-year-old cold case?"

"I'm investigating the murder of Captain Sal Vincenzo, and he was investigating that case when he was killed. Based on what I've gleaned from his recent notes, and documentation from the police investigation, I believe he was getting close to evidence that would blow the cold case wide open. We're working on the theory he was killed to quash his investigation into that case. Shortly after Vincenzo was killed, his home was burglarized, and the files he amassed were stolen. On top of that, a critical piece of evidence disappeared from the Area 3 evidence locker."

"Really."

"Sadly, yes."

"Hm…That's disturbing. Well, what would you like to know?"

"I've gone over everything in the Byrne murder case. Read all the reports, interviews, notebooks, and so on. One of Vincenzo's friends recently told me he was looking for something that would ruin Byrne. 'Ruin' is the word he used. I don't know if that was something Winslow was using to blackmail Byrne or if this is something new."

Wolff nodded. "I understand. Well, if this pertains to the blackmail Winslow was using against Byrne, Robert Wallingford was not very forthcoming about what it was. He refused to give specifics which we found quite frustrating. He said it would come out in his court testimony because he didn't trust revealing the physical evidence beforehand."

"He had physical evidence of some kind?"

"Wallingford told us he was given taped evidence by a private investigator who was dying of cancer. He wanted Wallingford to have it. He played it for Winslow, and the two of them concocted a scheme to blackmail Byrne."

"A tape…This information wasn't in any of the evidence files or in any of Vincenzo's notes," said Joe.

"No, it wouldn't have been because we granted Wallingford immunity on the blackmail case if he would testify against Byrne. He was not only an eyewitness to Winslow's murder, but also a witness to the motive for Winslow's murder. Our whole case hinged on his testimony."

"Do you have any idea who killed Wallingford?"

"No. Whoever did it knew how to cover his tracks."

"Vincenzo told his buddy he believed Wallingford's killer was a cop. It's something Vincenzo said in passing, but I haven't found anything to substantiate it."

"A cop?"

"Yeah. Speaking of cops, I want to alert you to corruption inside Area 3 regarding this case."

"Explain."

"I discovered a flash drive with Vincenzo's research in his home. I took it to the evidence locker myself and witnessed it being logged in. When I asked to have the information on it printed out, so I could have an official copy, it was carried by Sergeant Oatman, the officer in charge of the evidence locker, to my superior, Lieutenant Yvonne Briggs' office. In the process, the flash drive got switched with one that was blank."

"How do you know the one you entered into evidence wasn't blank?"

"Because the blank one didn't have my little mark on it. I've known Sergeant Bill Oatman for years. He wouldn't have made the switch."

"So, who do you suspect?"

"Someone higher up."

"And you're sure the original flash drive wasn't blank?"

"Just between you and me? I made a copy before entering it into evidence. That's how I have Captain Vincenzo's files. Only you, my partner, and I know that."

"I don't condone what you did, detective. But under the circumstances, it turned out to be a good move on your part."

"Someone has a long reach in this case if they can destroy evidence inside Area 3. I'm reluctant to enter anything else I might find into our evidence locker. What do you suggest?"

"Well..." considered Wolff. "If it's something that can be copied, like a flash drive, an audio or videotape, I would suggest making a copy and keeping the original in a safe place. If the copy disappears, you'll still have the original. If that happens, I want you to contact me right away. I'll make sure we get an investigation underway. We need to get to the bottom of this."

Joe left his meeting with Casey Wolff with her direct phone number and secure in the knowledge she would have his back regarding the submission of copies of evidence. The meeting also revealed that the damning evidence Vincenzo was looking for might have been in the form of something on tape.

Since he was downtown, Joe treated himself to a sit-down lunch at an excellent Russian restaurant on East Adams Street, one he and Destiny had patronized many times. When he walked in, he saw his Detective Commander, Dale Edwardson, sitting at a table by himself. Edwardson saw Joe and called him over.

"You dining with anyone?" Edwardson asked.

"As a matter of fact, no," said Joe. "I was downtown and decided to come here for lunch."

"Well, you can join me if you like. I'm not expecting anyone."

Joe wasn't about to turn down an invitation from his commanding officer, so he pulled up a chair. Joe suspected Edwardson was curious about how the investigation was going into Vincenzo's death. Joe was reluctant to discuss anything substantial with Edwardson, not knowing if he might be involved with Carson Byrne. They discussed the case, but Joe kept the details general and mentioned nothing about suspected corruption within Area 3. He didn't get the impression Edwardson was involved in the conspiracy since he didn't press Joe for critical details. Their lunch was cordial, and Joe felt good about him after they had finished. Maybe the circle of conspirators was small.

Once back at Area 3, he sat down at his computer to begin entering what he had learned from Casey Wolff into his computer. But shortly after he had begun, he was contacted by the duty sergeant about a thirty-year-old man who was found dead in an apartment in Lakeview.

Joe and Sam drove to the North Sheffield Avenue address, arriving at the same time as the Medical Examiner. They greeted Kendra, who stepped from the ME's van, and the three of them were directed by a uniformed officer to the fifth floor where the victim's apartment was located.

They began by questioning the man's girlfriend, Stephanie Pappas, who discovered his lifeless body in the bathtub. She was standing in the hall with Officer Alicia Howard, one of the responding officers from the 19th District.

"What was the name of the deceased?" asked Joe.

"Peter Christoph," Pappas responded, dabbing her eyes with a tissue.

"What was your relationship with him?"

"He's my boyfriend."

"Did he have any medical issues that you know of?"

"He had epilepsy, but he hadn't had a seizure for months. He thought he had them under control," she said, dissolving into tears.

"What kind of seizures would he have?" asked Sam.

"Grand mal."

"Do you know if he was taking his medication?"

"I don't know. I assumed he was, but...."

"What?"

"He always complained his pills made him feel tired."

Joe turned to Sam. "I'd better let Kendra know about his epilepsy."

He stepped inside the door and called, "Kendra!"

"What is it?"

"His girlfriend just told us the victim was an epileptic. Prone to grand mal seizures."

"Good to know. Thanks," she said and continued on her way into the bathroom.

Once Kendra had completed her work, she told them the preliminary cause of death was drowning. An autopsy would be conclusive.

Three hours after they arrived, Joe and Sam were on their way back to Area 3 so a call could be made to the police department in Galesburg, Illinois, where the deceased man's parents lived. The notification would be made by an officer from the Galesburg Police Department.

Joe wished he would not have to be called out on cases like this. If only he and Sam could concentrate exclusively on Vincenzo's case and let other detectives investigate all the new deaths. But that's not the way the detective business works.

Chapter Fifteen

During his ride home, Joe thought about what he had learned so far and what he could do to root out more leads. It occurred to him that meeting with his former drinking buddies could prove beneficial. He had given up seeing these cops once he decided to turn his life around and get into good physical shape, but it would be worth a trip to the bar for a chance to pick their brains.

When he arrived home, Destiny was busy working at her laptop. She saw him grab a bottle of water from the refrigerator and closed her laptop.

"What's this? No wine today?"

"No, I'm saving myself for tonight. I'm going out. You know those guys I used to drink with at Benny's a while back? Before I met you?"

"Yeah, you told me about them," she said with a note of curiosity in her voice.

"I thought I would join them tonight and see if any of them might know something about Carson Byrne. You know, the kind of stuff that doesn't show up in research on the net."

"You mean 'gossip,' don't you?"

"I prefer to call it 'rumor and innuendo.'"

"Okay," chuckled Destiny. "I'll remember that."

"You never know what you might learn from a bunch of cops sitting around drinking."

"I can only imagine." She paused. "On second thought, no, I can't. You're not going to get drunk, are you?"

Joe laughed. "Are you kidding? I'll have one scotch and something with no alcohol after that. I'll probably be calling for an Uber by eleven."

"Well, then, instead of calling for an Uber, call me. I'll pick you up, and we'll have a late supper somewhere. How about that?"

Joe slipped his arm around her and said, "That sounds great. Gotta place in mind?"

"Uh-huh."

"Gonna tell me?"

"Nope."

At 8:30, Joe arrived at Benny's Place, a bar often frequented by Chicago's finest. An old establishment with a neighborhood charm that had not been updated in years. The old wooden bar ran twenty feet down one side with stools in front and a mirror on the wall behind it. Wooden booths lined one wall, while well-worn tables and metal chairs filled the rest of the room.

When Joe walked through the door, he spotted the same group of guys sitting at their usual table: Mike Bridges, Mitch Williams, and Tony Edwards, detectives from Area 1, and Vince Murphy, a uniformed officer from the 18th.

When Mike, a former star linebacker for the University of Illinois, saw Joe enter, he exclaimed loudly, "Well, I'll be damned. The prodigal son hath returned!"

Greetings, quips, and laughter followed as Joe pulled up a chair and sat down. The old camaraderie was still there despite the fact Joe had not joined them for over a year.

"I hear you got yourself a 'significant other'," said Mike.

"I did."

"And she let you out of the house?" asked the freckle-faced Vince.

"No, I escaped."

"What she sees in an ugly guy like you, I'll never know."

"Isn't my money, that's for sure."

"Heard you bought a house, too," said Mitch.

"We did," said Joe.

"He probably can't afford to drink with us anymore."

"How did you know that?"

"We're detectives. We detect," said Vince. Laughter followed.

As they were yucking it up, Lucy, the barmaid, walked over to the table. "Hello, stranger. Long time no see."

"I see you're still here," replied Joe.

"Always. Double scotch on the rocks?"

"You still remember. No, make it a single. I'm out of shape."

"Gotcha." She walked back to the bar.

Joe turned back to the guys and said, "So, what else have you detected?"

"Heard you're handling your former lieutenant's murder. That right?" asked Mike.

"Yeah. Sam and I are pursuing leads. Vincenzo was working on a cold case when he was killed. You know the Carson Byrne murder case?"

"That was ten years ago," said Tony in his deep, authoritative voice.

"Yeah. Vincenzo arrested Byrne for killing Troy Winslow, who was supposedly blackmailing him."

"The eyewitness was found murdered the day before he was scheduled to testify. I remember all about that," said Tony. "Byrne walked."

"Byrne was behind it, but nobody could prove it," said Vince. "He was good at covering his ass."

"So, he got off?" asked Mitch.

"Yeah. Without its main witness, the state had no case," said Joe.

"So, what was Vincenzo investigating?" asked Mike.

"Who killed Robert Wallingford, the eyewitness. Wallingford was working with Winslow to blackmail Byrne, and supposedly he had something on tape that was being used to blackmail him. That's what Vincenzo was after."

"Audiotape or videotape?" asked Mitch.

"Don't know. It came from a PI," said Joe. "It could be on tape from a bug that was planted, for all I know."

"Don't you think Byrne would've destroyed it?" asked Mitch. "He cleaned up everything else."

"Apparently, Vincenzo didn't think so."

"So, what would've been on the tape?" asked Mike.

"Something that would've ruined him. That's what Vincenzo told one of his friends."

"Something scandalous," said Mitch. "What? Was he gay or something?"

"In this day and age, I doubt that would've ruined him," said Mike.

"Whenever he's seen in public, he always has a good-looking woman on his arm," added Vince. "The guy's a player."

"It would be my guess the tape was evidence of him taking a bribe," said Mike. "He's a public figure. What else could ruin him?"

"A payoff from someone important would do it," said Vince.

"I think he's a pervert," said Tony, taking a swig from his beer.

"Who's a pervert?" asked Lucy, setting down Joe's scotch.

"Vince," said Mitch.

Vince slowly raised his middle finger in response.

"Really? I knew there was something I liked about you, Vince. Refills, anybody?" Mike and Mitch both requested beers, and Lucy returned to the bar.

"So, why do you think Byrne's a pervert, Tony?" asked Joe.

"Those pretty girls he's with are just beards. If you ask me, he bats for the other team."

"Being gay doesn't mean he's a pervert," said Mike.

"Hey. Just sayin'."

"Whatever," said Mike. "Did you know Tony's retiring next month?"

"No, I hadn't heard," said Joe. "Congratulations, Tony."

"Thanks."

"You gonna move to Florida and open a bar?"

"Shi-i-i-t," chuckled Tony. "That'd be the day."

"He's gonna stay home and watch reruns of Hogan's Heroes," razzed Mitch.

"Gonna have to get a job, so I don't have to look at the old lady twenty-four-seven."

"Or she you."

Lucy returned with the beers, and after she left, Joe got up with his empty scotch glass and walked to the bar. Reaching in his wallet, he pulled a twenty and gave it to Lucy, saying, "From now on, give me apple juice on the rocks instead of scotch. Just between you and me, okay?"

"Sneaky. Okay. Your secret's safe with me." She took the twenty. "I'll bring your 'scotch' in a minute."

Over the next couple of hours, he downed two more apple juices with no one suspecting. When Lucy delivered the third one, he gave Destiny a call to come pick him up.

Twenty minutes later, Destiny walked through the door. Mitch noticed first. "Whoa! Look what walked in."

They all turned and looked. They watched as Destiny walked over, pulled up a chair next to Joe, and sat down. Everyone was speechless.

"Well, are you going to introduce me?"

"Of course." Pointing to them one by one, Joe said, "This is Mike Bridges, Tony Edwards, Mitch Williams, and Vince Murphy. Guys, meet Destiny Alexander."

After various clumsy greetings, Destiny said, "Nice to meet all of you. Actually, Joe's told me nothing about you."

"Probably for good reason," said Vince.

Lucy walked over to the table and asked, "Can I get you something?"

"No, thanks," replied Destiny. "I'm just here to pick up Joe."

As Lucy walked away, Destiny reached over, picked up Joe's glass. She took a sip and then tipped it up and killed it, much to the surprise of all the cops at the table. "Ah. That hit the spot," she said. The men's jaws dropped a little.

Sliding her hand up Joe's arm, she said, "You ready to go, honey?"

"Yeah." Joe made a show of looking at his watch. "Looks like it's about bedtime."

"It is." They stood. "Nice meeting you, guys," said Destiny. "Be safe."

"See you guys," said Joe.

The men uttered good-byes in return. As Joe and Destiny walked toward the door, Joe called out, "Thanks, Lucy."

"No problem, Joe. Come back soon."

Mike watched them leave and then turned back to the guys at the table. "Man! No wonder Joe stays at home."

Chapter Sixteen

On Saturday, Joe thought about what Mike had suggested: Byrne may have been caught on video taking a bribe. Joe searched Vincenzo's notes and could find nothing corroborating such a theory. But there was nothing that suggested anything else, either. He needed to find the identity of PT. Who would know? Who would be a good source of information? Then it dawned on him: Margaret Kummeyer, the reporter for the Tribune. She owed him for all the scoops he'd given her, so he decided to give her a call.

"Joe, to what do I owe the pleasure?"

"Can we meet somewhere? I need to talk to you, and I don't want to do it over the phone."

"Ooh, sounds serious."

"I want to pick your brain about something."

"Then, it's definitely serious. How about lunch today?"

"Suits me. Where?"

"We both live in the same area. How about the Whiskey Café on North Lincoln Avenue? Serbian food. You know it?"

"Yeah, as a matter of fact, we've eaten there before. Good choice."

"Twelve-thirty? I'll call for a reservation."

Joe pocketed his phone as Destiny walked into the room. "Sounds like you have a date for lunch."

"Yeah. Margaret Kummeyer from the Tribune. I'm hoping she can give me something on Carson Byrne I don't already know."

"Is she good-looking?" Destiny asked, kidding him.

"Not especially. Rather plain. She might be attractive if she'd bother to fix herself up, but she's one of those types who never wears makeup and always looks thrown together. Good reporter, though."

"So, I don't have to worry?"

Joe got off his stool and kissed her. "Nope. I'd invite you along, but—"

"I'd cramp your style?" she asked.

"You'd probably intimidate her. On second thought, I don't think anyone could intimidate Margaret. But you might cramp her style."

"I wasn't trolling for lunch with you. I've already made plans. Liz and I are going out to lunch."

"Where you going?"

"We're going to try out a vegan kitchen on North Broadway. One of her friends was raving about it. We'll see if it lives up to the hype."

At 12:20, Joe's Uber dropped him off at the North Lincoln Avenue address where the Whiskey Café was located. He spotted Margaret sitting in a booth farthest from the door. Looking up, she saw him and gave a little wave.

"Hello, Margaret. How are things?"

"Same old, same old. I see you bought a house."

"How is it everybody knows we bought a house?"

"Real estate transactions are published, you know."

"And you read that boring stuff?"

"I glance through them to see if there's anything interesting, and I happened to see your name there."

The waiter came with menus and glasses of water. "Could I interest you in a beverage of some kind?"

"I'll have a glass of Chardonnay," replied Margaret.

"A glass of Pinot Noir for me," said Joe.

They looked at the menus for a few moments, and then Margaret said, "I don't know about you, but I'm famished."

"I'm fairly hungry myself."

When the waiter came back with their wine, he took their orders: grilled chicken breast with mushrooms for Margaret and salmon for Joe.

"So…What's so urgent you need to pick my brain?"

"You can't write about any of this yet, okay? But you know I'm lead detective on Captain Vincenzo's murder."

"Yeah, I'm aware of that."

"He was investigating a ten-year-old cold case. The Carson Byrne murder case, and he was focusing on who killed Robert Wallingford. It's never been solved. We think that's what got him killed."

"Ah. You think someone associated with that old case shut him up?"

"Yeah. I've done a lot of research on Carson Byrne. We think Vincenzo was looking for a recording that Troy Winslow was using to blackmail him. A couple of things have been said about Byrne but haven't been confirmed. Any innuendo floating around about him?"

"There have been allegations of sexual abuse in the past, but those allegations have somehow evaporated. I don't know if he paid people hush money or what. But he was never charged with anything."

"So, women have filed complaints against him, and the complaints went away?" asked Joe.

"Evidently. Now, I can't verify any of it. It's rumor, and there's nothing solid I've ever been able to turn up."

Joe took a drink of his wine and thought, *If someone filed a complaint, there'd be a paper trail. Those things simply don't go away.*

Margaret saw he was thinking about something and asked, "What?"

"Oh...Is there anything else about Byrne that seems odd?"

"Well, he's never been married, but he's always seen in the company of beautiful women, and he's quite wealthy. So, one would assume he enjoys playing the field. At least he doesn't get married and divorced numerous times like some rich guys do.

"Any rumors about him being gay?"

"Well, he's never been married, so...but nothing has ever come out about him being gay. It wouldn't be good for his image if it did. He courts the Christian right as well as the black and brown communities quite successfully. He wouldn't want to alienate any of those constituents."

"He seems to guard his private life. You seldom see him in public. If you do, it's with one of his girlfriends or the kids on the sports teams he sponsors."

One thing I find unusual—he does take a lot of trips to Mexico."

"Mexico?" asked Joe.

"Yeah. Maybe he has a place down there or something. Who knows, maybe he likes the climate."

"It's got to be more than that."

"What happens in Mexico stays in Mexico?" joked Margaret.

"Drugs?"

"Not him. He's very anti-drug. He gives a lot of money to drug rehab programs for teenagers."

"One of my colleagues suggested the tape used to blackmail Byrne could have been a video showing him taking a bribe. Does that sound plausible to you?"

"He's a public figure. He's certainly open to being bribed, but I've never heard rumors of him being corrupt. But that doesn't mean he's squeaky clean, either."

"It was serious enough that he killed Troy Winslow over it."

"Hm. Whatever was on it must have been pretty bad for him to go that far."

Their food arrived, and the conversation turned to more pleasant things. The food was excellent, and once they had finished, the subject reverted back to Joe's investigation.

"There's other stuff going on here, Margaret. I'll give you the scoop once we've got all our ducks in a row. But someone is behind eliminating evidence in this case. Vincenzo's condo was burglarized, his laptop and all his research were stolen. And a flash drive with his documentation disappeared from the Area 3 evidence locker."

"No shit?"

"Yeah. Someone has a long reach and wants this covered up."

"Wow...but you're not going to let this go, are you?"

"Not hardly. And some heads are gonna roll when we're done."

"I hope so. Vincenzo was a good cop. Straight shooter. He deserved his retirement."

Joe tipped up his glass and drank the last little bit of his wine. Margaret noticed. "Another glass?"

"Thanks, but I only have one drink a day nowadays. I'm no fun anymore."

Margaret grinned, "Oh, I doubt that. I've seen Destiny Alexander."

The waiter came by, and Joe asked for the tab. He called for an Uber, and on their way out of the café, Margaret assured him everything they discussed was off the record. But she said she was looking forward to the scoop.

"You'll be the first I call, Margaret. As always."

"Cool beans, Joe."

Joe's Uber pulled up, and they parted company. As he rode home, Joe thought about what he had learned from Margaret. *Allegations of sexual abuse going away, periodic trips to Mexico. Maybe the payoffs had something to do with one or both of these things. But payoffs to whom?*

Chapter Seventeen

Back at work on Monday, Joe began researching if there were any complaints made against Carson Byrne. He found none. He decided to email the detectives who were part of Area 3 ten years ago to see if any of them remembered any such complaints.

An hour later, Gary Nelson walked up to Joe's desk. Dirty Gary, as he was known to more than a few, because he had eyes that would make the toughest guys flinch. "Got your email."

"Oh, yeah? You remember something about Byrne?"

"I didn't follow up on any complaints back then. But a friend of mine over in the 19th told me a complaint was filed against Byrne. About harassment or abuse or something. But I don't have the details. I mean, it was quite a few years ago."

"You have a name?" asked Joe.

"Yeah, but it won't do you any good. He's retired and playin' cowboy in New Mexico."

"Shit!"

"Not much help, I know. But if there was a complaint, evidently nothing came of it. Maybe it got withdrawn. I was working Special Investigations at the time, and I don't remember any call to check it out."

"You think if it came through, someone here might have buried it?"

"Somebody at the top, you mean?"

"Possibly."

"You never know. If somebody did, good luck proving it."

"Yeah. Thanks, Gary."

"See ya." And he turned and walked away.

Joe made notes and thought maybe he was going off on a tangent, and this business about a complaint filed against Byrne was taking time from the main thrust of his investigation. But maybe it would loop back and connect somehow. He had one more person to contact.

He walked to the desk of Duty Sergeant Rodney Brown, who was working in the same position ten years ago when Vincenzo and Smith were detectives. He thought perhaps Brown would recall something about Byrne. But the sergeant had a desk outside Lieutenant Briggs' office, and he didn't want Briggs getting any ideas. So, he sent Brown an email saying he needed to speak to him during his lunch break. Brown agreed to stop by Joe's desk when he was off.

Shortly after noon, a curious Brown showed up at Joe's desk.

"What's going on?"

"Let's step out in the parking lot," said Joe. "I need to keep this on the QT."

"You think there's spies in here or something?" joked Brown.

"You never know."

"Okay."

They walked out of the building and into the parking lot. The noonday sun was intense, and coming out of the air-conditioned building was not pleasant. Joe spotted a shaded area and walked over to it.

Joe asked an already sweating Brown, "I didn't want to ask questions within earshot of Lieutenant Briggs."

"Okay. This have something to do with your investigation into Captain Vincenzo's death?"

"Maybe. You were a duty sergeant ten years ago, right?"

"Right."

"So, do you remember any complaints filed against Carson Byrne? Seems there was one filed in the 19th, but it wasn't investigated through Area 3."

"I remember one…vaguely. Because somebody made it go away."

"Quashed it?"

"Uh-huh."

"That was right before I got here. Who was the lieutenant, then?"

"Crouse. Not long after that, he got promoted and became Commander when William Blackmore retired."

"Jerome Crouse, right?"

"Yeah, he's a big cheese now that he's retired. Consults for the mayor's office."

Joe picked up on the disdain in his voice. "You didn't like him much?"

"Let's just say I liked working for Lieutenant Vincenzo a lot better."

"You think it was Crouse who buried that complaint?" asked Joe.

"I don't know."

"Was it a sexual abuse complaint??

"I...don't remember. Sorry."

"That's okay. I just needed to know if the complaint came over from the 19th because I couldn't find any documentation on it. You think the order to bury it could have come down from Commander Blackmore?"

"Doubt it," said Brown. "He was a straight shooter all the way. Unless it came from the very top, and it bypassed him."

"Gotcha. Thanks, Sergeant. I owe you. Let's get back inside before we sweat out our clothes."

After eating his lunch, Joe called and spoke to the desk sergeant at District 19. Sergeant Ford remembered Joe, having spoken to him months before when the suspect who blew up Joe's Camaro was detained and interrogated there.

"Hello, Detective. What can I do for you?" asked Ford when Joe identified himself.

"I need someone who can conduct a search of your records for an investigation I'm working on. Can you put me in touch with the right person?"

"Uh...yeah. I can transfer you. Hold on."

The line went silent for a few seconds. Then an older male voice answered. "Sergeant Dennis."

"This is Detective Joe Erickson from Area 3. I'm investigating the death of Captain Sal Vincenzo, and I need someone to look up a complaint lodged against Carson Byrne in your office ten years ago. Your desk sergeant transferred me to you."

"Well, you got the right person. I can look that up for you, but it'll take a while. When do you need it?"

"It's a priority."

"All right. I don't suppose you have a date?"

"Sorry, I don't. But I can tell you it was probably made prior to July."

"That helps some. I'll try to get back to you sometime this week," said Dennis.

"That would be great. Thanks, Sergeant." Joe gave him his cell phone number and ended the call. He hoped there would be some documentation left in the files at the 19th.

Shortly after 1:15 p.m., Joe and Sam got called out to investigate the discovery of a body next to a self-storage unit on North Broadway. The victim was found by a renter picking up items from his unit. Although Joe felt compassion for the young man who had been shot to death, he was annoyed. The call had taken them away from their investigation into Vincenzo's death. *Why wasn't another team called upon to take the call? Their caseload was already full.*

Joe had been documenting the number of times he and Sam had been called out to investigate murders compared to other teams on their watch. They were called out three times when Nelson and Chen weren't called out at all, and Cardona and Murphy were called only once. Their investigation into Vincenzo's death was being stonewalled, and Joe was getting tired of it. He was getting ready to file a grievance with his union rep, something that would surely piss off Lieutenant Briggs. Joe knew she was complicit in the corruption going on, but he couldn't prove anything. At least, not yet. For now, he would have to go through official channels to get her off their backs and protect their investigation.

The Uber dropped Joe off at home around 5:30. When he came through the front door, he was greeted by Destiny and her friend, Liz, cooking up a storm in the kitchen. Liz brought her six-month-old Lhasa Apso puppy, who treated Joe with suspicion. Destiny kissed him and handed him a glass of Pinot Noir.

Looking at the pup, Joe said, "I see we have a four-legged guest."

"That's Autumn," said Liz.

Joe kneeled down and said, "Hi there, Autumn." He held out his hand, expecting the long-haired pup to come to him or at least sniff his hand. Instead, she just sat there, looking him over.

Liz chuckled. "Typical Lhasa. It takes them a while to check you out and see if you're worthy of their attention."

Standing, Joe said, "Must be a smart dog. I wouldn't trust me, either."

He was tired and really didn't want to interfere with their cooking, but their energy was infectious and buoyed his spirits.

Liz was the same age as Destiny, and they had been friends since high school. They sometimes worked out together, but she was not into martial arts like Destiny. Her husband, an attorney, was someone Joe didn't mind being around. Despite being rich, he was a fellow gearhead who loved high-performance cars and didn't mind getting his hands dirty working on them.

"I think I'll adjourn to the living room," said Joe.

"Do we intimidate you?" teased Liz.

"You do. I'm no match for the two of you."

"Well, at least you admit it."

"Hey, I know when I'm out of my league," he said with a smile as he left the room.

He sat down on the couch, kicked off his shoes, and began reading an article in one of his car magazines. He took a couple of drinks from his wine and continued reading. An hour later, Destiny was waking him up.

"Joe. Joe. Hey, babe," she said, giving his shoulder a little shake.

"Wh-What?"

"It's six-thirty. You've been asleep for an hour."

"Wow."

"I guess I don't have to ask how your day was, huh?"

"Busy," he said, looking up at her. "Mentally, it was tiring."

Destiny held up her phone and said, "Autumn checked you out and decided you were okay." She showed Joe a picture of him sleeping with Autumn curled up beside him. "Isn't that cute?"

"Cute. Jeez."

"I think you made a friend. You hungry?"

"I don't know yet. Probably."

"Liz and I made some really good food. It's ready whenever you are."

"Come here," he said, pulling her down on the couch next to him. They kissed. "The food will get cold," she said.

"We can heat things up, can't we?"

"Ohhhhh, yeah!"

Chapter Eighteen

J oe contacted the other homicide teams and found he and Sam had
been sent out thirty percent more often since they began investigating
Vincenzo's death. He knew that had to be the result of a directive from
Lieutenant Briggs through one of the duty sergeants. It wasn't coming from
Sergeant Rodney Brown because Briggs would have known he would refuse
to assign them overloads. It had to have been one of the other sergeants, but
Joe was not going to confront them. He wanted to go through appropriate
channels, so he filed a grievance with the union.

As part of a search for information on the charge filed against Byrne, Joe
contacted retired Captain Jerome Crouse and asked for a meeting. He agreed
to meet him at two o'clock that afternoon in his office at City Hall, where he
worked as a consultant to the mayor. Joe was after two bits of information:
the charge against Byrne and Crouse's reaction to his questioning. Joe didn't
know Crouse despite the fact he was functioning as Area North Commander
when Joe first became a detective. The Commander is an administrator
who doesn't have the kind of interaction with detectives that sergeants and
lieutenants do. When the Areas were reconfigured, and their Area North
office became Area 3, Crouse had already retired.

Later that morning, Joe received a call on his cell phone.

"This is Sergeant Jason Dennis calling from the 19th."

"Yes, Sergeant."

"Well, I searched our records for that complaint against Carson Byrne, and
I couldn't find any digital records. But I went through our paper files and
found something unusual."

"And what was that?"

"There was file folder on him. But it was empty. Nothing in it."

"How do you explain that?"

"I can't."

"So, do you have any guesses?"

"If I didn't know better, I'd say somebody didn't want a record of whatever was in there and removed it. But you didn't hear that from me."

"If someone wanted to destroy evidence, I wonder why they didn't take the entire file."

"Maybe whoever did it wasn't the sharpest knife in the drawer. Most of the time, criminals get caught because they're stupid, you know?"

"Yeah. Thanks for checking. I appreciate you taking the time."

"Just catch the guy who knocked off Vincenzo, okay?"

At noon, Joe and Sam drove down to the Loop. City Hall was located on North LaSalle Street, and Joe knew of a good restaurant nearby where they could have a decent meal before their meeting with Crouse at two o'clock.

The Reid Murdoch Building housed a restaurant that Joe liked, and he convinced Sam that if he ate there, his taste buds would have a "culinary orgasm." Sam was skeptical and would have been happy grabbing something at Burger King, but he agreed. He seldom ate lunch at a place with cloth napkins and tablecloths.

They spent an hour eating some excellent food, and Sam had to admit it was very good.

"You bring a date here," said Joe, "and you're going to have it made."

"Yeah, I'll have to try this place sometime. Taking them to McDonald's may be why they never go out with me a second time. You suppose?" he joked.

"Could be a clue."

Leaving the Reid Murdock Building, they walked the two blocks to City Hall and took the elevator to the floor where Crouse's office was located. Stepping through the door, they entered a small empty room that must have served as a receptionist's area at one time. On the wall facing them was another door that had light reflecting through the glass. Joe knocked.

Moments later, a distinguished man with silvery hair opened the door.

"Good afternoon," the man said. "Jerome Crouse." And he extended his hand.

Joe reached to shake his hand as he said, "Joe Erickson. This is my partner, Sam Renaldo."

Sam shook his hand, and Crouse invited them in and indicated two chairs for them to sit. Walking behind his desk, he looked at Joe and said, "I recognize you from the serial killer case. That was nice work."

Joe knew Crouse must have looked him up after he called. He would have wanted to know who he was dealing with. "Thanks," Joe replied.

Crouse sat and looked from Joe to Sam with his steely eyes. "So, you're investigating Sal Vincenzo's murder. Helluva thing. He was a good man."

Joe decided to forego pleasantries and get straight to the point. "We found Captain Vincenzo was working on a cold case he originally investigated with Nate Smith ten years ago. You probably remember…the Carson Byrne murder case?"

"I certainly do. The State's star witness was killed the day before he was set to testify. Bad deal. The case fell apart, and Byrne got off. It stunk."

"We think Vincenzo was on to something, and it got him killed," said Sam.

"Really?" said Crouse. "What was it?"

"We don't know…at least, not yet," said Joe. "He was looking into Robert Wallingford's murder at the time of his death. You probably remember something about that, don't you?"

Crouse looked at Joe as if trying to read his intention, and after a moment, he said, "That was a while back. But yeah. I remember something about it."

"You were Vincenzo's lieutenant at the time, right?"

"Right."

"Do you recall a request to investigate a complaint filed against Carson Byrne earlier that year? It was forwarded from the 19th?" Joe was zeroing in on Crouse's face, focusing on any micro-expressions, minute body language movements that are flashes of true emotion.

Crouse blinked quickly, several times. "I don't recall any such complaint. It wouldn't have been brought to my attention unless one of the detectives had an issue with it. And even then, you're talking, what? Ten years ago?"

"Yeah."

"The reason we ask," added Sam, "records of this complaint against Byrne have disappeared."

"Hm," muttered Crouse. "Disappeared? Are you sure this so-called complaint ever existed in the first place?"

"Oh, yeah. It did," said Joe as he studied Crouse's eyes. "Whoever destroyed the records was good, but he wasn't perfect. He forgot one important item."

Hearing that, Crouse's breathing changed. His hand went to his face, and he rubbed his chin with his finger. It was a tell, a pacifier that helps relieve stress. He looked at Joe and Sam said, "I assume that's privileged information."

"It is," said Sam.

"You see," Joe went on, "we think Vincenzo knew this, too. And on the night he was killed, he was meeting with someone who could link Carson Byrne to the information Troy Winslow and Robert Wallingford were using to blackmail him. Something that would ruin him."

"Someone found out about their meeting and placed a sniper to kill Vincenzo in order to end his investigation," said Sam.

"We're picking it up where he left off, at a somewhat disadvantage, I don't mind telling you. Someone burglarized Vincenzo's condo and stole his laptop and all of his research. We'll eventually find out who's behind it all. It's just a matter of time."

"Then heads will roll."

Crouse's eyes squinted very briefly in response.

"No matter who it is," said Joe.

Crouse squirmed ever-so-slightly in his chair and repositioned his hands. "As it should be," he said. "Is there anything else I can help you with, detectives?"

"What can you tell us about your former boss, Commander William Blackmore? He passed a couple of years ago, I believe," asked Sam.

Crouse thought for a few seconds, his eyes blinking quickly before they refocused on Joe and Sam. "A good administrator. I never had a problem with him. I thought he was a little too political for my liking. He seemed like a puppet for the upper administration, but that's just my opinion. Why do you ask?"

Joe was expecting that type of answer, a subtle deflection away from himself and onto a respected officer incapable of defending himself. Crouse's eyes suggested he was constructing a lie.

"Just curious," said Sam. "Did you ever have any issue with Vincenzo or his partner, Nate Smith, when you were their lieutenant?"

"Oh, hell no. Those two guys were my best team. Bulldogs, both of them."

"Good to know."

They spoke a little longer, and then Crouse glanced at his watch. "Anything else?"

Joe looked at Sam and then said, "No, I guess not. Thanks for your time, Captain. You've been most helpful." He and Sam rose from their chairs, preparing to leave.

"Anything I can do to help," Crouse replied, standing. "You want my opinion? You're heading down a dead-end street with this ghost complaint. Your time would be better spent finding Vincenzo's killer."

"You may be right," replied Sam. "But we'd be negligent if we didn't check it out."

Crouse walked around his desk and saw them out. "Take care, detectives," he said and smiled with his mouth but not with his eyes. A fake smile if Joe ever saw one. He sensed contempt in his face.

As they were walking to the car, Sam said, "He didn't feel too comfortable with our questions, did he?"

"You noticed all those non-verbals, too, huh?"

"Oh, yeah."

"And those micro-expressions of his. He was lying like a rug. I'll bet he and Carson Byrne are bosom buddies."

"And have been for years."

"You think he knows Yvonne Briggs?" asked Joe.

"In the biblical sense?"

"Jesus, Sam."

"It might be worth checking out, you know?"
"You're right. It may be worth checking out.
"I don't mind playing sleazy PI if it gets us somewhere."
"Okay. But no intimate pictures, please."

Chapter Nineteen

When Joe returned to his desk, he had an email message from the forensics lab. Tests on the syringe taken from Merlin Fitzgerald's room showed the syringe contained succinylcholine. The nurse imposter's objective was not to threaten Fitzgerald as Sam previously thought. The objective was clearly to end Fitzgerald's life. An overdose of "sux" is quickly absorbed by the body. It does not show up in a toxicology check unless the lab is specifically testing for it. His death would most likely have been attributed to his injuries. Why? They needed to question Fitzgerald again.

Joe stepped to Sam and said, "Did you get the email from the forensics lab?"

"Yeah. Why do you suppose he was trying to off Fitzgerald? What's that guy know, anyway?"

"They think he knows something. We need to talk with him again."

Joe called the hospital and found Merlin Fitzgerald had been discharged. They drove to his apartment located on West Agatite Avenue in Uptown. When they rang, Fitzgerald's wife answered the door. They identified themselves prior to being buzzed in. Both had their ID's out when the door opened, and they stated their names.

"I remember you from the hospital," she said to Joe. "What's this about?"

"We have some additional questions for your husband. Is he home?" asked Joe.

"He is. Come in," she said, opening the door for them.

"Who is it, Carol?" came a voice from inside the apartment.

"The police," she stated in a loud voice. "They have some questions for you." Turning back to Joe and Sam, she said, "He's sitting in the living room. Go on in."

They saw Merlin Fitzgerald sitting in a leather recliner. His face was no longer swollen, but it was still black and blue around his eyes and jaw, reflecting the severe beating he received at the hands of his assailant.

"Detectives," said Fitzgerald. "Forgive me if I don't get up."

"No need," said Sam. "We're here to ask you some additional questions based on some evidence we received."

"Oh? And what evidence is that?"

"Please sit down, won't you?" offered Carol, pointing to the couch. Did you catch the man who beat up Merlin?"

"No," said Joe. "But we believe he's the same person who posed as a nurse and tried to kill your husband in the hospital."

Carol gasped and looked at Merlin. "Why would anyone want to kill you, dear?"

"That's what we'd like to know," said Sam.

"What is it you know or have seen that's motivated this man to kill you?" asked Joe. "Assassins don't target people for no reason."

"Assassins!" cried Carol.

"That's who this man is," said Sam. "He tried to kill your husband on two occasions."

"We received a report from our forensics lab on the contents of the syringe. It was filled with succinylcholine, a muscle relaxant. An overdose would be fatal," said Joe.

"Merlin. What's going on?" asked Carol.

"Come on, Mr. Fitzgerald. You need to be up-front with us," said Sam.

"If I knew, I'd tell you. But I don't. I'm a property manager. Why would somebody want to kill me? I don't gamble. I don't cheat on my wife. I don't sell drugs. I'm a boring guy."

"Well, somebody is threatened by you. Evidently, they think you know something, and they want to shut you up. Now what could you possibly know that could be a threat to somebody else?"

"I don't know!"

"Did this assailant ask you anything while he was beating you?" asked Joe. "Was he trying to extract information from you?"

Fitzgerald thought for a minute and said, "I think I remember him asking me something about 'where's the tape,' and I thought he wanted to use it to tie me up, so I told him it was in my desk drawer. That's all I remember. Was I tied up with tape when I was found?"

"No. You weren't. Your hands and feet were bound with extension cords."

"I guess I was dreaming, then, wasn't I?"

"Do you remember him saying anything to you in the hospital room?" asked Sam.

"No, I was sleeping. I didn't wake up until the scuffle started."

Joe was getting frustrated with Fitzgerald's lack of candor. "I want to tell you something, Mr. Fitzgerald. A man has tried to kill you twice. What makes you think he won't try to finish the job?"

There was a silence.

Carol looked at her husband and back at Joe and Sam. "Do you think he will try again?" she asked, her voice shaking.

"He could. If he feels your husband is still a threat, then, yes. He could very well try again."

"I don't understand!" she cried. Looking at her husband, she pleaded, "Why Merlin?"

Joe and Sam looked at Fitzgerald as he watched his wife. Clearly, he cared for her, and he didn't want to cause her any more emotional pain. He looked at Sam and then at Joe and said, "All right."

There was a pause. Then Sam said, "All right, what?"

"The guy...the one who beat me up...was demanding to know who got Wallingford's stuff. I didn't even know Wallingford."

Joe looked at Sam and then to Carol. She looked like Wallingford was the name of some long-lost Ku Klux Klan member uncle.

Fitzgerald saw her reaction and quickly said, "I told him all his things were turned over to an auction house, but he didn't believe me."

"You said you didn't know Robert Wallingford?" pressed Sam.

"I didn't, really. He lived in an apartment complex I managed. When he was killed, I had to get his apartment ready to rent again after the police released it. But I didn't take anything."

"The man that tried to kill you might think you did," said Joe.

"What's Merlin supposed to do?" asked Carol through tears. "Some guy may still want to kill him?"

"Go into hiding? Carry a gun wherever I go?" said an angry Fitzgerald.

"No," said Sam. "I wouldn't advise that."

"THEN WHAT?" screamed Carol.

Joe needed to calm them down, so he quietly said, "Listen to me. Please. Whoever this guy is, we need a description, so it would be helpful if you'd work with one of our forensic artists to create a composite sketch for us to go on. Maybe we can run it through facial recognition and get a hit."

"I haven't seen all of his face. How can you do that?"

"But you've seen enough to create a partial sketch, and what you didn't see, the computer can use algorithms to fill in the rest."

"Can you manage your properties from home?" asked Sam.

"For the most part, but sometimes I need to meet one on one with residents."

"Then, I would suggest you go with your assistant or a friend. The offender would be less prone to do anything if you were with another person."

"The security in this building—is it good?" asked Joe.

"Yes," said Fitzgerald. "The security cameras outside and inside the building all work, and I'm changing the access code on our door every week."

"Do either of you own a firearm?" asked Sam.

"No."

"Well, don't go out and buy one. If you want to own a firearm, you need to be trained in how to use one first. We've seen too many accidents involving people who don't know how to use one properly."

"So, you have no idea what the guy was looking for?" asked Joe.

"No, he never said what it was."

"You said he asked, 'Where's the tape?' When he first attacked you, right?"

"Yes."

"But he tied you up with an electrical cord." Joe looked at Sam. "I think he was asking where you were keeping a 'tape recording.' He wanted Wallingford's copy of either an audio or videotape."

Fitzgerald looked confused. "I don't know anything about any recording."

"What's this tape recording?" asked Carol.

"Ten years ago, Troy Winslow, along with Robert Wallingford, were blackmailing Carson Byrne. We believe they had a tape recording with compromising information that could ruin Byrne politically. Both Winslow and Wallingford were killed, and it's believed a copy of that tape is still out there. Police Captain Sal Vincenzo was murdered while on the trail of that tape recording."

"My god," said Carol. "I read about him. That's why he was killed?"

"Uh-huh. He was our former lieutenant. So, we're vested in finding this man. He might have been involved in our lieutenant's murder, too."

"When would you like me to meet with your police artist?" asked Fitzgerald.

"We'll arrange it and email you her contact information. It's all done by computer now, so she may be able to do it right here at your dining room table," said Sam.

On their way back to Area 3, Sam said, "I'll bet the offender was really enraged when he asked, 'Where's the tape?' and then opened the drawer and found a roll of masking tape."

"Yeah. And he took out his rage on Merlin," replied Joe. "We need to find this guy."

Back at Area 3, Joe contacted their forensic artist and let her know about the need for her services. He sent Merlin Fitzgerald an email with her contact information so he could set up a meeting to create a composite sketch of the man with Peter Lorre eyes.

Chapter Twenty

After his two days off, Joe was back in the office with a fresh outlook on things. He had an idea he wanted to pursue and spoke with Sam about it. Sam agreed it was worth checking out, and before long, Joe had pulled up the Chicago Public Library's website and was logging in to gain access to the Chicago Tribune's Historical Archive, where he could read articles about the Carson Byrne trial.

After successfully logging in and searching for the date of the first day of the trial, he found an article covering the anticipated beginning of the trial. It didn't reveal much. Then he scrolled to the next day and found an article reporting on the trial's first day. As he read, he saw the name of the assistant prosecutor, and his jaw dropped. "Paul Titus." Could Paul Titus be the "PT" that Vincenzo was going to meet the night he was killed?

Joe called to Sam, who was coming back from the conference room carrying a cup of coffee. "Sam! Come here!"

"What?" asked Sam, spilling coffee over the side of his cup.

"Look what I found. I think I may have found 'PT.' Look." And he pointed to the name on his screen. "Paul Titus was an assistant prosecutor on the Carson Byrne murder case."

"You think he's still working with the State's Attorney's Office?"

"I'm going to find out. I'll let you know."

"Nice work, partner."

Joe's call to the Office of the State's Attorney was answered, and he asked to speak with Andrea Butterworth, the person who assisted him with research about the Byrne case previously. He was transferred, and she picked up.

"Andrea Butterworth."

"Good morning, Andrea. This is Detective Joe Erickson from Chicago PD again. Remember me?"

"Yes, as a matter of fact, I do. What can I help you with today?"

"I have a simpler question for you. The assistant prosecutor on the Byrne murder case was Paul Titus. Is he still employed with the Office of the State's Attorney?"

"Let me check." Joe heard her fingers hitting the keyboard, and after a minute, she said, "No, I'm sorry. He no longer works here."

"That's what I needed to know. Thank you, Andrea. Much appreciated."

"No problem."

Well, that didn't go as well as Joe had hoped. Now, he would have to track down Paul Titus, and he wondered if Titus was still practicing somewhere in the city. He searched the internet for "Paul Titus, attorney" but got only old hits. He looked Titus up in the Illinois State Department of Professional Regulation and found he still maintains his state license to practice. Then he checked the state's driver's license database. He found Paul Titus's driver's license, but it had expired three years ago. He did have a state-issued ID in lieu of a driver's license. Odd, but there could be a reason for that. On it was his last known address. Joe wanted to make a phone call to arrange a meeting, but no phone number could be found.

Joe alerted Sam, and they made a trip to Paul Titus's last known address on North Mozart Street. They pulled up to a nicely kept brick bungalow. Joe rang the bell, and after a moment, a voice came across the speaker.

"Who is it?"

"Detectives Erickson and Renaldo, Chicago PD," stated Joe.

"State your business, please."

"We have some questions for Paul Titus regarding a trial he worked on ten years ago."

"Can I see your IDs, please?"

Joe and Sam held their IDs up close to the doorbell unit, and a few moments later, they heard the door lock release and the voice say, "Come in."

They entered a foyer and turned right, entering a front room where they were met by a bearded man in his fifties sitting in a wheelchair.

"I'm Paul Titus. Pardon me if I don't get up," he quipped.

"That's quite all right," said Sam.

"I'm Joe Erickson. This is my partner, Sam Renaldo."

"Come on into the living room and make yourselves comfortable," said Titus, spinning his wheelchair around and wheeling it into the next room. "Have a seat."

"I suppose you're wondering why I'm on wheels. Everybody does. It's MS. I've had it a long time, but it's been taking its toll on me, and it put me in this damned chair three years ago. But…what do you do? It could be worse."

Mr. Titus, we—" Joe began.

"Paul," interrupted Titus. "Call me Paul."

"Okay. Paul. We're investigating the murder of Police Lieutenant Sal Vincenzo. Maybe you read something about it."

"Yes, I did."

"Vincenzo was investigating elements of a cold case—the Carson Byrne murder case from ten years ago. According to his daily planner, he was meeting with someone he noted as 'PT' the night he was killed. We've been trying to figure out who 'PT' may have been, and we were wondering if it might have been you."

"Sorry, but I'm not the PT you're looking for."

"You're not?"

"No."

"I see."

"We were thinking since you were assistant prosecutor on the Byrne murder case, Vincenzo was seeking information from you," said Sam.

"He never contacted me. Sorry. I don't leave the house much. Don't have a driver's license anymore. It's even tough to get around in a taxi when you're in a wheelchair."

"Never thought of that."

"Neither did I until I found myself stuck in this thing."

"I have another question for you, if you don't mind," said Joe.

"Shoot."

"You wouldn't happen to remember anyone else with the initials 'PT' associated with the Byrne case, would you?"

"Oh, man...Uh...Not offhand. But Wallingford had a girlfriend named Patty. I don't remember what her last name was. You could probably find out. It might be worth checking."

"Patricia?"

"Could be. That was ten years ago, so my memory's a little hazy, you know?"

Joe handed Titus his card. "If you happen to remember what her name was, give me a call, okay?"

"Yeah. Who knows, in the middle of the night, it might pop into my head."

"You can always call and leave a message. Day or night."

"I keep a notepad on my nightstand. If I remember it, I'll write it down. A habit I picked up a long time ago."

Joe looked at Sam. "You have any more questions for Paul?"

"No, I think we covered it."

"You still maintain a practice?" asked Joe.

"Yeah, I still practice part-time from home. Consulting, wills, divorces. Enough to keep me busy. I get referrals from my old firm."

Glancing around, Sam said, "Nice house."

"It belonged to my parents. I inherited it from my father when he passed. My parents left me pretty well off. There are a few advantages to being an only child."

"I'm an only child, too," said Joe. "Can't say as I have any advantages."

"Looking at you, I'd say you have a lot of advantages."

Feeling a little sheepish, Joe replied, "Yeah. I suppose I do. It's easy to take things for granted."

"Thanks for your time, Paul," said Sam, rising from the couch. "You have a card? I may need legal advice sometime."

Titus reached in his shirt pocket and pulled out his card. "Here you go. Be glad to help. Just don't expect me to represent you in court."

"Understood."

"We appreciate your help," added Joe. "Maybe Patty will be the person we're looking for." As Joe and Sam made their way to the front door, Titus followed in his wheelchair.

"Good seeing you. Hell, it's good seeing anybody," said Titus, a sad smile emanating from his face.

Back at Area 3, Joe logged into the Chicago Tribune archives again and began searching for Robert Wallingford's obituary. When he found it, the obituary listed Patricia Thorpe, his fiancé, as a survivor. Patricia Thorpe—PT. Could she be the 'PT' Vincenzo planned to meet with on the night he was killed? Only one way to find out. He would have to track her down. Given the many Patricia and Patty Thorpe names in the Chicago area, finding the right woman was going to take some time. He needed to find the original files on Robert Wallingford's murder and hope there was an address for Patricia Thorpe. With any luck, she might still be living there.

After lunch, Joe found the file on Wallingford's murder and began searching for information on Patricia Thorpe. He found Vincenzo and Nate Smith had interviewed her as a part of their investigation into Wallingford's death. Her address was on West School Street in the Avondale neighborhood. He also saw that she was employed as a member of the service staff at Saint Xavier University.

Joe and Sam drove to the West School Street address. They looked at the list of the apartment's residents but didn't see Thorpe listed as a last name. They buzzed the manager and identified themselves. Once they were inside, they were met by a squat, middle-aged man with a pock-marked face. He seemed very concerned with their presence.

"Is there something wrong?" he said as he approached them.

"Nothing to be concerned about," said Sam. "We're looking for information on someone who may live here. Or at least she did a few years ago."

"Okay, well. What's her name?"

"Patricia or Patty Thorpe."

"Oh. She doesn't live here anymore. She did several years ago, but she moved out."

"I don't suppose you'd have a forwarding address, would you?" asked Joe.

"No. That was quite a while back. If I did, I would've tossed it by now. I have enough junk in my files. You can't keep everything, you know?"

"You don't keep a file on your residents?" asked Joe.

"The company probably has records, but I don't have anything that old on the premises."

"Your name would be?"

"Roy. Roy Carter."

"What's the name of the company you mentioned?"

"Starlight Properties."

"Oh. They manage my apartment complex, too," said Sam. "They have a lot of apartment complexes around the city."

"All right," said Joe. "Thanks for your time, Mr. Carter."

"Yeah. Good luck finding her."

Sam handed Carter his card. "If you happen to run across her file, give me a call."

Carter took his card and was reading it as they left. Out on the street, Sam said, "So, what do you think?"

"I think our next step should be to contact Saint Xavier University and find out if Patricia Thorpe still works there."

"First thing tomorrow."

"Yeah."

Chapter Twenty-One

When Joe came into the office the next day, he got online and brought up the Saint Xavier University website. He knew that privacy laws would prevent the university staff from giving out information about employees over the phone, so he and Sam would have to travel to campus and speak with someone in Human Resources. He found the Human Resources Department was listed in the Human Resources Building. *Hm*, he thought. *Guess I don't have to write that one down.*

Joe and Sam drove to the south side of the city where Saint Xavier University is located on West 103rd Street and South Central Park Avenue. The attractive campus surrounds Lake Marion. Joe printed a campus map and saw the Human Resource Building was on the northern part of the campus next to the baseball field. Not hard to find.

Upon entering the building's main office, they were greeted by a woman seated at a desk inside the door. They showed their IDs and asked if they could speak with someone who could answer a question about an employee.

"Let me get the Associate Director for you," she said, and she walked to one of the adjacent offices and went inside. A moment later, a middle-aged woman in a gray business suit came out and greeted them.

"I'm Marilyn Russell. May I help you?"

After showing her their IDs and introducing themselves, Joe said, "We're investigating a case, and we'd like to speak with a person who may be employed here. Could you verify her employment with the university?"

"Why don't you come into my office," she replied. And she turned and walked down a short hall and through a door with her name on it. Joe and

Sam followed. Once inside, she closed the door.

"Please, have a seat," she said as she walked behind her desk and sat down.

"This individual is not in any trouble," Joe clarified. "We believe she may have some information that could prove valuable in a case we're working on."

"I see," said Russell. "Normally, we don't give out information about employees."

"But you list your faculty by name on your website, don't you?"

"We do."

"So, your employees are public information then, aren't they?"

"Well…"

"This person is a service worker, or at least she was several years ago. It could be that she's no longer employed by the university. That's what we need to know. You don't list service workers on your website."

"That's correct. We don't."

"We could get a warrant for this," said Sam. "But that would take time, slow down our investigation, and we would eventually get the information anyway. Your cooperation would be appreciated."

After a moment, she asked, "All right. What's the person's name?"

"Patricia Thorpe. T-h-o-r-p-e," said Joe.

Russell worked her keyboard and then paused. "Patricia Thorpe. Yes, she's currently employed with us. She works in building maintenance."

"A custodian, in other words," said Sam.

"In other words."

"Could you tell us where she may be working today?" asked Joe. "We'd like to speak with her."

"Let me make a call." She picked up her campus phone book and looked for a number. Then she picked up her phone and dialed.

"Hello. This is Marilyn Russell in Human Resources. I need to know if Patricia Thorpe is working today and what building she's working in."

There was a silence. She looked from Joe to Sam and then to her computer screen as she waited. Finally, her eyes lit up.

"The library. Thank you. She's working today at the library. You know where that is?"

"I do. Thank you," said Joe, rising from his chair.

"We appreciate your cooperation," added Sam.

"You're welcome," said Russell, but they could tell by her tone she was not pleased about giving out the information.

Upon entering the large brick library building, they walked to the student manning the checkout desk and asked to speak with a supervisor. She returned with a thin, bespectacled man in his early sixties.

"Yes?" he asked in a soft-spoken voice.

They produced their IDs and introduced themselves. "Could we talk over there?" asked Joe, indicating a space by the reference books.

Taken somewhat aback, he said, "Most certainly."

They moved in between two rows of reference books where Joe and Sam quietly spoke with him. "We would like to speak with a maintenance person by the name of Patricia Thorpe. We were told she's working in the library today."

"Patty? Yes, of course. I saw her earlier, upstairs. I...hope she's not in any kind of trouble."

"She isn't," said Sam. "We simply want to ask her some questions."

"Regarding an investigation we're working on," added Joe.

"I can take you up to the second floor where I saw her half an hour ago, but she could be elsewhere by now."

"I'm sorry. You are..." asked Sam.

"Oh, I'm Victor Beckwith. I'm the reference librarian."

"Thank you, Mr. Beckwith."

"If you'll be good enough to follow me, gentlemen." They followed him past the reference aisle and back to a staircase that led to the second floor, where he spotted Patty Thorpe dry-mopping the tile floor. "That's her, right over there," he said, pointing in the direction of a slender woman with dark hair.

Joe and Sam walked toward her and stopped a few feet away. She looked up from her mopping as the two detectives produced their IDs. Joe asked, "Patty Thorpe?"

CHAPTER TWENTY-ONE

Her angular face acknowledged them with a surprised look, and she said, "Yes?"

"I'm detective Joe Erickson, Chicago PD. My partner, Sam Renaldo."

"Okay," she said with an incredulous smile. "So, what do you want with me?"

"We're investigating a cold case. The murder of Robert Wallingford."

"Oh, for god sakes," she said. "That was years ago."

"Ten, to be exact," said Sam. "You were involved with Robert Wallingford back then?"

"We were seeing each other. Yeah."

"We'd like to ask you a few questions."

"Look," she said, leaning on her mop. "This isn't the time or the place. I'm working, and I can't take time out of my day for an interview. I've got a job to do."

"I understand. What's a good time for you to meet with us?" asked Joe.

"I get off work at four-thirty, and I'm usually home by five. How about then?"

"Sounds good. What's your address?"

She gave Joe and Sam her address, and they agreed to meet at her apartment at 5:15 p.m. That was after Joe and Sam were off duty, but they needed to follow the lead so they would put in a little overtime.

Late that afternoon, Joe and Sam drove to Thorpe's South Kildare Avenue apartment complex in the predominantly white, blue-collar neighborhood of Archer Heights. They arrived shortly after 5:20 p.m. The drive from Area 3 was long since Archer Heights is located seven miles southwest of the Loop.

They rang her doorbell, and it opened, revealing Patty Thorpe holding a bottle of beer.

"Come in," she said. "Have a seat on the sofa. Can I get you a beer?"

"Thanks, but no thanks," said Sam. "Still on the clock."

"We're fine, thanks," replied Joe.

Thorpe sat in a matching chair perpendicular to the sofa. The apartment was small and decorated with inexpensive furnishings, but the place was clean and neat. A huge flat-screen television hung on the wall opposite the sofa. A framed picture of her and a man sat on a small table along with some knickknacks.

Referring to the framed photo, Joe asked, "Is that you and Robert Wallingford?"

"Yeah, that's me and Bob. At my parents' farm downstate. Happy times," she said with a joyless smile. Then she looked back at Joe and Sam and asked, "What do you wanna know?"

Taking the lead, Joe said, "Bob and his acquaintance, Troy Winslow, were blackmailing Carson Byrne. And—"

She set her beer down hard on the end table. "Troy Winslow was a piece of garbage. The thing about Bob was, he wasn't very good about choosing his friends. It was Troy's idea to blackmail Byrne, not Bob's. He talked Bob into getting involved in that scheme of his. Thought they could get rich quick."

"Okay," said Joe. "We know about Winslow's rap sheet for petty crimes. Our question centers on the tape they were using against Byrne. Did Captain Vincenzo contact you and set up a meeting to discuss something about a tape?"

"Oh, god." She bent forward, elbows on her knees, and leaned her head on her hands. Beginning to shake, she sniffed back tears. After a moment, she sat up, wiped tears away from her cheeks, and took a deep breath.

"Captain...Captain Vincenzo...he called me and wanted to know some stuff. And I told him I didn't want to meet with him anywhere we could be seen together. So, I picked that school late at night." She reached over, picked up her beer, and took a couple swallows. "He was already there when I pulled up—we told each other what kind of cars we'd be driving so I knew it was him. I opened my door, and when he got out of his car...." She took a deep breath. "Someone shot him!" Tears rolled down her cheek, and she was trying her best to hold it together.

"What did you do?" asked Sam.

"I...I panicked. I...thought I was going to get shot, too. So, I got back in my car and drove away as fast as I could. I...Oh, god...I know I shoulda checked to see if I coulda helped him. But I was too scared. I feel so guilty about...."

"You couldn't have helped him. The shot was fatal. He was dead before he hit the ground."

Joe paused to let that sink in before he asked, "Did you mention your meeting to anyone?"

"No. Of course not."

Her shaking hand tipped the bottle up to her lips, and she finished it. "Excuse me," she said, getting up and going to the kitchen. She returned with another beer and some tissues and sat down. Holding up her beer, "You sure you don't want one?"

"We're sure," said Sam.

She put the bottle down and then used a tissue to blow her nose.

"I'd like to pursue another line of questioning, if I could," said Joe. "What information were you going to give to Captain Vincenzo that night?"

"Bob was given a videotape from his uncle, a private investigator. His uncle had a recording of Carson Byrne. I don't know what was on it, and Bob never told me. His uncle was dying of cancer of the pancreas, had just a few days left to live. Bob told me his uncle wanted him to hand it over to the police after he passed."

"A videotape?" asked Sam, glancing at Joe.

"Yeah. It was a videotape," said Thorpe.

"What was this PI's name?"

"Van Andel. I don't know his first name."

"Do you know if Bob kept a copy of the videotape?"

"Not that I know of."

"What happened to Bob's things after he was killed?"

"He didn't have much. I picked over what I wanted, and I guess some auction house probably came in and took the rest."

"His parents take anything?" asked Joe.

"I doubt it. He didn't have anything they would've wanted. He wasn't the kind of guy who would have memories or sentimental stuff layin' around."

"Lived a Spartan existence would you say?" asked Sam.

"You could say that. If it wasn't useful, he wouldn't have it."

"Did he do things that put his life in danger? Take chances? Make risky choices? Things like that?" asked Joe.

"Other than choosing some questionable friends, no. He was a fun person, but he wasn't somebody who had a death wish. He would've eventually owned half a farm downstate. He could've invested all that money and simply enjoyed himself. <u>We</u> could've enjoyed ourselves. And Carson Byrne had him killed because Troy Winslow was an idiot."

Ten years had not erased any of the bitterness Patty Thorpe felt over the death of her boyfriend. And the years of bitterness had taken a toll on her looks as well. She looked so attractive in the photograph with Wallingford. And now, ten years later, she looked hard, worn out. Joe felt sympathy for people like her, those who could never get past the death of a loved one. He knew people who seemed to be able to cope with tragedies in their lives and others who could not. She was one who could not. Shame.

Joe looked at Sam, who acknowledged they were done. "Thank you, Patty. Your time is most appreciated." Standing, he reached in his pocket and handed her his card. "If you can think of anything else, feel free to call me."

On their way to the car, Sam said, "Too bad she didn't have a copy of that videotape. I'd love to see what's on it."

"Yeah," said Joe. "You and me both."

Chapter Twenty-Two

Two days later, Joe got a call from Detective Pete Rafferty from Area 1. He said, "I'm here at a crime scene, and I have your card in my hand. I found it inside the apartment of a homicide victim a few minutes ago. Thought I had better call you about it."

"Really. Whose apartment is it?" asked Joe.

"It belongs to the victim, Patricia Thorpe."

Joe was stunned and couldn't speak for a few seconds. Finally, he said, "What happened to her?"

"She was found tied in a chair and beaten to a pulp. The ME says it looks like the cause of death was manual strangulation."

"Oh, man."

"My question for you is, how did she get your card?"

"My partner and I interviewed her as part of an ongoing investigation three days ago."

"Three days ago."

"Yeah. When did this happen?"

"Two days ago, the way it looks. Her supervisor at the university called and asked the police to do a wellness check since she'd been absent for two days and hadn't called in."

"Did the place look like it was searched?"

"Yeah, as a matter of fact. Somebody turned the place upside down. How'd you know?"

"I think the offender was looking for the same thing we are."

"What would that have been?"

"Don't know for sure. We have a general idea, but it would only be speculation at this point."

"Speculate for me."

"Could be a copy of a videotape from a ten-year-old cold case."

"Okay."

"Who's the ME?" asked Joe.

"Meloni."

"He's good. Hopefully, the evidence techs will turn up something."

"Hopefully."

"I'd appreciate it if you'd keep us in the loop on this one," said Joe.

"Yeah. We'd appreciate the same."

The phone call ended, and Joe sat staring at his computer screen for the better part of a minute, trying to grasp how someone could have known he and Sam had spoken to Thorpe. Then he got up and walked to Sam's desk.

When he saw the expression on Joe's face, he asked, "What's happened?"

"Patty Thorpe's dead. Beaten and strangled two days ago."

"What?"

"I just got a call from a Detective Rafferty from Area I, who's on the scene. Her place had been tossed. He found my card and wanted to know what she was doing with it."

"Somebody's thinking she had the tape or knew where it was."

"Sounds like it. But how did someone know we questioned her? Or that she had knowledge of the videotape? You think we were followed?"

"Good question. I think we should check the car for a tracker."

"Yeah. Let's do it."

Joe and Sam went out to the squad car they were using and went through it from top to bottom. After an exhaustive search, Joe said, "Well, there isn't any tracking device. It's got to be something else."

Sam asked, "Did you input any of your notes from our meeting with Thorpe into your department computer?"

"Yeah. I transcribed my notes about our meeting with her at the university and again first thing the next morning after our meeting at her apartment."

"That's got to be it."

"What do you mean?"

"She was killed the next day. I'd be willing to bet someone's been hacking into our computers. They didn't need to follow us. They've been reading our notes. Hell, they could've been one step ahead of us all along if they've been reading our notes."

"Now, that pisses me off," said Joe.

"You think it's Briggs?"

"I don't know."

"You think she's computer savvy enough to pull this off?"

"It takes some degree of sophistication to do that. Could be an associate of hers. But she could let him into the system by giving him her login and password. Then he could hack his way into our accounts."

"How do we find out?" asked Sam.

"Probably can't without raising suspicion."

"So, what do we do?"

"From now on, my transcribed notes are going into my computer at home. I'd advise you to do the same."

"Yeah. But we can't stop entering information, or they'll think we're on to them."

"Right. So, we keep our entries general and leave out specifics like who actually knows something or what the good leads actually are."

"So, if we had noted Patty Thorpe as a dead end, maybe she'd still be alive."

"Right."

"Son-of-a-bitch!" exclaimed Sam. "Somebody's gonna pay for this."

"They will," assured Joe. "They will."

"We're going to have to coordinate all this, you know."

"Should be no problem. We can talk about it as we drive. And use private email."

"Okay."

When they went back inside and sat down, it wasn't fifteen minutes before they got called out to investigate a body found in an alley on North Clark Street in Andersonville, not far from the Swedish American Museum.

When Joe and Sam got there, uniformed officers from the 20th District had closed off the area. They walked up to the officer managing the onlookers and showed their IDs. He lifted the yellow tape and let them through.

At the mouth of the alley, they met another uniform, Officer Larkin, who Joe recognized from working cases with him in the past.

"What've we got, Officer?"

"Kid. Perry McGuire, seventeen. Looks to have died just a few hours ago. A passerby saw him and called 9-1-1. He was dead by the time we got here."

"Foul play?"

"Doesn't appear to be. Looks like he just sat down and died."

"You got the person who called it in?" asked Sam.

"Yeah. She's sittin' in my squad car."

As Joe and Sam were walking to Larkin's squad car, the ME's van pulled up. Jen Clybourn, one of the newer medical examiners stepped out. She was young, with only a year of experience with the Cook County Medical Examiner's Office. She was easy on the eyes, too.

"I'll speak with the ME," said Sam.

"I'll bet you will," replied Joe. "I heard her significant other plays for the Bears."

"Where'd you hear that?"

Joe smiled and left Sam standing as he continued walking to the squad car. His interview with Emily Parris was of no help. She simply glanced, saw the teenager slumped over in the alley, and called 9-1-1. End of story.

When Jen Clybourn completed her examination of the body and emerged from the alley, Joe and Sam approached her. Pulling off her mask, she said, "I don't have a preliminary finding for you, detectives."

"Time of death?" asked Joe.

"Four to six hours ago," she replied. "As far as cause, an autopsy will have to determine that. A seventeen-year-old doesn't just die for no reason. There were no marks, bruises, needle punctures. No tell-tale signs of anything."

"He have a wallet on him with a driver's license?" asked Sam.

"He did," she said, "You can have it in a few minutes. I'm almost done here."

When she had completed her work, she handed Sam the bag with his wallet. He took down the information. The only thing left to do was to make the notification. Helluva way to end the day.

Chapter Twenty-Three

The next time Joe was on duty, he and Sam got called into Lieutenant Briggs' office. She said she had some information that could be pertinent to their investigation of Vincenzo's death.

When they entered her office, she said, "Shut the door."

Sam closed the door, and she asked them to sit down. Joe anticipated this had something to do with the grievance he filed about excessive work being assigned, but it turned out to be something else.

She began, "I just heard that Roosevelt Harris, aka Rosie Harris, was released on parole from Statesville ten days prior to Vincenzo's death. Captain Vincenzo arrested him and helped send him up on a charge of second-degree murder. Harris vowed to kill Vincenzo if he ever got out of prison."

"Interesting," said Joe.

"And he's here in Chicago?" asked Sam.

"He is. I have an address," she said. "Apparently, he was seen at the apartment of a former girlfriend a couple days ago. You may want to check it out." She slid a slip of paper with an address written on it over to Sam.

"So, you think someone may have used Harris or paid Harris to kill Vincenzo in order to stop his investigation into Robert Wallingford's murder?" asked Joe.

"I don't know what to think, Detective Erickson. I only know that Rosie Harris vowed to kill Captain Vincenzo if he ever got out of prison. He got out, and now Vincenzo's dead."

Briggs was getting hot under the collar. Joe knew she didn't like him and opening his mouth any more would just make things worse. He sensed she knew about his grievance. He could tell by her eyes. There was hate in those eyes.

"All right," said Sam. "We'll check it out."

"Good," she replied to him and him only. She refused to look at Joe. "You're dismissed."

Joe and Sam left her office, and as they were walking back to their desks, Sam said, "I don't think she likes you."

"The feeling's mutual."

"You want to check out this address?"

"Yeah. Get it out of the way. But first, I want to read up on Rosie Harris."

As Joe was reading Rosie Harris' file, he found he was a huge man: six-foot-five, two-hundred-eighty pounds. A habitual criminal, Harris was a suspect in the murder of a drug informant, James "Jimmy Fingers" Figueroa. When Vincenzo and Nate Smith went to arrest him, he tried to shoot Smith in the head with a nail gun. Vincenzo pulled his service weapon and shot Harris, seriously wounding him. Harris recovered, was tried, and found guilty of second-degree murder in the death of Figueroa. After the guilty verdict was read, Harris had to be restrained when he exploded at Vincenzo, vowing he would kill him if he was ever released. Harris was sent to the Statesville Correctional Center, a maximum-security state prison, in Crest Hill, Illinois, where he served seventeen years of a twenty-year sentence.

One thing Joe read that caught his eye was the fact that Harris joined the US Army at age eighteen. After one year, he was given a bad conduct discharge for assaulting his superior officer. That aside, Joe suddenly realized Harris would have expertise in firing an assault rifle.

Getting out of his chair, Joe walked to the conference room to get a cup of coffee. Stepping into the room, he saw Sam filling his cup.

"I just saw something interesting in Rosie Harris' file," said Joe.

"So did I. You first."

"Rosie Harris spent a year in the army before he got a bad conduct discharge. He would've been an expert on how to fire an assault rifle."

"I realized that, too. Brilliant minds think alike, man."

"He might be the trigger man, but my gut's telling me he's not the brains behind it."

"Yeah. Somebody could have known about his hate for Vincenzo and used him to take him out."

Joe nodded in agreement. "You up to bringing him in?"

"Coffee first."

Fifteen minutes later, Joe and Sam were on their way to an address on West Adams Street in the West Garfield Park neighborhood, the most dangerous community area in the city. Because of Harris' record of violence and the threat from the neighborhood, Sam called for backup from the 11th District. The street was lined with two-story brick apartment buildings built in the early years of the twentieth century. They were met by a cruiser with Officers Washington and Jones joining them as backup in case they needed it. They parked around the corner, two buildings away from the actual address. Walking to the front of the building, they opened the iron gate. Washington took up a position next to the steps while Jones moved to the back of the building. Joe and Sam climbed the steps to the entrance door and rang the bell for the apartment of Latrice Williams, Harris' girlfriend.

"Chicago PD," said Joe. "We need to speak with Roosevelt Harris."

They were buzzed in. Once inside, Washington remained on the first floor while both Joe and Sam carefully made their way up the steps to the second-floor apartment of Latrice Williams. They stopped in front of Apartment 2B and rang the bell. Expecting possible trouble, they stood to the sides of the door.

"Just a minute," came a woman's voice from inside.

Suddenly the door flew open, and gunfire erupted from inside. Joe and Sam stepped back farther from the door. At the same time, the door to Apartment 2C opened, and a man with a gun stepped out. Sam had his back to him, but Joe saw him and fired twice, dropping him before he had a chance to fire his weapon.

Sam threw himself inside the open door of Apartment 2A, rolling on the floor and firing at a woman holding a gun. The woman ducked behind a couch, and Sam put three rounds into the couch where he thought she was hiding. As he did, a man came out of the bedroom, gun in hand.

"DROP IT!" yelled Joe, who had stepped into the room. The man froze. "I SAID DROP IT, ASSHOLE!" The man decided today was not his day to die and dropped the gun. "Hands on your head!" The man complied.

"Behind the couch," said Sam, warning Joe about the woman. Sam moved toward the couch, prepared to react to what could be lurking behind it. After seeing the woman, he looked at Joe and shook his head. His bullets had hit their mark.

At that point, they were jolted by a loud voice from the hall. "POLICE! FREEZE!" And then a shot rang out.

"You got this?" asked Joe.

"Yeah," said Sam.

Joe checked the hall and saw Officer Washington stepping toward another shooter who was lying on the floor, and Officer Jones racing up the back steps.

Joe ducked back into the room where Sam had his gun on the offender. Joe moved to the man, kicked away his gun, and cuffed him. Marching him out into the hall, he sat him down while he checked the offender he shot to see if EMTs needed to be called. They didn't. He looked at Washington, kneeling over the man he'd shot.

"We need a bus for him?" asked Joe.

"Too late for that," said Washington.

"Jones was on his radio, calling in the shooting to his sergeant at the 11th District. Detectives would be called in from Area 4 since the 11th fell within their boundaries. Joe made a call to Area 3 to let his duty sergeant know what had happened. "I'm sure Lieutenant Briggs will want to know we are both fine," said Joe with a hint of sarcasm.

Joe tapped Jones on the shoulder. Referring to the prisoner, he asked, "Can you keep an eye on this guy? I need to talk with my partner."

"Sure thing," replied Jones, looking down at the offender. "This punk isn't going anywhere."

Joe and Sam stepped outside on the front steps. People had heard the gunshots and were beginning to gather outside the iron fence. But they still had some semblance of privacy for their conversation.

"You think this was a setup?" asked Joe, his voice full of contempt.

"No shit, Sherlock!" said Sam, steaming. "That bitch wanted us dead."

"Yeah. Sure looks that way, doesn't it?"

"We need to talk to somebody about this."

"Who? Who do we trust? How far up does this go? Is the Commander involved?"

Sam just shook his head. "So, what do you suggest?"

"We don't trust anyone. We can't prove anything at this point. Briggs gave us the address of Harris' girlfriend. So, what? We can't prove it was a setup, unless the shooter in there talks, and chances are he doesn't know anything."

"This sucks," said Sam.

"There's one thing I think we should do."

"Yeah?"

"Surveil Briggs," advised Joe. "See what she does and who she sees when she's not on duty. It might reveal something.

"I'm all in for that."

"It means trading off working nights like we did when we kept watch on the Fielding's yacht last year."

"I don't mind if you don't."

"Okay, let's start this Friday and see what kind of social life she's got. You or me?"

"I'll take Friday."

"Okay. I'll let Destiny know. I don't think we need to watch her on weeknights, do you?"

"Not to begin with. Let's see what we get from her weekend activities."

They went upstairs, and Joe grabbed Officer Washington so he could explain to him and Sam what would be happening since he was the only one who had experience with an officer-involved shooting.

"Get ready for a lot of red tape."

"I can hardly wait," said Sam.

"I'm a rookie, man. I don't need this shit!" said Washington.

"You can bet an Investigative Response Team is already on its way to interview us. After they investigate the shooting, the team will submit a report based on their findings."

Washington looked at Joe. "Okay. But there's more, right?"

"Yeah. You'll have to submit a formal statement to COPA, the Civilian Office of Police Accountability. COPA will want that within twenty-four hours, so write it up ASAP while it's fresh in your mind. They'll determine if the shooting was justified."

"Justified! That muthafucka was raisin' his gun to shoot me. I had to fire on him!"

"Calm down," said Sam. "You had no choice. Neither did we."

Joe went on to explain, "Next step is a meeting with them. You'll be represented by counsel provided by the FOP to ensure your rights are protected."

Joe could see Washington's emotions were still running high.

"Listen, it's a formality, something you have to do. We all have to do it. Just tell them what happened. Simple as that."

"They hard asses?" asked Sam.

"Depends who you get, I suppose. But I went through this last year when I had to shoot an armed offender. After it was all said and done, they found the shooting was justified."

"Anything else?" asked Washington.

"Paid administrative leave," said Joe. "We'll all be on desk duty for a while."

Before the investigations began and the media showed up to write their stories, Joe called Destiny to let her know what happened.

"Before you hear about this on the news, Sam and I were involved in a shooting today."

"Omigod! Are you alright?" she asked.

"We're both okay, and the two officers who were acting as backup are okay, too. We've arrested one, so we may find out some facts from him."

"What happened?"

"It's too complicated to explain on the phone. Suffice it to say we were ambushed. I'll tell you more about what happened when I get home, okay?"

"Okay. Call me when you're on your way.

"I will."

"Love you."

"Love you, too."

They were interviewed by Detectives Larson and Coates from Area 4. They gave a complete picture of who they were seeking and what happened, emphasizing the address was provided by their lieutenant, Yvonne Briggs. The ME required their service weapons, so Joe had to hand over his Glock. It wasn't the only handgun he owned, so he would have to use his backup Glock for several weeks.

Joe explained everything again to the IRT team with special emphasis on the address given to them by their lieutenant. This interview took even longer than the one with Larson and Coates. The IRT people wanted a lot of detail for their investigation, so they could get a full and accurate picture of what happened.

Joe had been interviewed by the IRT team only one other time—last year when he shot and wounded Vernon Leo Becker, a neo-Nazi involved in a human trafficking operation. He had to fire in self-defense when Becker drew down on him. And during all his years as a police officer, he had to kill only one offender, Barry Henderson, a double murderer who tried to kill him during an investigation in Iowa. Ending the life of another human being, no matter how despicable, sickened him, and the fact it was done to preserve his own life gave him little solace.

When everything was winding down, Joe turned to Sam and said, "Did you notice someone conspicuously absent?"

"Briggs?"

"Yeah. Vincenzo would have been here making sure we were okay and interacting with the detectives from Area 4. Letting them know if he could be of assistance."

"So much for caring about your detectives."

When Joe got home, Destiny had a bottle of Pinot Noir waiting and something with a wonderful aroma emanating from the oven.

"How are you feeling?" she asked, pouring his favorite wine.

"Pretty lousy and pretty lucky."

"You need to explain that."

"Lousy because I killed someone, lucky because I'm alive."

Destiny stopped pouring the wine and looked at him, realizing it was more serious than she originally thought. "You had to kill someone?"

"Yeah. So did Sam. We were fired on and had to defend ourselves. One of the uniforms had to take a third guy out."

"My god."

"We were set up."

"What?"

"By our lieutenant," he said through clenched teeth.

Joe..."

"She gave us an address where a suspect could be found. Supposedly, his girlfriend's place. And when we got there, we got ambushed—from inside the apartment and the one across the hall. They were waiting for us. Four of 'em."

"But your lieutenant?"

"We think she's somehow connected to the killing of Vincenzo. I don't know if she's covering for someone or what. But she's definitely involved with the missing evidence on the flash drive. Of course, we can't prove it."

"What are you going to do, Joe?"

"Keep our heads down. That's all we can do until we have some tangible evidence. Do our jobs as best we can while we're on administrative leave and keep our heads down."

Destiny handed Joe the glass of wine. "So, other than that, Mrs. Lincoln, how was the play?" she asked with a wry smile.

Joe chuckled at the irony. "Clever girl."

She took her glass and clinked his. "It could have been worse."

"It sure could have."

She leaned over and kissed him. "Good to have you home...in one piece."

Chapter Twenty-Four

Being on administrative leave is challenging. Detectives are still expected to work their cases, but they cannot leave the building and work the streets. Everything has to be conducted from their desks.

The next morning, Joe and Sam set up a Zoom meeting with the 11th District to question the offender, the sole survivor of the ambush, who was taken into custody inside the apartment the day before. They wanted to question him to determine who set them up.

Andre "Boog" Brundage, 30, had a rap sheet for minor offenses going back to age seventeen. He lived in the same building where the ambush went down. He did not ask to have an attorney present when he was questioned. To get the best deal he could, he chose to cooperate and answer their questions.

"Shit, man. I was just there to protect Latrice, that's all."

"What do you mean?" asked Joe.

"See, Latrice, she said she owed two grand to this loan shark, and she didn't have it. And the dude was sending a coupla mawgs to make her pay up. She said they would kill her if she didn't have the money, you know?"

"That's what she told you, huh?" asked Sam.

"Yeah. So, she asked a few brothers for protection."

"A couple of "white guys." That's what you're saying?"

"Yeah. Get taken out over two lousy grand. Come on, man. That ain't right. Couldn't let that shit happen."

"How well did you know, Latrice?" asked Joe.

"Well, enough."

"What's that mean?"

"It means, I was willing to help her out if she asked."

Joe and Sam questioned him further, but it was clear that he didn't know anything that would be helpful.

After the interview, Sam said, "Sounds like Latrice Williams pulled these guys in based on a lie."

"Yeah, and we were the 'mawgs,'" said Joe. "Somebody probably paid her to set us up, and she recruited several accomplices to assist her based on a bullshit story."

"And the real story died with Latrice Williams."

"Yeah. Another dead end."

At 1:30 that afternoon, Joe met with the Civilian Office of Police Accountability as required to explain the shooting the previous day. He was represented by counsel provided by the Fraternal Order of Police.

Since Joe had experienced a COPA investigation one other time, he knew what to expect. He felt his explanation of the events would prove his shooting was justified. He wanted to make sure they knew it was Lieutenant Briggs who gave them the address, and that fact was on the record.

The meeting was cordial. Joe delivered a narrative of what happened in as much detail as he could. Questions were asked, and he gave them answers that clarified those questions and provided insight from his point of view, including his opinion they were set up. That was discussed. Knowing that COPA worked closely with Internal Affairs, he hoped someone in IA might pick up on Briggs' possible involvement. It was a long shot.

However, his counsel from FOP took a definite interest in his implication and wanted to know more after the meeting had concluded. Joe let him know that nothing could be proven at this point, but as they continued to investigate Vincenzo's murder, evidence implicating police personnel could be unearthed. Joe felt he could give him only enough details to satisfy his curiosity. He didn't know him and didn't want to trust him with too much information. For all he knew, he could be a friend of Briggs.

Joe and Sam wanted to find Rosie Harris to discover if he had a hand in setting up the ambush. Joe contacted Harris' parole officer and was told that Harris currently lived on North Orleans Street in the Near North Side neighborhood. The parole officer said Harris had been meeting all his obligations since his release. In addition, he told Joe that Harris had a spiritual awakening while in prison, where he converted to Islam and changed his name to Yusuf Al-Faruq.

They needed to interview him, but it would have to wait until they were off administrative leave. Years ago, administrative leave for an officer-involved shooting amounted to three days and a call to a psychiatrist. Today, it is thirty days, desk duty, and everything under a microscope.

* * *

Thirty days later, and all three cleared in the shootings, Joe and Sam drove to the North Orleans Street address. They had sought backup from the 18th District, not knowing if they would be confronting another armed response. The neighborhood on the Near North Side was considerably better than what they faced previously. Two squad cars from the 18th met them a block away from the address, and Officers Norton and McElravy were ready to assist them if necessary. Joe and Sam explained the situation, and the four established a plan of action.

They walked to the front of the building, where they entered a small vestibule. Joe rang the apartment labeled Al-Faruq.

"Who is it?" came a female voice across the intercom.

"Chicago PD. We need to speak with Yusuf Al-Faruq."

To Joe's surprise, they were buzzed in, and they climbed the steps to Al-Faruq's apartment on the second floor. Officer Norton remained on the first floor while McElravy accompanied them.

When they reached Apartment 2B, Officer McElravy placed himself at the end of the hall. Joe and Sam drew their weapons and rang the bell to 2B. Standing back, they waited for a response. Moments later, the door opened as far as the chain would allow, and a woman wearing a hijab appeared in the opening.

"Are you the police?" she asked.

Holding up their IDs so she could see them, Joe answered, "Detectives Erickson and Renaldo, Chicago PD." The woman looked carefully at the IDs and then lifted the chair from the door and opened it fully.

"Come in."

Still holding their firearms down next to their sides, they entered the room and saw a large man sitting in a recliner. He was dressed in a white thobe, the long, ankle-length robe worn by many Muslim men. He had a full beard, and his head was covered by a black kufi skull cap. He rose when they entered.

Seeing their guns, Al-Faruq said, "You can put those away, gentlemen. You have nothing to fear from me. Please. Sit down." His voice was calm and controlled.

Joe and Sam returned their service weapons to their holsters and took seats on the couch.

"You can leave us, Amani." The woman turned and walked out of the room.

"I suppose you're here to question me about something. What would you like to know, detectives?"

"Where were you yesterday?" asked Sam.

"I was here." Lifting his thobe and showing his ankle, he revealed a monitoring device. "As you can see, I can't go nowhere without somebody knowin' about it."

"Did you know Captain Sal Vincenzo was murdered recently?" asked Joe.

"I heard about that. He arrested me and sent me to prison, you know."

"We do. We also know you vowed to kill him if you ever got out. You remember that?"

"I do. I certainly do. Is that why you're here?"

"Partly."

"Well, you have to understand that I was different back then. Angry and hateful. I was a bad person. I admit that. But finding Allah when I was in prison, it turned my life around. I'm a different man today, detective. I'm not Roosevelt Harris anymore. That man is gone. I'm Yusuf Al-Faruq, now. I've found inner peace.

"So, you had nothing to do with the shooting at an apartment on West Adams Street in West Garfield Park a month ago?" asked Sam.

"I don't know nothing about any shooting."

"No?"

"What about Latrice Williams?"

"Latrice? Oh, man. I haven't talked to her since I went inside. How is she?"

"Killed. A month ago."

"Oh, no." He paused for a moment and asked, "West Adams Street, you say?"

"Yeah."

"Amani!" he called out. "Come in here." Shortly afterward, the woman came into the room.

"You used to live on West Adams Street in West Garfield Park, right?"

"Uh-huh," replied Amani.

"What was the address?"

She told Joe and Sam the address, but it wasn't a match to the address where the shootout took place.

"I had to leave that neighborhood if I was going to survive," she said.

"What happened to Latrice?" asked Al-Faruq. "You said she was killed?"

"Yeah. In a shootout with police last month," said Sam.

Al-Faruq slowly shook his head. "She always was crazy. Never thought she'd do somethin' like that, though...Too bad."

"Were you approached by anyone to do a job after you got out of prison?" asked Joe.

Al-Faruq paused. He looked uncomfortable and twitched in his recliner. Leaning forward, he looked at Joe and Sam. "I got this phone call, see. From some guy. Don't know who it was. Axed me if I wanted to make twenty g's. Axed what I had to do, and he says, 'pull a trigger.' Told him no, wasn't interested, and hung up."

"Any idea who it might have been?"

"White guy. 'At's all I know."

"What were you doing the night of June third?" asked Joe.

"Amani? What were we doin' the night of June third?"

"Let me check the calendar." She went into the kitchen and, when she returned, said, "We were at the Mosque that night. Night prayers."

138

CHAPTER TWENTY-FOUR

"Ah. Tahajjud," said Al-Faruq. "Keeping vigil."

"And there are people who can verify you were there?"

"About a hundred or so," said Amani.

"You can ask the Imam. He can vouch for us."

Joe looked at Sam, who gave a nod. "I think you've answered all our questions."

As they were going out the door, Al-Faruq said, "Peace be with you."

And Joe automatically replied with his ingrained Catholic response, "And also with you." *That was interesting*, he thought, smiling to himself. Looking down the hall at Officer McElravy he called, "We're good." McElravy joined them as they took the stairs down to the first-floor hall where Officer Norton was waiting.

"Thanks for the assist," said Sam. "You're a lot luckier than the two officers we asked to back us up last month."

"Yeah? What happened?" asked Norton.

"We got ambushed."

"As Joe and Sam walked to the car, Sam asked, "You think we need to interview the Imam at the mosque?"

"No," replied Joe. "I think Al-Faruq has an alibi. He's being monitored. They'd know if he removed it or ventured outside his prescribed area."

"So, you're thinking he didn't have anything to do with any of this?"

"I think someone's using him as a red herring to throw us off the track."

"Or get us killed."

Parroting Lieutenant Briggs, Joe said, "I just heard Roosevelt Harris was released on parole." He paused. "Heard from who? That's what I'd like to know."

"How about nobody?"

Chapter Twenty-Five

After work on Friday, Sam began surveilling Lieutenant Briggs. He staked out her residence and waited to see if there would be any activity. By 7:00 p.m., nothing had happened except he had eaten his sub sandwich and polished off a can of Red Bull.

Then, shortly after 7:30, a blue Cadillac pulled up in front of her home. Sam reached for his Nikon and prepared to shoot photos of the driver and whatever happened next. The driver stepped out, and there was no mistaking it was former Captain Jerome Crouse. When he rang the bell, the door swung open, and he was greeted by a smiling Yvonne Briggs, who kissed him on the mouth before he disappeared inside.

Shooting at three and a half frames a second, Sam got everything, including the kiss. He looked at the digital image of the kiss on the camera and felt his stomach churn. *Wait until Joe sees this,* he thought.

He decided to call Joe rather than just send him the images. He not only wanted to reveal the connection between the two, but also see his reaction.

"Sam? What's up?"

"Hey, Joe. I got something you need to see. Are you home? Or should I say, are you busy?"

"No, we're not doing anything tonight. Stop over."

"Okay. It'll be about half an hour."

Sam drove thirty minutes to Joe and Destiny's house in the Lincoln Square neighborhood. The porchlight was on, and he felt energized as he trotted up the steps and rang the bell. Joe answered the door.

"Come in."

"Hi, Sam," said Destiny. "Can I get you something to drink?"

"No, thanks."

"Let's go into the living room," said Joe, and he led him to the couch, where they sat down. "Were you watching Briggs tonight?"

"I was, and I want to show you what I saw." Removing the camera from around his neck and turning it on, he pulled the screen out for viewing. As he was pulling up the last few photos, he said, "I think I may have discovered a possible link to something interesting. You remember when I said I wouldn't mind playing sleazy PI?"

"Uh-huh."

He handed the camera to Joe and pointed, "Use this to advance the photos."

Joe looked at the first photo and said, "Jerome Crouse?"

"Yeah. Keep scrolling."

"When Joe saw the kiss, he said, "Aw, Jesus!"

Sam chuckled, "Yup."

"Well, I don't need any bedroom fantasies in my head. I'm already seeing a shrink."

Sam laughed. "Seriously, though. Crouse was Vincenzo's lieutenant when he was a detective sergeant, wasn't he?"

"He was. And he was promoted to captain shortly before Vincenzo was promoted to lieutenant," said Joe.

"Yeah."

"You think we need to take a look at Crouse and see if he's somehow connected to Carson Byrne?"

"I do," said Sam. "Crouse is a consultant in the mayor's office. Byrne's an alderman. They could still have a connection."

"Crouse could be influencing Briggs to make decisions to derail our investigation into Vincenzo's murder. And when we continued to make progress, they decided to set us up. He's still trying to protect Byrne."

"So, what the hell is there to protect after all this time?"

"Whatever it is, it's the key to this whole thing. And if we want to solve this, we have to find out what it is. Otherwise, we're just chasing our tails."

Joe handed the camera back to Sam. "Email me those pictures."

"You can download them directly from my camera to your computer before I leave if you want." And he pulled a cable from his jacket pocket and dangled it in front of Joe.

"You came prepared."

"Always."

Destiny, who had been listening in the kitchen, stepped into the room. "Sorry for butting in, but I couldn't help overhearing."

"Go ahead," said Joe.

"If Crouse, Briggs, and Byrne are involved in some kind of conspiracy, who do you think is responsible for killing your sources? Someone tried to kill Merlin Fitzgerald, and they succeeded in killing Patty Thorpe. You have a hitman in the mix."

"Yeah, the one who shot me," said Sam.

"My money's on a connection to Crouse, not Briggs," said Joe. "When the time is right, we could set up a sting and nail the guy. See if he sings to save his ass. We have DNA from under my fingernails that could prove he was the guy in Merlin Fitzgerald's hospital room."

"Maybe we'll get lucky, and the evidence techs will find something at Patty Thorpe's crime scene, too," replied Sam.

"But we need to find that videotape. We've got to locate it if it's out there."

"It appears someone thinks it is," added Destiny. "And they're determined to get it before you do."

"I also think we need to start feeding Briggs disinformation regarding our investigation, not just keeping it from her. We have to show part of what we're doing and create a fictional account for the rest. We can't have any more people killed in a search for the videotape."

"You guys are going to have to carefully coordinate that," said Destiny.

"We can do it from home and then transfer the details to our computers at work," said Sam.

"Okay," concluded Joe. "I think we got this. "Let's get those photos downloaded."

They rose from the couch and entered the kitchen, where Joe's laptop was sitting on the island. Sam downloaded the photos from his Nikon to Joe's laptop.

"Sure I can't get you a drink? Or something to eat?" asked Destiny.

"No thanks. Another time." Picking up his camera, he said, "I have to get home. Great house you have here."

Joe and Destiny thanked him, and Sam left. Joe turned to Destiny and said, "Now we have two things to prove: who killed Vincenzo and who's involved in this conspiracy."

"When you come to a fork in the road, take it?" she asked with the hint of a smile.

"I'm taking the fork leading to Vincenzo's murder. It should eventually lead me to the other."

"It'll be a long and winding road."

"Wasn't that a song?"

"Yeah. And a great one."

Chapter Twenty-Six

Saturday was a day off, but Joe decided to keep working from home. After his jog and breakfast, he worked from his laptop, looking at Vincenzo's notes. He reviewed Vincenzo's research and once again came across the name of the private investigator, Frederick Van Andel.

Joe began thinking about Van Andel and whether he may have made a duplicate of the original videotape. He was dying of cancer. That's why he passed the tape along to his nephew, Robert Wallingford, in the first place. Question is: would he have retained a copy? What reason would he have if he was dying? But there is always the chance he may have kept a copy somewhere.

Joe looked up the obituary and began reading. Apparently, Van Andel had no children. According to the obituary, his wife, a brother, and his parents preceded him in death, he was survived by two sisters, Elise Pemberton of Cicero, and Carol Fitzgerald of Chicago. *Carol Fitzgerald?! Merlin Fitzgerald's wife?*

Joe went to the Illinois Driver's License database and looked up Elise Pemberton with a Cicero address. When her license pulled up, he saw her photo. *Holy shit!* It was the same red-haired woman he saw with Carol Fitzgerald at the hospital the day they found the nurse imposter in Fitzgerald's room.

Joe attempted to find a telephone number for Pemberton but evidently, she had elected to forego a landline and go cellular. To interview her, he would need to make a visit to her home in Cicero, a city of 80,000, sixteen miles west of Chicago. He copied the address from her driver's license and decided to call Merlin Fitzgerald to get her phone number. Fitzgerald picked up on the second ring.

"Mr. Fitzgerald, this is Detective Joe Erickson calling."

"Yes, sir."

"I was not aware that your wife was a sister to Frederick Van Andel, the private investigator who provided the videotape that Winslow and Wallingford used to blackmail Carson Byrne."

"Well...that's something I didn't want known."

"It would have been helpful to our investigation had you made us aware of that."

"I'm sorry."

"Well, you can make up for withholding information by telling me who inherited Van Andel's possessions after he died," said Joe in a voice that was conciliatory.

"He didn't have anything we wanted other than a few photos my wife was interested in. His furniture was junk. But Elise, my sister-in-law, she took a lot of personal items like his books and stuff like that."

"You have a phone number for her?"

"Uh, yeah. Hold on...I've got it right here...somewhere. Uh, here it is. 708-555-3841."

"Thank you."

"Any leads on who tried to kill me?"

"We're getting closer. Hopefully, it won't be long until we know who it is. Out of curiosity, did you ever meet with our forensic artist about creating a composite image of your attacker?"

"Uh...No, I didn't."

"Why not?"

"Something came up. I had to cancel."

"And you didn't make another appointment?"

"Not yet."

"It would be very helpful if you did."

"Yes, I know. I'll do that. First thing."

Joe ended the call and decided to speak with Sam before he made a call to Elise Pemberton. It was Sam's day off as well, and Joe didn't know if he wanted to hear about work today, but he was going to call Sam anyway.

"Hey, Sam.

"Yeah."

"I know it's your day off, but you want to hear about some work stuff?"

"Why not?"

"I just found out that Merlin Fitzgerald's wife is the sister of Frederick Van Andel—you know, the PI that—"

"—had the original videotape. Yeah, I know who he was. Sister, huh?"

"Yeah."

"You said Fitzgerald knew more than he was saying. Seems he was probably trying to protect his wife."

"And her sister that accompanied her to the hospital."

"Oh, the henna-head. Yeah. You think they know something?"

"I think the sister, Elise Pemberton, could maybe *have* something. She collected some of Van Andel's possessions after he died. It's a long shot, but I'm thinking he may have kept something of interest."

"You want to check that out Monday?"

"Yeah. I'm going to call her. She lives in Cicero. I want to set up a time to pay her a visit."

"Sounds good. We'll need to cover our trip to Cicero, somehow."

"Yeah, I know. It's over fifteen miles away."

"Maybe it would be better to do it this weekend when we're off," said Sam.

That was an interesting suggestion, especially coming from Sam. He was always protective about his days off.

"I'll tell you what. Why don't I call her and see what she says. Maybe I can set something up today or tomorrow. I'll text you."

"Cool."

Joe called Elise Pemberton and hoped his call would not be interpreted as one of those obnoxious solicitation calls. Fortunately, she answered.

"Hello."

"Ms. Pemberton, this is Detective Joe Erickson calling from Chicago PD. We met briefly outside Merlin Fitzgerald's hospital room."

"Oh, yes. I remember. How can I help you?"

"Our investigation is progressing, but we have some questions. Since you're Frederick Van Andel's sister, we would like to pursue a line of questioning regarding Mr. Van Andel and wondered if you would have time to meet with my partner and me this weekend."

"Oh, dear. I don't know what I could tell you about Fred. He and my late husband didn't really hit it off, so we were estranged for many years. Once my husband passed, and later when Fred got sick, we became closer. But he never talked to me about his work."

Joe pressed on, saying, "There are questions we have that I'd rather not go into on the phone. Is there a time when it's convenient for us to meet with you?"

"Well...I guess I could meet with you this afternoon."

"What time works for you?"

"How long do you think this will take? I have Bingo at six."

"It depends. No more than an hour. Probably less."

"How's three o'clock, then?"

"Three o'clock it is," said Joe. He confirmed her address and thanked her for her cooperation.

Then Joe texted Sam with the time and said he would need to pick him up around two-fifteen to allow for traffic. Sam agreed.

They arrived at Elise Pemberton's well-kept brick bungalow on South 54th Avenue in Cicero a few minutes after 3:00 p.m. They climbed the brick steps to the front door and rang the bell. A few moments later, the red-haired woman Joe saw in the hospital opened the door and invited them in.

"I remember you when I came to the hospital with my sister."

"Thank you for seeing us," said Joe.

She led them through a living room crammed with knickknacks, pictures, and anything else that could take up space to a dining room table that had, at its center, a three-tiered food tray displaying artificial fruit.

"Please, sit down," she said.

"Like I told you on the phone, we have a few questions regarding your brother."

"Okay."

"Your sister told us you kept a number of your brother's personal effects after he died. Would any of those items happen to be videotapes?"

"Why, yes. He had a large collection of science fiction movies and books. He was a big fan of science fiction."

"Did he have any other videotapes? The kind he would have used to record things himself. You know, like TV programs?

"I don't know. I just boxed everything up from his apartment. I didn't examine everything. Why do you ask?"

"We think he may have a copy of a surveillance he made before his death. If he did, it could be pertinent to a case we're presently working on."

"Oh."

"Where are those videotapes now?" asked Sam.

"Downstairs in the family room."

"I wouldn't ask this if it wasn't extremely important," said Joe. "But...would it be possible for us to look through those videotapes to see if there could be one related to our investigation?"

Pemberton thought for a moment and said, "The family room is a mess, but if it'll help your investigation, I guess it would all right." She rose from her chair. "Follow me."

Joe and Sam followed her through a door and down a set of stairs into a finished basement. The main room served as a family room that sported a couch and chair, a fifty-four-inch TV, and several bookcases, one crammed with books and another lined with videotapes.

Pointing at the videotapes, she said, "Have at it." Then she sat down in the chair, picked up knitting needles, and began working on a knitting project. Joe and Sam started examining the videotapes. All of them were commercially available VCR tapes. Fortunately, Pemberton had them arranged according to collections.

Van Andel's collection of sci-fi movies was extensive. While Joe was not a huge fan of science fiction, he knew film well enough to recognize classics like *Metropolis*, *Silent Running*, and *The Day the Earth Stood Still*. Both he and Sam pulled out a few of them and checked to be sure the box matched the actual tape.

Then as Joe was looking over the Star Trek movies, he saw two copies of *Star Trek II: The Wrath of Khan.* Joe thought *That's odd. Why two copies?* He pulled out the first one and looked it over. Nothing unusual. He put it back and removed the second. As he looked at the tape, he noticed something. A recordable VCR tape has a small plastic tab over a square indentation that allows the VCR machine to record on the cassette. Such a tab is missing on a commercially recorded tape to prevent recording. The small square indentation under the tab on this videocassette had been filled in with small pieces of cardboard and covered with a piece of scotch tape.

"Hey, Sam." Pointing to the modification, he said, "Look at this."

"Huh. Looks like somebody wanted to copy over this tape."

"Yeah." Joe got up, crossed over to Pemberton, and showed her the tape. "Excuse me. Did you copy over this videotape?"

"Me? I haven't even played any of these tapes since I got them from Fred's place. Just dust them once in a while."

Joe and Sam went through all of the tapes, looking for any others that may have been altered. They didn't find any. Just this one. Satisfied, they approached Pemberton.

"I think we may have found something," said Joe. "But we won't know until we watch this video. Do you have a VHS player here?"

"Sorry, I don't. Only a DVD player," said Pemberton, getting up from her chair. "So, you want to take that with you?"

"We do," said Sam. "We're going to need a VHS player so we can see what's been recorded onto this video cassette."

"Recorded? I don't understand."

"It's a duplicate of one you already have. We suspect something may have been recorded over it. If it's what we're looking for, it may need to be retained and admitted into evidence," said Joe.

"I suppose it's all right. I can't watch any of 'em, anyway."

On their way to the car, Joe said, "I don't have a VHS player. Do you?"

"Yup," said Sam. "Looks like we're going to my place."

They drove to Sam's apartment, a place Joe had never been. Entering his living room, Joe was amazed when he saw that Sam's entertainment system took up one wall. It was made up of a seventy-inch flat-screen television on top of a cabinet containing several different players, Bose surround sound, multiple receivers, and carefully placed speakers and sub-woofers. It was a film buff's dream home theatre system.

"I had no idea you were into this kind of equipment," said Joe. "This is some serious stuff."

"You like your cars. I like my home movies," said Sam. He pressed some switches and put the cassette into a VHS player. A moment later, the movie began playing its musical introduction. The sound quality was amazing, like being in a movie theater.

"You may as well have a seat. He could have recorded something anywhere. Besides, this is the best of the Star Trek films."

They watched the first several minutes, and right after the bridge was destroyed during the training session, new black and white video footage cut in. The quality was not the best, but it was clear enough to show a naked Carson Byrne with a naked boy about ten years of age.

"Oh…my…god," muttered Joe.

"I see now why it was worth killing for," said Sam.

They watched in silence as Byrne engaged in sex with the child. It was sickening, and Joe had to look at the floor and only glance at the screen occasionally, hoping it would soon be over. Finally, it was, and the Star Trek movie cut back in and continued playing. Sam stopped the tape.

"You need to see it again?"

"Are you kidding?" said Joe.

"Just wanted to know if I should rewind it." And he pressed "rewind" on the remote.

"Think we can find the identity of the boy?"

"From ten years ago or more? It'll be tough," said Sam. "But maybe sex crimes can do something with it."

"Byrne's a monster, a child molester. And to think he's been getting away with this for years with the help of people like Crouse and Briggs."

"Vincenzo was like a bloodhound, you know? He was on the trail, and

Byrne knew he would never stop until he found this video. Van Adel was clever enough to conceal it. But Vincenzo would have found it eventually."

"What do you think Vincenzo's reaction would have been if he'd found this video?" asked Joe.

"Same as ours. Outrage."

"What would he have done?"

"Ruin him with it," said Sam.

"I've got a way to do that. And I think we can catch who's been stealing evidence at the same time," said Joe. "Let's hold on to this video before we turn it in for evidence. And I want to make copies of the sex part of the tape—one on a video cassette and three on flash drives."

"I have the equipment to do that. I'll take care of it tomorrow."

"Good. I'll need two of the flash drives. And can you make the video cassette look old?"

"Age it? Sure, I can do that."

"Great."

"You have a plan, don't you?"

"Damned right."

Chapter Twenty-Seven

On Monday, Joe contacted the Office of the State's Attorney and asked for a meeting with State's Attorney Casey Wolff.

"May I ask what this is about?" Jada Robinson, her assistant, asked.

"Tell her I discovered a copy of the videotape. She'll know what that means."

"Hold on, please."

After a minute, she came back on the line and said, "How soon can you get here?"

Joe drove to the State's Attorney's Office, and when he entered the outer office, Jada Robinson picked up her phone and alerted Casey Wolff. Moments later, Wolff's door opened.

"Detective Erickson. Good to see you. Come in."

Joe was invited to sit, and as she rounded her desk, she said, "I was told you found a copy of the blackmail tape?"

"We did," said Joe. "We learned one of Frederick Van Andel's sisters took some of his possessions after he died, one of them being his science fiction videotape collection. To make a long story short, we found the video in question embedded within a VHS tape of a Star Trek movie."

"What was on it?" she asked eagerly.

"It clearly showed Carson Byrne havin' sex with an underage boy about ten years old."

Wolff's jaw literally dropped, and she was silent for a few seconds. "My god," she whispered.

"That was my reaction, too."

"I need to see this reprehensible video. Not that I want to, but I need to confirm it's him."

"Of course," said Joe, and he handed her a flash drive. "My partner made a copy for you on a flash drive so you could view it."

"Once I confirm it's him, you can arrest him. But you'll need to enter the original tape into evidence."

"That's the problem," said Joe. "It will disappear from our evidence locker. What I'd like to do is to enter into evidence a fake. But before that, I'd like to initiate a little sting operation in order to set up the person who's been tampering with evidence."

"Okay. I assume you have a plan for that?"

"I do. I have a good idea who's responsible. So, I'm having my partner place the sex video on a separate VHS tape and then age it so it looks ten years old. An exchange won't be possible. But it would be possible to tamper with it. Someone could erase it or render it unwatchable."

"Chain of custody will be critical," said Wolff.

"I can work with Sergeant Oatman who's in charge of the evidence locker. He can check the video after each person checks it out. If it comes back scrambled or destroyed, we've got our offender."

"Can you wait a few minutes, Detective?"

"Sure."

Wolff took the flash drive and inserted it into her computer. She watched the video for about one minute and then clicked off and removed it.

"I've seen enough. I'll watch the rest at home. If I'm going to vomit, I'd rather do it in my own bathroom. Go ahead and arrest Carson Byrne and place that videotape into evidence."

"Thank you."

"And keep the original in a safe place."

"It already is."

Joe left the Office of the State's Attorney and called Sam on his cell phone. Sam picked up on the third ring.

"Where are you?"

"Work. Where are you?"

"Returning from the State's Attorney. I'll be there shortly. I've cleared everything. Once we have the fake videotape, we can arrest Carson Byrne."

"I've got it. I finished it last night."

"But first, we need to get a VHS player for the evidence locker."

"Okay. Let me see if I can locate one with a built-in monitor."

"That would be best. You know where to get one?"

"Yeah, I do, but it's going to take a few minutes."

"While you're out getting one of those, I'll explain to Bill Oatman what we're doing. This little sting operation should nail our evidence thief."

"Okay," said Sam. "Then we can make the arrest this afternoon."

When Joe pulled into the Area 3 lot, he saw Sam waving to him. He walked over and asked for the keys.

"I need to go pick up the VHS recorder. I found one from a dealer I know. He says it's in excellent condition. I told him if it eats a tape, I'd have his ass in a sling. He claimed it rewinds and fast forwards without a problem."

"Perfect," said Joe. "I'll let Oatman know everything."

"Okay. This place isn't too far away. I should be back in half an hour."

Joe went straight to the evidence locker. Sergeant Oatman was on duty, and Joe asked if he could speak with him in confidence.

"What's going on?" asked Oatman.

"You know this issue we've had with missing evidence on the Vincenzo case?"

"Yeah."

"Sam and I are about to make a high-profile arrest, and we're going to be entering a piece of evidence into your custody. With permission from the State's Attorney, it's a copy of the original videotape. We suspect someone will try to tamper with it. We're going to bring you a video player so you can play the video after each person returns it after checking it out. If it comes back scrambled, broken, or does not have my mark on it, note who had it and let me know right away. We need to know who's been tampering with evidence in this case. Evidence that's in your custody."

"I want to know that, too. I sure as hell don't want somebody tryin' to blame me for fuckin' up."

"Good. Sam will be bringing a video player down here in a few minutes. He'll set it up and show you how to run it. Are you okay with this?"

"Hell, yes."

Joe and Oatman shook hands. "I have a feeling we're going to nail someone."

"Hope so."

Joe gave him his cell phone number so Oatman could call him should the tape come back scrambled or broken. Joe went back to his desk and entered generalized notes into his computer. He had talked these over with Sam, who would be entering comparable notes into his files as well.

Ten minutes later, he got a call from Sam. "Did you work everything out with Oatman?"

"Yeah, he's on board."

"Okay. I'm in the parking lot, and I have the unit. I'll come in and take it straight to the evidence locker."

"He's expecting you. I'll run interference in case someone we don't want might get eyes on the video player."

Joe met Sam at the entrance. Fortunately, Briggs did not come out of her office while they covered the space between the entrance and the evidence locker. Sam set up the video player for Sergeant Oatman and explained to him how to operate it. Like many people his age, he owned one in the past, so he was familiar with playing VHS tapes.

"Don't worry, Sam," Oatman said. "You and Joe can count on me."

"I know we can," said Sam, giving him a slap on the shoulder.

Sam walked to Joe's desk. "We're all set up with Oatman. You want to go pick up our esteemed alderman?"

"Yeah, let's do that," said Joe. You have the tape?"

"Uh-huh."

"Let's hope the alderman's in his office and not on vacation in Mexico."

Joe and Sam drove to Carson Byrne's office and double-parked outside with their lights flashing. They entered Byrne's office and presented their IDs to his receptionist, who told them he was in. Before she could ask their business, they barged past her into his office. He was on the phone when they entered.

Showing their IDs to a surprised Carson Byrne and his assistant, Joe said, "Hang up the phone, Alderman."

An indignant Byrne hung up the phone, stood, and protested, "What's going on here? How dare you?"

"How dare you, sir?" said Sam as he grabbed Byrne's arm and began cuffing him. "You're under arrest, Mr. Byrne."

"For what?"

"Predatory criminal sexual assault of a child to begin with," said Joe.

An intimidating, middle-aged man entered his office, and Sam shoved his ID in his face. "Chicago PD. Who are you?" Sam saw the bulge under his jacket and grabbed him by the arm, shoving him up against the wall.

"Mr. Byrne's bodyguard," said the man.

Sam disarmed him and said, "I hope you have a concealed carry license for this."

"I do."

"Let me see it."

Sam turned him around, and Joe saw his eyes. Sam looked at his concealed carry license and handed it back to him.

"Take a good look at his eyes," said Joe. "Look familiar to you?"

Sam looked and said, "Yeah. Lorre eyes." He turned the man around and cuffed him.

"What do you mean 'lorry-eyes'? What's that supposed to mean?"

"It means your eyes gave you away, Mr. Zelenko," said Sam. "Those gnarly hands of yours. And I see you bite your nails. Bad habit."

"Are you crazy?"

Sam began reading him his rights as he marched him out of the room.

Byrne's assistant stood dumbfounded in the doorway. Byrne looked at her and ordered, "Call my attorney, Cindy!"

"Mr. Byrne—"

"NOW, GOD DAMMIT!" screamed Byrne. Cindy ran out of the room like a frightened rabbit.

Joe read Byrne his rights, and then they walked both men out of the office

156

and to their car. On the way to Area 3, Joe called Al Hendricks, who headed up the sex crimes unit, and let him know what they had. He said he would meet them when they got in.

"You have the 'evidence'?" asked Joe.

"Check the glove compartment," said Sam.

Joe opened the glove compartment and looked at the videotape. He was astonished at how well Sam had aged it. The cardboard of the case was discolored and worn around the edges, while the tape itself was dusty in the indentations, and the label was smudged, scraped, and worn. Joe thought, *Wow, Sam could moonlight as a master forger.* He looked over at Sam and said, "Nice work, partner." Sam nodded and smiled.

Once they arrived at Area 3, they took Byrne to the conference room for questioning and Zelenko to a holding cell. Immediately, Byrne lawyered up and threatened to have Joe's star for this apparent affront to his dignity and reputation. Joe chose not to respond. Instead, he called Margaret Kummeyer at the Tribune.

"Greetings, Joe," she said in her usual teasingly provocative voice.

"Greetings to you, Margaret. What if I told you I had evidence of one of the biggest stories of your career? What would that be worth to you?"

"I don't do sexual favors."

"I don't accept them."

"How about my everlasting gratitude and a drink at GWilliquors?"

"Sounds good. Meet me there at five o'clock."

"Wow. This must be fucking big."

"Margaret, it's fucking huge."

Joe knew that Byrne could afford the best lawyers money could buy. He might be able to quash the videotape in court, but Joe wanted to ruin him in the eyes of the public in case he could beat the rap legally. He knew Margaret could do that. And there was no way that Margaret would reveal her source.

Sam entered the videotape into evidence, and Sergeant Oatman knew the sting was on. He watched the videotape to make sure it was in good condition. His reaction was one of disgust, and he told Sam, "It's a wonder it doesn't self-destruct." He rewound it to get it ready for the next person who needed to view it and then locked it up.

Al Hendricks met Joe after Byrne had lawyered up. Joe explained they had a copy of the VHS videotape that Frederick Van Andel had provided to the blackmailers of Carson Byrne. Telling him what was on it, Hendricks wanted to view it so he could see the victim. Joe told him the tape was in the evidence locker, and he would have to have a VHS player to view it. Hendricks said he would bring one to work the next day.

When Lieutenant Briggs heard Joe and Sam had arrested Carson Byrne, she came barreling out of her office like a Doberman Pinscher in attack mode. "What the hell do you two think you're doing arresting an alderman?" she growled.

"You mean arresting a child molester," snapped Joe."

"A what?!"

"Maybe you should watch the videotape we have showing him having sex with an underage boy, Lieutenant!"

That stopped her dead in her tracks. "You have a tape of him doing that?"

"Yeah. It's now in the evidence locker."

"I'll want to see it."

"Get in line," said Sam. "I think Al Hendricks has first dibs."

"We'll see about that," she snarled. "The next time you make a high-profile arrest like this, I want to know about it ahead of time."

"Your predecessor didn't require us to inform him of our arrests," replied Joe.

"That's right," said Sam. "We were just following what we believed to be established protocol."

"Well, I don't care what Lieutenant Vincenzo did. From now on, if you make this kind of arrest, I want to know about it. Is that understood?"

"Understood."

"Would you prefer a phone call, email, or a text?" asked Joe with a deadpan expression.

"Or face-to-face?" added Sam.

With a look that would kill lesser men, she replied, "Face-to-face, detectives."

CHAPTER TWENTY-SEVEN

"Understood," Joe replied.

"Thank you, Lieutenant," replied Sam.

Briggs turned and went back into her office.

"You think she's calling Crouse?" asked Sam.

"Undoubtedly."

"Honey. Honey, there's been a development," said Sam, imitating Briggs.

"Oh, Jeez. Don't do that!" chuckled Joe. "It isn't funny, you know."

"You're telling me. Have you thought about doing surveillance on Crouse to see who he might be hanging out with?"

"I've been thinking about it, but it might be more productive if we nail his squeeze. It might throw him off-balance, so he makes a mistake."

"You think Vincenzo pegged him as the shooter in the Wallingford murder?"

"I think there's a good chance he was the triggerman. He could have identified himself as a detective, showed his ID to Wallingford, gained his trust, and then popped him. And Byrne was in a position to pay him handsomely for the hit. I'm going to do some background work on him and see what turns up."

Joe and Sam began questioning Stan Zelenko, but he refused to talk and asked to speak to an attorney. He was photographed, and Joe got copies of his mugshot to show Merlin Fitzgerald to see if he could identify him as the man who beat him up or as the nurse who tried to inject him with succinylcholine.

The day ended with no one checking out the videotape. By the time Byrne's attorney arrived, it was too late for him to make bail, and he was forced to be held in custody overnight. It infuriated him.

Joe called Destiny and told her he would be late getting home. Then he took an Uber to GWilliquors, a bar on Randolph Street, to meet with Margaret Kummeyer. He and Margaret had a symbiotic relationship in that he would occasionally act a source for her as long as it would not compromise an investigation. Sometimes it would result in a scoop for her, and sometimes she would agree to hold a story if it would jeopardize an investigation.

Joe got to the bar early and grabbed a stool at the bar. For a Tuesday, the place was quite busy, and no booths or tables were available. He ordered a Guinness and waited. Three swallows into his drink, he felt a tap on his shoulder. Swiveling on his stool, he saw Margaret with an amused look on her face.

"How many of those have you had?"

"First one."

"Likely story." She looked over her shoulder and pointed, "That booth is clearing out. You want to grab it?"

"Yeah." They moved to the booth and sat down before anyone else moved in.

"Can I get you something?" Joe asked.

"A glass of Chardonnay would be nice."

Joe went to the bar and got her a glass of Chardonnay, and returned to the booth. Setting it in front of her, he said, "Your server will be with you shortly."

"I thought you were my server," she said, blinking her eyes behind her glasses.

"I guess I am, in a manner of speaking." And he removed a flash drive from his pocket and pushed it across the table.

"What's this?"

"We arrested Alderman Carson Byrne today. This is the evidence. I thought you might like to view it before you write your 'shocking article' for tomorrow's edition. What time do you go to press?"

"What was he arrested for?"

"Predatory criminal sexual assault of a child."

"Omigod! Are you kidding me?"

"Watch the video, and you'll see him in action."

"Oh, no…no, no, no. You're not telling me…?"

"Yeah, I'm telling you, Margaret. But you didn't get the footage from me."

"You know I never reveal my sources."

"It's the video footage that Troy Winslow used to blackmail Carson Byrne ten years ago. Byrne killed him for it. Winslow concocted this scheme along with Robert Wallingford. Wallingford acquired the videotape from his uncle, a private investigator, who filmed it. He gave it to Wallingford before he died. He wanted him to take it to the police."

"How did his uncle get it?"

"He must have managed to get a spy camera into Byrne's bedroom. I don't know any details about it."

"Too bad. He must have suspected something or been working for somebody."

"We'll probably never know. Anyway, Wallingford witnessed Byrne killing Winslow, and that's what got Byrne arrested. Before Wallingford could testify about it in court, Byrne had him killed, and the videotape went missing. Captain Vincenzo was investigating Wallingford's murder because he originally arrested Byrne for Winslow's murder. He told me he wanted to solve this cold case before he retired. We think Vincenzo was killed because he was getting close to solving it."

"And this was all because Byrne was trying to cover up his sexual activities with young boys?"

"Four murders that we know of," said Joe. "And we can't prove any of them. At least, not yet. You can't print that, of course."

"I know. I'll stick with the perversion angle. That should suffice, don't you think?"

"Oh, yeah. It'll suffice. For now."

Margaret got up to leave. "Sorry, but I have to run. I need to get my editor's approval to run this. And he may need to run it up the chain."

Chapter Twenty-Eight

While other newspapers ran a small article about Alderman Byrne's arrest, the Tribune upstaged them all with Margaret's front-page exposé on his arrest, the scandalous charge, and its possession of a sex tape. Local television stations picked up on the Tribune's article, and reporters swarmed Byrne's office and home.

Back from jogging, Joe found a copy of the Tribune Destiny left on the table. She had coffee ready and poured him a cup. "You might want to check out the Trib before you hit the shower. You're mentioned by name."

Oh-oh, he thought. "I am?"

"Uh-huh. Go ahead and read it. I'll make you breakfast."

"Thanks." He picked up the paper and saw the front-page article with Margaret Kummeyer's byline. "Way to go, Margaret!" he said with a smile as he sat down at the island and began reading.

"Should I assume she got a scoop from someone I know?"

"I think you can assume that."

"She's going to owe you big-time."

"Mm-hm."

Joe finished reading the article as Destiny placed his breakfast of whole wheat toast buttered with roasted red pepper hummus and a glass of tomato juice in front of him.

"That's quite an article. She didn't have to mention Sam and me as the arresting officers, though. What do you think of the article?"

"It's devastating. He'll be ruined politically."

"That's what I wanted. If he somehow weasels out of a conviction, and we can't prove he was behind Vincenzo's murder, at least he'll be a pariah in this city."

"Did you give her a copy of the sex tape?"

"I did."

"Aren't you concerned someone will find out it came from you?"

"She'll never reveal her source. Besides, it could have come from someone besides me. Who knows who might have a copy of it?"

When Joe got to the office, Sam was already there. He handed Joe a large cup of Starbucks coffee.

"Good morning. What's new?" asked Joe, tongue firmly planted in cheek.

"I take it you read the Trib this morning?" asked Sam.

"Yeah."

"How the hell did Margaret Kummeyer get that kind of a scoop?"

"She must have had a good source."

"Uh-huh. I don't suppose you still have those two flash drives I gave you?"

"Kasey Wolff has one, and I seem to have temporarily misplaced the other one. But if I look hard enough, I can find it."

"I thought so."

Out of the corner of his eye, Joe saw Lieutenant Briggs carrying a box toward her office and Sergeant Ackerman, who works outside her office, carrying a small flatscreen television.

"Look to your left," said Joe.

Sam caught a glimpse of Briggs. "Looks like she's preparing to watch the videotape this morning."

"Uh-huh. I wonder if she's read the Trib."

"Oh, I'll bet she has. How much you want to bet we'll get called into her office?"

"Only a fool would take that bet," chuckled Sam.

After logging in, Joe called down to the evidence locker to check in with Sergeant Oatman.

"Evidence Locker, Sergeant Oatman."

"Joe Erickson."

"How you doin'?"

"I wanted to give you a heads up about Lieutenant Briggs. I saw her carrying in a box, and Sergeant Ackerman was following her carrying a small TV this morning. She'll be requesting the VHS tape at some point."

"I anticipated that. I've already got it ready to go."

"Great. Thanks, Sergeant."

Shortly after 8:00, Joe and Sam were called into Lieutenant Briggs' office. The VHS player was not set up yet.

The first words out of her mouth were, "Why did I have to read about sensitive evidence about Carson Byrne in the Tribune this morning?"

"I don't know, Lieutenant," replied Joe.

"I have no idea," said Sam.

"Now, I want to know how that reporter was privy to so much information. Did that leak come from one of you?"

"Lieutenant Briggs," Joe began. "Margaret Kummeyer has more scoops than Baskin-Robbins."

Briggs' eyes went cold. "You think this is funny, Detective?"

"Not at all. She scoops other reporters all the time. She's their best investigative reporter. She must have sources all over the city."

"I've wondered how she does it myself, Lieutenant," added Sam. "This isn't the first time she's done this."

"Well, I'd better not find out the leak came from either of you," snarled Briggs.

There was a pause, and after a few seconds, Sam spoke up. "You're not going to congratulate us on our collar, Lieutenant? Big fish."

Joe had to bite the inside of his cheek to keep it together when he heard Sam's question.

A vein in Briggs' forehead pulsed as she looked back and forth from Sam to Joe. Then, she begrudgingly said, "Congratulations...Now get back to work." She turned her back to them and walked to her desk and continued connecting the VHS recorder to the TV.

Joe and Sam walked out of her office. Once they were in the hall, they looked at each other and burst into laughter.

"I can't believe you could ask that with a straight face," said Joe.

"I wanted to get under her skin," said Sam.

"I think you succeeded."

"Did you see her face when you said that 'Baskin Robbins' line?"

"Yeah. It was colder than a dish of Daiquiri Ice."

When Joe got back to his desk, he made a call to Merlin Fitzgerald's cell phone. His call went to voicemail, so he left a message stating it was very important he call him. In the meantime, Joe began researching Stan Zelenko, Byrne's bodyguard.

Stanley Raymond Zelenko was born in Des Moines, Iowa, forty-one years ago. He graduated from high school in Des Moines and joined the U.S. Marine Corps shortly after graduation. He spent six years in the Marines and served multiple tours in the Middle East. His Facebook account was not very active. But it showed he was a member of the National Rifle Association, Sportsman's Alliance, and the Safari Club International.

Joe ran him through the system and found Zelenko did not have a criminal record. Checking various systems, he found he had a FOID (Firearm Owners Identification) card, a concealed carry license, an Illinois driver's license, a hunting license, and owned a two-year-old Ford Mustang. Nothing unusual other than the fact he liked to hunt and probably owned guns. But with six years as a Marine coupled with his hunting background, he would know his way around high-powered rifles, making him a likely suspect for the triggerman in Vincenzo's shooting.

A few minutes after ten o'clock, Joe got a call from Lieutenant Briggs, who wanted to see him and Sam. Joe called Sergeant Oatman.

When they walked into her office, she had the VHS player hooked up and the television monitor on.

"Have you seen this videotape?" she asked angrily.

"Yeah, we've seen the footage," said Joe.

"Well, maybe you can explain this," she said as she pushed "Play" on the video player. What played was a scrambled, snowy mess that showed virtually nothing.

"Yeah. I can explain it," said Joe. "You used a demagnetizer on it."

"What are you—"

"Shut the fuck up!" said Joe. "Arrest her," he said to Sam.

"How dare you!"

Joe put on a pair of gloves and started going through her desk.

"You're under arrest for destroying evidence," said Sam.

Are you crazy?" Then she called out, "SERGEANT!"

Sergeants Brown and Ackerman, who sit at desks outside the Lieutenant's office, came running in to find out what was wrong. Both were horrified to see Sam cuffing Briggs and reading her her rights.

"What the hell's going on?" asked Ackerman.

"We've just arrested Lieutenant Briggs for suspicion of destroying evidence. To be more precise, for destroying a videotape with this," said Joe, pulling a demagnetizer device from her drawer.

"Do us a favor and get Lieutenant Bell in here from Property Crimes. A supervisor needs to run this up the chain of command," said Sam. "NOW, PLEASE!"

Sam knew Zachary Bell had previously worked as a detective in homicide and vice before moving to property crimes, and Bell would be able to handle this issue temporarily.

Ackerman left to get Lieutenant Bell while Sergeant Brown stepped in and looked on, watching Joe place the demagnetizer and the videotape into evidence bags.

"You're going to pay for this, Erickson," growled Briggs.

"You're the one who's going to pay, Briggs. Destroying evidence is the least of your worries."

Sam marched her to the conference room, where she demanded to speak with an attorney as well as the Commander.

Sergeant Brown left as Sergeant Oatman stepped into the room. Moments later, Lieutenant Bell entered and walked up to Joe. "My god! You've arrested Lieutenant Briggs. Is that right?"

"We have. We suspected her of switching evidence once before, and today she destroyed a videotape with this demagnetizer," said Joe, holding up the demagnetizer in the evidence bag.

"Are you sure about this?"

CHAPTER TWENTY-EIGHT

Joe looked over at Sergeant Oatman and said, "Sergeant."

Oatman stepped forward and said, "This videotape was in perfect condition when I brought it up for her to watch. If something happened to it, it happened in here."

"What was on the videotape?" asked Bell.

"Evidence showing Alderman Byrne having sex with a young boy," said Joe.

"And she destroyed it?" said a horrified Bell.

"She did, but the videotape was a copy we used to catch whoever was destroying evidence. We have the original in a safe place."

"Thank god for that. I'll call Commander Edwardson and bring him up to speed on what just happened. Think she's working for Byrne?"

"We think there's a conspiracy to keep Byrne's sexual proclivities secret. Captain Vincenzo was investigating it and became a victim of this conspiracy. Briggs was a part of it."

"Omigod...think she'll talk?"

"We'll see." He handed the bagged evidence to Sergeant Oatman. "It's all yours, Sergeant."

"I'll get this logged in," said Oatman, and he left for the evidence locker.

While Joe and Sam were preoccupied with arresting Lieutenant Briggs, Carson Byrne made bail and quickly made himself unavailable for comment. His attorney, Richard Whittier of the high-powered firm of DeForrest, Brown, and Whittier, called the charges "spurious" and proclaimed, "Mr. Byrne will soon be cleared of these malicious and false allegations."

Stan Zelenko's attorney got him released. He could only be held for twenty-four hours without charges. Peter Lorre eyes and bitten fingernails were hardly grounds to charge him with anything, and Merlin Fitzgerald had not returned Joe's phone call. Joe tried calling him again to see if he could come in and try to identify Zelenko as his assailant, but his call went to voicemail. He would have to follow up tomorrow. Joe was hoping they could collect something to get Zelenko's DNA, but he refused offers for food and drink. Smart.

Commander Edwardson met with Joe and Sam that afternoon, and they went into detail about how the flash drive logged into the evidence locker got switched after it was handled by Briggs. And after the discovery of the sex tape, they decided to create a sting to catch Briggs destroying evidence. Joe mentioned he discussed this with the State's Attorney, who suggested entering a copy into evidence rather than the original since Joe didn't know who to trust or how high this conspiracy might go.

"So, you suspected that I could be involved in this?" asked Edwardson, who was clearly offended by their lack of trust.

"After our lunch together, I was pretty sure you were not a part of this, Commander. But I couldn't be sure that one of your superiors wasn't dirty. I couldn't take that chance."

"All right, I guess I understand. If I was in your shoes, I'd be suspicious of me and everybody else up the chain. This entire goddamned thing stinks."

Joe let out a sigh of relief after hearing Commander Edwardson's response. He needed him on their side now, as well as his continued support as their investigation moved forward.

Joe and Sam continued to discuss where their investigation was heading but didn't mention they suspected former Captain Jerome Crouse, not knowing whether he was one of Edwardson's pals. Commander Edwardson commended them for their diligence in rooting out corruption within the department and their work on the Vincenzo investigation. He said he was going to meet with Lieutenant Briggs next since he was her supervisor and said he was interested in hearing her side of the story.

Joe wished he could be a fly on the wall during that meeting. Instead, he would be on his way home, planning what he needed to do tomorrow in order to get one step closer to solving Vincenzo's murder.

Chapter Twenty-Nine

With Lieutenant Briggs on suspension, the sergeants were carrying on until someone was appointed temporary homicide lieutenant. Sam brought in the original Star Trek videotape evidence discovered during the search of Frederick Van Andel's videos, and Sergeant Oatman logged it in and placed it in the evidence locker.

"Just in case, did you make a copy?" asked Oatman, half-seriously.

"There better not be a situation this time," said Sam.

"I don't think you have to worry about that now that Briggs got pinched."

"Let's hope not. But I'd still be checking."

"Oh, don't worry. I will be."

While Sam was in the evidence locker, Joe researched retired Captain Jerome Crouse. Crouse was fifty-seven years old, divorced with no children. He spent six years in the US Army infantry, where he completed US Army Sniper School...*Whoa!* Joe sat up and read it again. Crouse was a trained sniper? *Holy shit!* thought Joe. *He could easily have been the triggerman lying in wait for Vincenzo at the elementary school.* The round that killed Vincenzo hit him in the middle of his chest—a perfect shot for a trained sniper.

"Hey, Sam!" called Joe. "Come here."

"Whatcha got?"

"You've gotta see this."

Sam walked over, and Joe said, "I started looking into Crouse, and look what I found." He pointed to the screen.

Sam looked over Joe's shoulder. "Are you kidding me? He was a sniper?"

"A trained sniper. He may have kills to his credit since he served during

Desert Storm. I was looking at Zelenko for the hit on Vincenzo, but now...."

"I'd put my money on Crouse, but both he and Zelenko have infantry experience. Either one could have done it. Somehow, we need to narrow it down to one or the other," said Sam.

"Yeah. First, I need to contact Merlin Fitzgerald and see if he can recognize Zelenko's mugshot. Let me try calling him again."

Joe called Fitzgerald's cell phone, and once again, his call went to voicemail. He tried calling their landline, and after four rings, the answering machine kicked on. He hung up. Looking at Sam, he said, "I don't like this."

"What do you want to do?"

"Let's go to their home and see if they're all right. I hope to hell we don't find another Patty Thorpe scene."

Joe and Sam drove to the Fitzgeralds' apartment on West Agatite Avenue in Uptown. They buzzed but did not get an answer. Joe buzzed a random resident.

"Yes?"

"Chicago Police Department. Could you buzz us in, please?"

"A moment, please."

A minute later, a silver-haired man in his seventies appeared at the door. Joe held up his ID so he could see it, and the man opened the door.

"I'm Detective Joe Erickson. My partner, Sam Renaldo. We're trying to reach Merlin Fitzgerald, but we're getting no answer, and he's not answering his phone. Do you know him or his wife?"

"I live down the hall," said the man with an Eastern European accent. "They went to Florida."

"Florida? Since when, do you know?"

"A few days ago. They have a daughter who lives down there. Fort Lauderdale, I think."

"Would you happen to know her name?"

"I do not. Sorry."

"Do you know when they'll be back?"

"No. I saw them when they were walking out with luggage, and I asked if they were taking a vacation. To make conversation, you see. His wife said they were going to Florida to visit their daughter. That's all I know."

"Well, thank you for your time, Mr...."

"Kovalenko. Dmitry Kovalenko."

"Mr. Kovalenko. We appreciate it."

"Did something happen? They are not in trouble, are they?"

"No," said Sam. "We're just following up on an investigation. It can wait until he gets home."

On the drive back to Area 3, Sam asked, "You think they took a trip to Florida because they're afraid to stay here in Chicago?"

"I wouldn't be surprised. Beaten to a pulp once and nearly killed by injection another time. That would motivate a lot of people to get out of town. I'll keep trying to call him. Maybe he'll get tired of hearing my messages and call me back."

"Contact his assistant and see if he can give you an alternate email address."

"Good idea. I knew there was a reason I liked having you around."

Back at Area 3, Joe called their forensic artist to see if Fitzgerald had met with her before he left. He had not. Joe then contacted Dennis Coben, Fitzgerald's assistant, and obtained another email address for Fitzgerald. He sent him a message with a mugshot of Stan Zelenko attached and asked if he could identify him as his assailant.

Shortly after, a call came in from the Office of the State's Attorney. The news was not good.

"Detective Erickson, this is Jada Robinson from the Office of the State's Attorney.

"Yes, Ms. Robinson."

"Carson Byrne's attorney managed to get the videotape evidence suppressed. I'm sorry."

Joe's heart sank. "So, he walked?" asked Joe.

"We had no choice. The videotape was the only evidence we had. Unless we have the identity of the boy in the video, and he's willing to testify against Byrne, we have no case."

"Wonderful," mumbled Joe.

"If you can dig up more information, let us know. We want him behind bars as much as you do."

"Thank you. My best to your boss."

Furious, Joe had to go for a walk to cool down before he told Sam. Out in the parking lot, he called Destiny to tell her the news.

She reassured him, "You still exposed him for what he is, Joe. Everyone knows. And he's going to be an untouchable socially and politically."

"I know, but his victims deserve justice."

"Maybe there's still a way to tie him to the murder of Vincenzo. That way, you can put him away for good."

"I'll do my best."

"I know you will. That's all anyone can ask."

"I guess. See you later."

After speaking with Destiny and going for a walk, Joe had calmed down. He entered the building and let Sam know about the call from the Office of the State's Attorney.

Sam's disgust was palpable. "So, the molester's going to get away with it, huh?"

"No. We're not going to let him. There's more evidence out there. We can put him away for assault or put him away for murder. I prefer the latter. Let's put our effort in that direction."

"You may be right. Put him away for life rather than ten years."

"Let's keep an eye on Crouse and Zelenko. See where they go, who they see, what they do. Maybe we can turn up something," said Joe.

"We got the connection between Crouse and Briggs that way. We may be able to turn up something else if we keep our eyes peeled. Who do you want?"

"I'll take Crouse," said Joe. "I wonder if he'll still be seeing Briggs, now she's in big trouble."

"That might be enough to put some distance between them, but you never know about love," quipped Sam.

"Love. I'll let you know. You want to go Fridays, Saturdays, and Sundays, or should we do more days?"

"Let's do weekends and see what happens. We can go from there."

"Good, because I'm not doing every night stuff ever again."

Chapter Thirty

Shortly before one o'clock, two days later, Joe received a phone call. The caller was transferred to his phone from the department's main desk.

"Is this Detective Erickson?" the male voice asked.

"Yes, this is Detective Erickson. How can I help you?"

The man's voice revealed he was nervous and uncomfortable calling. "My name's Greg Campbell. I read your name in the Tribune about arresting Carson Byrne."

"That's correct." There was a pause. Sensing Campbell wanted to tell him something, he said, "Do you have information regarding the case?"

"Well, you know the videotape that was referred to? In the paper?"

"Yes?"

"Well...the boy in that video...he was my son."

This took Joe aback. He needed to be sure this guy was for real and not some crackpot. "All right, how do you know it's your son?"

"I paid a private investigator named Fred Van Andel to find out if my son was being sexually abused by Carson Byrne. He provided me with videotape evidence that he was."

Whoa! This guy's for real. "Mr. Campbell, I think we need to talk in person. Are you here in Chicago?"

"I am."

"What about your son?"

"He's a student at Princeton. He's taking a summer course at the moment."

"Would you agree to come in and speak with us?"

"I can do that."

Joe set up a meeting for him the next day at eleven o'clock. After he got off the phone, he walked to Sam's desk. He wasn't there, but Joe knew he was in the building. Walking to the conference room, he spotted him getting a cup of coffee from the Keurig.

"The young guys winning you over to their coffee?" asked Joe.

"The coffee in the pot is sludge. What's up?"

"You're not going to believe this, but I just got off the phone with the father of the young boy on the videotape."

"And it wasn't a crank call?"

"Oh, no. He told me he hired Fred Van Andel because he suspected Byrne of sexually abusing his son. Van Andel showed him video proof that he was."

"Oh, man. What a thing to see."

"No kidding."

"Did he do anything about it?"

"I didn't ask. I set up a meeting with him tomorrow at eleven. If we're lucky, we might be able to nail Byrne for abuse after all."

"You think his son would testify? He'd have to in order to convict Byrne."

"Yeah, I know. But dredging up those old memories could be traumatic."

* * *

The next morning Yvonne Briggs was arraigned on charges of tampering with evidence and obstruction of justice, both felonies in Illinois. Not only was she looking at losing her job and possible imprisonment if convicted, but also forfeiting her pension. She pled not guilty and was released on bond. Joe was sure he would be called as a witness for the prosecution once the trial was underway. He looked forward to it.

A few minutes before eleven o'clock, Joe got a call saying Greg Campbell had arrived. Joe alerted Sam, who went to secure the conference room while Joe went to meet Campbell.

Greg Campbell was a handsome, well-groomed man in his late forties. His blonde hair fell over his forehead, giving him a youthful, Kennedy-esque look.

"Mr. Campbell?" asked Joe.

"Yes," he said as he turned to see Joe. "You're Detective Erickson, I take it?"

"I am." After shaking hands, Joe led him to the conference room where he introduced him to Sam.

"Have a seat. You want anything? Water, coffee, soda?" asked Sam.

"I'm fine, thank you," said Campbell, unbuttoning his sport jacket and easing into his chair.

"Thank you for coming in," said Joe. "When did you first become concerned your son might be the victim of sexual abuse?"

"Andy was always an outgoing kid. Funny. Gregarious. Then he started withdrawing to his room and seemed distant. He wasn't interested in being with friends. Wasn't excited about swimming anymore, and he loved swimming on the swim team."

"So, what made you think it was sexual abuse?"

"I went into his room when he wasn't there and saw some of his drawings. Some of them were sexual in nature. Not something a ten-year-old would be drawing."

"What made you suspect Carson Byrne?"

"He sponsored Andy's swim team, and I noticed he attended all their events. He also had the boys over to his house to swim in his inside pool. And it was after one of these outings that Andy's behavior began changing."

"So, what did you do?"

"I got suspicious, so I hired a private investigator to look into it. I didn't want to accuse a city alderman of something if he was innocent. And I didn't want to pull Andy from the swim team if something was happening elsewhere."

"Did Byrne have another swim party at his house? After you hired the PI?" asked Joe.

"He did."

"And Andy attended?"

"Yes."

"Were you there?"

"No, I couldn't be there, but other parents were."

"Why couldn't you be there?

"I was called in on an emergency surgery."

"You're a doctor?"

"Anesthetist."

"Did you pick him up after the party?" asked Sam.

"No, the parents of one of his friends picked him up, and I went to their home to get him once I got out of surgery."

"I take it you're a single father?" asked Joe.

"I'm divorced. I got custody of Andy. His mother had…issues. I'd rather not go into it."

"That's fine. How long did it take for Van Andel to get back to you?"

"A week after the party. He asked me to come to his apartment, and that's when he…showed me the videotape."

"And…"

"I cried, Detective. I couldn't believe someone could do something like that to my ten-year-old son."

"And what did you do about the abuse?"

"I met with Byrne and told him I knew what he did to Andy. He denied it, of course, so I gave him a digital copy of the tape. After that, he asked me what I wanted. I gave him a choice: stay away from those kids, or I would go to the police."

"Why didn't you go to the police?"

"Because I didn't want to put my ten-year-old son through a highly publicized trial. I just wanted to get him into therapy as soon as possible. A trial could have done permanent damage to him psychologically."

"What did Byrne do?"

"He dropped his sponsorship of the swim team and stayed away from the boys. I picked up the sponsorship myself."

"What about Andy?" asked Sam.

"I got him into therapy right away."

"So, Andy's therapy was successful, I assume?"

"It was. A year of therapy did wonders. But it continued for three more years."

"Byrne's attorney got the videotape evidence thrown out, so the state has no case against Byrne at the present time. The only way we can convict Byrne is if Andy would be willing to testify against him in court. Do you think he'd be willing to do that?"

"Omigod," murmured Campbell. "I don't know. I...."

"I know it would be hard. And I understand if he would choose not to do it," said Joe. "But...would you at least ask him?"

"Yeah. I'll bring it up."

"That would be good. Thanks. I doubt if Byrne ended his sexual proclivities. We need to take him down once and for all. He's had three people killed to prevent that tape from surfacing. One was our former lieutenant, Sal Vincenzo. We want him one way or the other."

"He was responsible for that, too?" asked Campbell.

"We have pretty good indications he was, but we don't have the definitive evidence yet," said Joe.

"He's a bad guy, and we want to see that he pays for his crimes," added Sam.

When the interview was over, Joe and Sam showed him out and urged him to call them when he heard back from his son. Once he was gone, Sam turned to Joe and asked, "What do you think?"

"I hope his son is psychologically strong enough to testify. And it just gave me an idea to flush out our sniper. But first, we need to narrow down who it is."

"Any ideas about that?"

"Maybe."

Chapter Thirty-One

Early Friday evening, Joe began surveilling Jerome Crouse while Sam began watching Stan Zelenko. Shortly after 6:30 p.m., a black Nissan pulled up in front of Crouse's residence. Crouse came out and got into the backseat before it took off. Joe assumed he had called for a Lyft or Uber ride.

Joe followed the Nissan to Yvonne Briggs' apartment, where he went inside. At 9:00 p.m., Joe called Sam.

"What do you have?"

"A lot of excitement. Zelenko had a pizza delivered."

"Crouse caught an Uber to Briggs' apartment and arrived shortly before seven. No activity since," said Joe.

"Oh, I'll bet there's been activity."

"Probably commiserating about her indictment."

"Horizontally."

Joe laughed. "You're sick."

"I am. I admit it."

"Check in later."

A few minutes before midnight, Joe received a call from Sam. "Nothing happening here, Joe. What about you?"

"Nothing here either. Ready to call it quits for the night?"

"Yeah. Maybe something will shake loose tomorrow night."

"Maybe. Talk to you tomorrow."

Joe drove home and parked his undercover car in the garage, where it would be ready for tomorrow night's surveillance. Because Crouse was a former cop, he could have spotted an unmarked car's strobe lights mounted behind the grill or in the visor and become aware of their presence. That's why Joe and Sam chose undercover cars for their surveillance. They were cars seized in drug busts and other crimes and had no emergency lights or radios.

The next day at work, Joe and Sam discussed what to do about Zelenko and Crouse. In addition to surveillance, they needed information to help narrow the scope of their investigation.

"We didn't get much when we interviewed Zelenko the first time," said Sam. "Maybe we should question him again. See if he can provide us with anything."

"Agreed. Maybe we should get a warrant drawn up for his apartment in case we need it," said Joe.

"I'll get one ready."

Half an hour later, they were on their way to Carson Byrne's office. Once they arrived, they entered and met his receptionist, who recognized them immediately. She stood when she saw them and gave them a wary look.

"Good morning," said Joe in a friendly tone. "We'd like to speak with Stan Zelenko. Is he here?"

"He is. Let me get him for you." She picked up the phone and pressed a button. "Mr. Zelenko, there are two detectives here who wish to speak with you." There was a pause. Then she looked at Joe and said meekly, "He says he's busy."

"Tell him we'll wait as long as it takes."

Back into the phone, she said, "They said they'll wait as long as it takes."

Joe could hear his response over the phone, and it wasn't pleasant. She hung up the phone and said, "He'll be right out."

Seeing the nameplate on her desk, Joe said, "Thank you, Audrey." She tried to smile but didn't succeed.

A moment later, Zelenko emerged from a hallway. "What's this about?" he asked in a belligerent tone.

"We have a few questions," said Joe.

"Why didn't you ask them when you took me into custody the other day?

You made me sit in a cell all day."

"That was because you lawyered up," said Sam. "We have to play by the rules."

"Rules."

"Look, we can do this here, or we can take you back to our office again. What's it going to be? You can have your attorney present if you want."

After a short pause, Zelenko said, "Follow me." Opening his jacket for them, he said, "If you'll note, I'm not carrying."

They followed him down to a small meeting room with a table and chairs, where they sat down.

"Ask away. Let's get this over with," said Zelenko.

"All right," said Joe. "Where were you on the night of June third?"

"June third. On June third, I was in Wyoming hunting black bear."

"And you can prove that?"

"Do I need to?"

"If you want to be eliminated as a suspect in the murder of Sal Vincenzo. Yeah, you do."

"Okay. What do you want? Plane tickets? Hunting permit? Photos of me with the bear I took? Name and address of the hunting guide?"

"Those things would suffice," said Sam.

"Jesus," said Zelenko under his breath.

"You're an avid hunter," said Joe. "You own a seven-millimeter rifle?"

"Why do you ask?"

"Humor me."

"Yeah. A Remington 700. It's my bear rifle. Great for long-distance kills."

"Mind if we run it through ballistics?"

"Yeah, I mind. Why would you want to do that?"

"Because a seven-millimeter rifle fired the fatal round that killed Captain Vincenzo."

Zelenko was becoming more and more agitated as the questioning went on. "I had that rifle with me in Wyoming. I used that rifle to take down my bear."

"Then why not let us test it? To eliminate it as the murder weapon," asked

Sam.

"Because I don't want the police or anyone else messing with my guns!"

Joe pushed back his chair, as did Sam. "Thank you for your time, Mr. Zelenko." Joe left his card on the table. "I expect your verification information sent to my email address within a day, or we'll be back, and you won't like it. Oh, and you can expect a warrant for your rifle in the next few days as well."

Joe and Sam left Byrne's office listening to a barrage of profanity. Out in the car, Sam said, "You think he was bullshitting us?"

"I don't know," said Joe. "My gut's telling me he was being honest about that hunting trip. I'm going to do some internet sleuthing and see if I can verify anything he said. But I also think he's our guy for the attempt on Fitzgerald's life."

"And the asshole who shot me."

"Lorre eyes. And did you notice his fingernails?"

"Yeah. Gnawed down."

"I'm thinking he could have been the one responsible for Patti Thorpe's murder, too. Byrne's kept his circle small—Zelenko, Crouse, and Briggs. I don't see anyone other than Zelenko killing Thorpe and trying to kill Fitzgerald. He's their hatchet man."

"Zelenko wasn't in the picture when Wallingford was killed. He came later," said Sam.

"We know Byrne killed Winslow. Wallingford saw him do it. I think Crouse took out Wallingford. He could have used his identity as a cop to get access and put a bullet in him. His knowledge of forensic evidence made it easy for him to cover his tracks."

Back at his desk, Joe began searching black bear hunting in Wyoming. He found Stan Zelenko had purchased a Wyoming state bear hunting license this year and renewed a black bear bait site with the Wyoming Game and Fish Department. Seems he could be telling the truth. He needed to wait for Zelenko's email documentation.

In the meantime, Sam went to Judge Warner's office to deliver a warrant for the search of Zelenko's residence and the seizure of any seven-millimeter rifles. Given the circumstances and their experience with Judge Warner, Sam was confident he would sign the warrant.

Joe's phone rang, and it was Greg Campbell.

"I spoke with Andy about testifying in court about what happened to him. We talked for quite some time, and he told me he would do it. He said he didn't want Byrne to abuse any other kids."

"That's great news," said Joe. "But given the circumstances, I think we need to keep this quiet for the time being. I don't want to arrest Byrne quite yet."

"Why's that?"

"We have another case we're investigating that ties into this one, and I think it would be best to eliminate it before we go ahead."

"Okay," said Campbell. "There's something else."

"What's that?"

"Andy thinks he knows of one other kid that Byrne abused during that time. He still keeps in touch with him. He said he's going to contact him and see if his suspicions are true. Then he'll see if he might be willing to testify as well."

"It would be a good thing if there was more than one person testifying to Byrne's abuse," said Joe. "Please keep me apprised, and I'll let you know about the other case."

Joe knew he could be putting Andy's life in danger if word got out about him testifying against Byrne. He could wind up like Wallingford on the eve of the trial. He needed to figure out a way forward, and it would hinge on nailing Crouse. And that gave Joe an idea. He would need to think about it to see if he could turn it into a viable plan.

That evening, Joe drove his undercover car and parked around the corner a block from Crouse's home. About 7:30, Crouse's blue Cadillac left his condo and traveled east. Joe followed it to Byrne's home, where it pulled through the gates. Joe drove past, circled the block, and parked a discreet distance away. Shortly after he shut the car off, he got a call from Sam.

"I see your guy wound up here, too."

"Zelenko's here?" asked Joe.

"Sure is. Looks like a meeting of the minds to me."

"Briggs?"

"I doubt it. She's poison. He wouldn't want to be associated with her from now on."

"Maybe they're just here for a friendly community swim," kidded Joe.

Sam laughed. "More like circling the wagons."

"When you were downtown getting the search warrant signed, Greg Campbell called. His son has agreed to testify against Byrne."

"Great. Then we can arrest him."

"I want to talk to you about that," replied Joe. "But not on the phone. I have an idea."

"Okay…"

"I'll check in later. Drink your Red Bull."

At 9:50, things seemed to break up at Byrne's place. A Mustang driven by Zelenko drove out of the gates and turned left onto the street, followed by Crouse's Cadillac, which turned right. Joe let Sam go by and then pulled out to follow Crouse. Crouse drove to an American Legion Post, where he spent the next two hours. At midnight, he left the Legion Post and drove to his condo.

Sam checked in as Joe was driving home. Joe reported Crouse's activity, and Sam said that Zelenko went to a bar on North Sheffield Avenue and arrived home a few minutes ago with a girl on his arm.

"That meeting with Byrne must have energized his testosterone."

"Evidently," said Sam. "At least someone will have a warm bed tonight."

"Get yourself an electric blanket. They're cheaper."

"But a lot less fun."

Chapter Thirty-Two

Sunday was the first of two days off for Joe and Sam, but Joe was still up early jogging as usual. He was running his idea through his mind and trying to formulate it into a plan, thinking about the potential problems, risks, and logistics associated with it. By the time he got home, he felt he had made substantial progress in establishing a plan to set up Vincenzo's shooter.

Entering the house, Destiny greeted him by handing him a bottle of water. "Have a good jog?"

"I did. Got a lot of thinking done. I'd like to run something past you later."

"Something?"

"A plan."

"Ah, so you're putting together a plan. What kind of plan?"

"A complicated one, but I think it could work. I'd appreciate your input."

"Well, you certainly know how to get a girl's attention."

Joe finished his water and headed for the shower. Twenty minutes later, he was dressed and walking into the kitchen. Seeing Destiny had made coffee, he poured himself a cup and sat down at the island.

"Do you have anything planned for your day off?" asked Destiny.

"I haven't thought about it. Work's been occupying my mind so much, I haven't had a chance to think about anything else."

"You need a break. Something to get your mind off the case, give it a rest so you can come back to it with a fresh perspective."

"Did you have something in mind?"

"Uh-huh."

"What?" asked Joe skeptically.

"How would you like to go for a cruise on Lake Michigan with the Affannatos on their yacht today?"

Joe smiled. He spent a lot of time on the fly deck of the Affannato's yacht surveilling a neighboring yacht last year. Loretta Affannato was a friend of Destiny's mother, and Loretta warmly welcomed him and Sam aboard, and her cooperation helped in bringing down a human trafficking operation.

"I'd like that," said Joe. "Sounds like fun. I'll finally get to meet Mr. Affannato."

"Gino—you'll like him. He's quite a wit. She'll have lunch for us onboard, and then we'll sail out of the harbor for a cruise out on the lake. Should be relaxing."

"You always come up with great stuff to do," he said, kissing her on his way to get a second cup of coffee.

"I try. What do you want for breakfast?"

"I saw some bacon seitan in the fridge yesterday. How about Eggs Benedict?"

"You making the Hollandaise sauce?"

"I don't mind."

"Then, you do that, and I'll do the rest."

After breakfast, Joe opened his laptop to see if Stan Zelenko had sent him the documentation for his Wyoming hunting trip. So far, he had not. But since it was early, and it was Sunday, he wasn't that concerned he had not received it yet.

Pulling up a new Word document, Joe began entering his plan, piece by piece, onto a new page. He wanted to move it from his head into something he could review and revise as it continued to evolve. The more he wrote, the more he thought. And the more he thought, the more he wrote. As he composed, he became lost in his work, oblivious to time.

When he finished thinking it through and writing it down, Joe felt as though his plan had come together. It would take considerable planning, and timing would have to be spot-on, but he was convinced it could work. Now, he wanted to get Destiny's opinion. He closed the laptop and went into her office, where he found her working on her emails.

"Want to hear my plan?" he asked.

Turning in her chair, she said, "I would, but have you seen the time? We need to head for the harbor in a few minutes. Joe glanced at the clock on her wall.

"Oh, I guess I lost track of time."

"You can tell me when we get home. Love to hear it." She closed her laptop and rose from her chair. Handing Joe the keys to her Mercedes, she said, "Why don't you bring the car around, and I'll lock up."

When they returned early that evening from an enjoyable time spent with Gino and Loretta Affannato, Destiny said, "Now, doesn't it feel good to get away and get your mind off work?"

"It does," said Joe as he sat down and opened his laptop.

"What are you doing?" asked Destiny.

"Checking my email."

Putting her hand on the top of his laptop, she said, "No, you're not. You can check it tomorrow morning. I know you. You'll be checking work stuff."

Joe removed his hand from his laptop and said, "Okay. It can wait. I have tomorrow off, too."

"You want something to eat?"

"Not after what Loretta fed me today."

"I'm going to have a glass of wine. You want one?"

"Well, I guess I can get away with a second one this once."

Destiny opened a bottle of Merlot, poured two glasses, and handed one to Joe. "What do you think of this?"

Joe tasted the wine and said, "Nice. What is it?"

"A Merlot I read about in a wine magazine. Thought I would get a bottle."

They sat down on the couch to enjoy their wine. "What do you want to do tonight?" asked Destiny.

"After talking to Gino about old hardboiled detective fiction, I wouldn't mind watching a Bogart movie."

"Which one? *The Maltese Falcon* or *The Big Sleep?*"

"I think I'm in the mood for *The Maltese Falcon.*"

Joe put in a DVD of *The Maltese Falcon*, and they sat close on the couch, sipping their wine and watching Humphrey Bogart, Sidney Greenstreet, Mary Astor, and...Peter Lorre.

* * *

After his morning jog, and after he had eaten breakfast, Joe checked his email. And there it was. A message from Stan Zelenko. Opening it, he read Zelenko's curt message: "Here's what you wanted." Short and to the point. Joe checked the attachments. Included were a copy of the invoice from his hunting guide, a photo of him posing with a dead black bear, a hotel receipt from Casper, and a scan of his plane tickets. All the dates created a solid alibi for Zelenko on the night of Vincenzo's shooting.

Joe forwarded Zelenko's email to Sam with the message: "Looks like Zelenko is off the hook. This leaves Crouse."

When Destiny entered and saw him staring at his laptop, she said, "Are you going to share that plan of yours with me?"

"Yeah. Pull up a seat."

Chapter Thirty-Three

Back on the job first thing the next morning, Joe was sitting at his desk logging in to his computer when he felt a tap on his shoulder. It was Sam.

"I got your email. You work at home on all of your days off?"

"Can't help it. A case doesn't take days off. It follows me around like a stray dog."

"Did you feed it?"

"I did. I devised a plan to nail our killer. I ran it past Destiny, and she thinks it'll work. But it's going to require a lot of planning and coordination."

"So, tell me about it."

"It's rather involved, so rather than explain it now, I think we should meet with Lieutenant Bell. I'll explain it and see if he gives it his blessing."

"Is he in?"

"I don't know. I haven't checked."

"Well, let's check. You can't keep me in suspense like this."

Joe stood and said, "Let's go." Lieutenant Bell had been appointed Acting Lieutenant of Homicide since Lieutenant Briggs' arrest. He previously worked as a detective sergeant in homicide before transferring to Property Crimes. Given his previous experience with Bell, Joe felt good about laying out his plan.

They walked to the closest sergeant's desk and asked Sergeant Joel Pierce if Bell was in his office.

"Yeah, he's in there," said Pierce. "Go ahead and knock."

Joe knocked and opened the door. "Are you busy?" he asked.

189

"Come in," said Bell, rising from his chair. "How are you coming on the Vincenzo investigation?"

"That's what we want to talk to you about," said Joe. "We've come up with a plan to flush out Vincenzo's killer, and we want to run it past you." Joe wasn't some hotshot who arrogantly took sole credit for ideas. He preferred to take a "we" approach that included his partner.

"Let's hear it."

"One of Carson Byrne's victims has agreed to testify against him for sexually abusing him when he was a pre-teen—a swimmer on a team that Byrne sponsored. He's the boy in the videotape that Byrne's attorney got tossed out."

"My god. I'm astonished you managed to find him."

"Fortunately, his father came forward. He hired the PI that got the video in the first place. Anyway, this kid is now twenty years old, and we think if his identity gets out, Byrne will try to have him killed. Just like he did with Robert Wallingford."

"Okay, go on."

"I think we should set up a sting. A fake residence across from an abandoned building where a sniper can pick off the kid. Of course, the kid will be a dummy sitting on a couch in front of a window. And we'll use an undercover cop to pose as the kid going in and out of the apartment. We think we know who the shooter is."

"Who is it?" asked Bell.

"Former Captain Jerome Crouse," said Joe.

"Jerome Crouse? Our former Commander?"

"Yeah. He was a trained sniper in the army. And he's been in cahoots with Carson Byrne, Yvonne Briggs, and Byrne's bodyguard, Stan Zelenko. We've observed them meeting, and we suspect Zelenko in the death of one person and the attempted murder of another. This was all in an attempt to keep the sex tape from surfacing."

"But it did anyway."

"It may have ruined Byrne in the court of public opinion, but he can't be prosecuted unless we have a witness. He wouldn't hesitate to eliminate a witness," said Sam. "He did it before."

"Where is this kid who wants to testify?"

"He's a student at Princeton. But his father lives here in the city."

"So, you want to set up an address for him here, have one of our undercover guys pretend to be him, act as bait for the killer, and then arrest the killer after he shoots a dummy? Is that it?"

"Yeah," said Joe. "I plan to keep Crouse under surveillance while Sam watches the abandoned building. We should be able to arrest him after he takes the shot."

"And what if it isn't Crouse? What if it's somebody else?" asked Bell.

"We nail him and make him talk," said Sam. "It has to be one of Byrne's inner circle: Crouse, Briggs, or Zelenko. But Crouse was trained as a sniper in the army."

Bell leaned back in his chair and thought for a moment. "There's a hell of a lot that can go wrong with this, you know that? For instance, how are you going to let Byrne know there's a witness?"

"We have enough to arrest him for predatory criminal sexual assault of a child," said Joe. "When we bring him in, we can let someone drop something to him or his attorney so he can find the kid's address."

"What if they do some checking? Like go looking for a Facebook page?"

"We'll have to have someone create one using our undercover guy's face and some of this kid's information," said Sam.

"It sounds like you've got this figured out." There was a pause while Bell contemplated making his decision. "Okay. Get everything planned out, and I'll try to get an undercover guy that looks twenty years old who'll agree to this. Let me know when you have everything in place and ready to go. I'll want to go over it with you. But I'm going to talk to the State's Attorney about this and let her know we have a witness. She needs to know what's going on."

"Good idea," said Joe. "Thanks, Lieutenant."

"Thanks," said Sam.

They all stood, and just as Joe and Sam were turning to leave, Bell said, "Guys. Don't screw this up. Because it'll all come back on me."

"We'll do our best, Lieutenant," said Joe.

Leaving Bell's office, Joe let out a deep breath, thankful that Bell had bought into his plan. They would still have been able to arrest Byrne if he had rejected the plan, but it would have been necessary to keep Andrew Campbell in a safe house before he testified against Byrne. And they would not have been able to tie Crouse to Vincenzo's murder. Joe wanted both Byrne and Crouse for Vincenzo's murder, and he would do whatever he could to make that a reality.

Joe sat down with Sam, and they began working out the details of the plan.

"What do you want me to do?" asked Sam.

"The first thing we need to do is to find an apartment opposite an abandoned building."

"How do I go about that?"

"Why don't you call the realtor Destiny and I worked with when we bought our house. She's great. Mention our names, and I'm sure she'll help you out. She'll have a better way to search for an apartment than we do."

Joe gave Sam her contact information. "I'll begin working with Greg Campbell to create a searchable background for our undercover officer who'll be posing as his son."

"Think he'll go for it?"

"I can sell him on it. If this goes the way it should, his son may not have to testify. It's better to get Byrne on a murder rap than sexual assault."

Sam went back to his desk to make a phone call while Joe called Greg Campbell to let him know what they were doing and what he needed his son to do.

"Does Andy have a Facebook page?"

"He does."

"Here's what I need him to do. I need him to change the fact that he's from Chicago. Have him change his hometown to Raleigh, North Carolina, instead. And then, he has to remove all photos of you, and any references to Chicago, like photos, favorites, and so on."

"Why is this necessary?"

"Because we're going to create a false Facebook page for an undercover officer standing in for your son.

"I don't understand."

"We are in the process of setting up a sting operation. We believe that Byrne will have someone make an attempt to kill the witness before he can testify against him. It happened once before, and we anticipate it will happen again. We're going to create a false identity for an undercover officer who's going to stand in for your son, and that includes creating a Facebook page using photos of our undercover officer."

"Look, if my son is in danger of being killed, I don't—"

"Your son will not be in danger. If this goes the way we hope it does," explained Joe, "your son may not have to testify. We may have Byrne on a murder charge rather than sexual assault. I'd much rather have him prosecuted for murder."

"Okay. I get it," said Campbell. "I'll have him do it."

"Do you have a Facebook page as well?"

"I do."

"Then, I'm going to need you to do the same thing. Remove all of Andy's photos and any references to his attendance at Princeton. You can put them back once we're done. We're creating an identity for Andy, living and going to school here in Chicago."

"You're going to all that work?"

"We are. We're dealing with smart people. They'll do the research to track down and locate Andy, and we have to make this look good. We may need a photo with you and our undercover officer to post on your Facebook page—father and son picture."

"Okay. Whatever you need."

"Thanks," replied Joe. "Let me know when you and Andy have finished cleansing your social media pages so we can proceed."

"Will do."

"Does Andy have an Illinois driver's license?"

"No. He has a New Jersey license now."

"Okay. Good to know. Talk to you soon."

Knowing Crouse had the ability to check the Illinois driver license database, they would need to create an Illinois driver's license for their undercover officer to complete the ruse.

Joe got on Andy Campbell's Facebook page and began looking around. He was pretty active, given the number of memes and photos. But there were only a few pictures of him and his father, and only a few that Joe could identify as obvious Chicago locations. The rest were with friends and funny pictures, memes, and cartoons. He couldn't see his posts, as they could only be viewed by friends.

Joe found Greg Campbell's Facebook page. He was not a very active poster, given the number of photos that showed up. There were a few photos of him with Andy, but mostly memes and images that had to do with words of wisdom, medical advice, and quotations from humorists like Mark Twain and Robert Benchley. It shouldn't take long for him to remove identifying images.

When Joe got home, Destiny gave him a hug and asked, "How was your day?"

"You could say, 'the game's afoot.'"

Chapter Thirty-Four

T wo days later, Joe was coming back from his appointment with Dr. Lemke when he saw Sam smiling widely and walking toward him in a fast-paced strut.

"What's with you?" asked Joe.

"I think I found a place. Or I should say, your realtor found us a place. I did an online search of the property, and it looks promising. Want to go take a look?"

"Yeah."

"Let me call the realtor and see if she can arrange for us to see it."

The site's only ten minutes from Area 3 offices on Belmont." Phone calls were made, and an hour later, Sam and Joe were pulling up to an older red brick building that had served as apartments for many years. Another brick building across the street was undergoing a major renovation with its sidewalk blocked off and large dumpsters filled with construction debris.

Sam made a call to the building manager before they entered the vestibule of the apartment complex. They were met by Martha Henninger, a matronly woman in her fifties. After introductions, Henninger took them up to the vacant third-floor apartment that was ready for leasing.

"I don't understand why a man like you would be interested in this apartment," said Henninger as she opened the door to let them in.

Not wanting to let her know it could potentially be used for a police operation, Sam said, "I'm going through a divorce. I need a place that's inexpensive."

"Sorry to hear that," replied Henninger.

"Mind if we look it over?" asked Joe. "I'm a friend of his. I'm here for moral support."

"Please do."

The apartment was of the age and condition that attracted college students and individuals who could not afford higher-quality accommodations. What interested Joe and Sam was the front window that faced the building across the street. It was large enough to place a couch in front and to situate a dummy squarely in the window frame.

Looking around the apartment, Sam found a folding chair in the bedroom closet, brought it into the main room, and placed it in front of the window.

"I'm going to sit here," said Sam. "Why don't you go across the street and check out the grass-man's position in that building."

"Gotcha," said Joe.

"Grass-man?" asked Henninger. "I don't understand."

Joe left to let Sam explain "grass-man" to her. It was slang for sniper, but Joe was sure Sam would come up with a suitable explanation. He crossed the street and walked up to one of the workers. He showed his ID and said, "I need to get inside this building to look around."

"You'll have to speak with the boss," said the worker. "Come with me."

Joe followed him to a small building that functioned as a command center for the project. He opened the door and said, "Cop wants to talk to you." Then he left.

Joe stepped inside, showing his ID. "I'm Detective Joe Erickson. I need to get inside the building you're renovating."

Getting off his stool, the burly, middle-aged man offered his leathery hand. "Walt Mueller. You want what?"

Shaking his hand, Joe said, "I need to get into the building you're working on so I can get a view of the apartments across the street. I'm especially interested in the third floor. Is it possible to get up there?"

"What's this about?"

"I really can't say. It's part of an ongoing investigation, and I'm not at liberty to talk about it. Sorry."

"Okay. Yeah. I can take you up there." He reached to a wall behind him and grabbed a hardhat and handed it to Joe. "You'll have to wear this." Then he picked up one off his desk and put it on. "Follow me."

Mueller escorted Joe inside the building and up several flights of stairs to the third floor. The building had been gutted and new sheetrock installed, but not finished yet, and doors had not been hung. As they walked down what seemed to be a hallway, sawdust, and gypsum from sheetrock were ground into the floor.

"What do you want to see?" asked Mueller.

"I want to look out a window to get a view of the building across the street," said Joe.

They came to a doorway, and Joe stepped inside. He saw a window, went over to it, and looked out. He studied the window of the apartment across the street, but he wasn't straight across from it. It wasn't an angle to shoot from.

Returning to the hall, he walked down to the next doorway and stepped to the window. It provided a perfect, straight-on view of Sam sitting in the window. Pulling out his phone, he took a picture to show him. It would be easy pickins' for a sniper to take out someone sitting on a couch behind that window. He called Sam.

"Turn and look out the window."

"Okay," said Sam, and he turned to look out.

Joe waved to him from the window across the street. "You're dead. It was an easy shot."

"Good. Then we've got our location."

"Now, we just need the department to lease the apartment for a month. That's up to Lieutenant Bell to work out the details," said Joe. "Hopefully, he's getting our guy from undercover lined up."

Joe asked Mueller about the kind of security the construction company had on the building during the night. After he showed Joe the perimeter chain-link fence and heavy-duty chain and padlock on the gate, Joe felt getting into the site wasn't something that a motivated person with a little imagination couldn't overcome.

Back at Area 3, Joe and Sam informed Lieutenant Bell they had found a location for their sting operation. Bell agreed to put through a request to acquire the apartment for thirty days. He also informed them he spoke to the State's Attorney, and she was on board. In addition, he had found an undercover officer, Austin Northrup, to play the role of Andy Campbell. Bell showed them Northrup's photo, and he looked the part. His age, coloring, and general appearance made him an acceptable likeness for Greg Campbell's son.

"He'll come in tomorrow and meet with you guys," said Bell. "You can brief him on what you need him to do. We're in the process of getting him a driver's license and creating a Facebook page. Is the apartment furnished?"

"No, we'll have to have some furniture brought in," said Sam.

"Okay, I know someone who can do that. What do we need? Livingroom and bedroom?"

"Yeah. He's going to live there. And we'll need a realistic dummy to prop up on the couch."

"Okay."

"I think I may have a source for that," said Joe, remembering Wally Kozlov, his acquaintance who makes human body parts for film, Halloween, and various freaks who want such stuff. Wally provided Joe with his disguises when he was tracking serial killer David Eugene Burton. Given his interest in the bizarre, Joe was pretty sure Wally would take an interest in this project.

Back at his desk, Joe gave Wally a call. The phone rang four times before Wally picked up.

"Yeah, whadda ya want?" greeted Wally with his typical edgy voice.

"Joe Erickson calling."

Suddenly, Wally's attitude abruptly changed. "Joe! How ya doin'? Long time."

"Yeah, it's been a while."

"You still hangin' out with that Destiny chick?"

"Still hangin' out."

"Well, zip up. She's probably tired of lookin' at it!" With that, Wally convulsed into gales of laughter. Once he had regained control of himself, he asked, "What can I do for ya?"

"I need a dummy for some police work."

"Step out on Michigan Avenue and swing a dead cat. You're liable to hit a few." He laughed again, and then said, "I suppose you mean a mannequin?"

"Yeah," said Joe. "I need one that will sit on a couch, but the back of the head needs to look like the undercover police officer we have working with us. And it may end up being shot in the head with a high-powered rifle."

"Ohhhhhh. Interesting. Well, I've got mannequins. No problem there. But I'm going to need to see your undercover cop to give you the right look."

"I can show you a picture."

"No, I've gotta see him in person."

"Okay. I guess I can bring him by. Any time after twelve-thirty still okay?"

"Yeah. Same address. You know the routine." Then he hung up. That was Wally. He had virtually no filter and spoke whatever entered his mind. Destiny found him highly entertaining when she met him. Joe wondered if Austin Northrup would respond the same way. After all, Wally was an acquired taste, and not everyone is capable of tolerating such quirky personalities.

When Joe got home, he asked Destiny, "How would you like to visit Wally Kozlov's place again?"

"Omigod, I'd love to. You have business with him again?"

"Yeah. He's agreed to supply the mannequin we're going to use in the sting operation. And he wants to see the undercover officer before he figures out the head."

She chuckled. "I'll bet it won't be any run-of-the-mill mannequin, knowing him."

Chapter Thirty-Five

J oe and Sam were called into Lieutenant Bell's office the next morning, where they saw a young man standing with him. He had long, light brown hair and a full beard and mustache. Dressed in a t-shirt and jeans, he could have passed as a musician in a rock band.

"Joe, Sam, meet Austin Northrup," said Bell. "Austin, this is Joe Erickson and Sam Renaldo. You'll be working with them on the sting operation you were recruited for."

They shook hands and exchanged pleasantries. Northrup's smile was at odds with his dark, intense eyes. Joe thought his beard made him look older than Andy Campbell's twenty years, but without the beard, he could look younger and pass for Greg Campbell's son.

"Why don't you go in the conference room and lay out the plan for Austin," said Bell. "You can fill him in on all the particulars and what you need him to do."

They moved to the conference room where Joe and Sam gave Northrup an overview of the Carson Byrne murder case from ten years ago, the killing of witness Robert Wallingford and Captain Sal Vincenzo, as well as the attempted murder of Merlin Fitzgerald and the arrest of Lieutenant Yvonne Briggs. Then they explained the discovery of the sex tape, the arrest of Carson Byrne, the suppression of the tape evidence, and the subsequent release of Byrne.

"At this point, we thought we were screwed in terms of prosecuting Byrne, but then I got a call from the father of the boy on the tape," said Joe. "And his son agreed to testify against Byrne in a criminal sexual assault case. But we think we can get Byrne and his circle for murder instead. That's where this sting comes in."

"I get it," said Austin. "So, given the track record of Byrne killing witnesses, you're betting on him doing it again."

"That's right," said Sam. "We believe former Police Captain Jerome Crouse may be the shooter. He was trained as a sniper in the army, so it would be natural for him to be the triggerman in Vincenzo's death."

"We've acquired the use of an apartment across the street from a building that's undergoing renovation. It's a perfect place for a sniper to set up at night and assassinate the witness who's come forward," said Joe.

"And you want me to be the witness living in the apartment, I assume."

"Yeah," said Sam. "There's construction going on during the day, so there won't be an attempt during working hours, but there will need to be activity in the apartment in case they reconnoiter the place."

"Got it. What about the time after the construction ends?"

"We think he'll try after dark when he can gain access to the construction site without being seen and then make his escape after the shot."

"Speaking of the shot..." began Northrup.

"We've got you covered," said Sam.

"We'll have a mannequin sitting on a couch which will be placed in front of the window," clarified Joe. "You'll have to set it up and then spend the night in the bedroom or the kitchen, so you won't be seen. Then you'll need to lay it down sometime after midnight and turn out the lights."

The kitchen can't be seen from the window, so you can cook and eat in there safely," said Sam.

"Okay. Got it."

"We need to take a photo with you and Greg Campbell. His son, Andy, is the witness. We'll be creating a false Facebook page and a driver's license for you under the name of Andrew Campbell. Being a former cop, if Jerome Crouse does some background searches on Andy, you'll show up. And the guy who's creating the mannequin wants to see you in person so he can build a facsimile of your head.

"How old is this Andy person?"

"He's twenty."

"I don't look twenty anymore."

"I think you'll look a lot younger if you're clean-shaven," said Joe. "Your long hair is fine. He's a college student, so the long hair fits. Besides, you won't be seen up close."

"I can shave. No problem there. Does he have a Facebook page? If so, I'd like to check him out."

"Yeah. I can show you after we're done here."

"So, you said you want to take some photos. When do you want to do that?"

"I'll make a call to Greg and work out a time when we can get together. In the meantime, we can meet with the guy who's creating the mannequin this afternoon if your schedule allows.

"Sure. I can do that."

"A third person will be going with us. She gets a kick out of the guy. He's...how shall I put this...a harmless eccentric."

"O-kay."

"Do you have any questions?" asked Sam.

"I'd like to see the apartment."

"Sure. One of us can take you there. We'll have to get the keys first. Should only be a couple of days before we take possession. Anything else?"

"Not at the moment. It sounds like a pretty easy operation on my part. But I'm sure I'll have some questions once we get going."

"Why don't we go to my computer, and I'll pull up Andy Campbell's Facebook page," said Joe. "Then, at 1:30, we can meet at the little shop of horrors and have Wally Kozlov figure out your head."

Northrup looked at Joe. "Little shop...?" Rather than explain, Joe handed him a piece of paper with Kozlov's address in Greektown. "Here's the address."

"For the mannequin?" asked Northrup.

"Uh-huh."

After checking out Andy Campbell's Facebook page, Northrup left, saying he would meet Joe and "the third person" at Kozlov's address. Joe called

Destiny to tell her they were meeting at Wally Kozlov's at 1:30, and she said she would meet them there.

Joe arrived at Wally's building shortly after 1:15. Destiny was waiting for him at the door, speaking with Austin Northrup. Northrup had shaved, and he looked a lot younger.

"Well, you two got here early," said Joe.

"You never know how traffic is going to be," said Destiny.

"True," said Northrup. "I have a thing about being late."

Joe rang the bell, and a moment later, a terse voice came over the speaker. "Yeah?"

"It's Joe Erickson."

"Okay." His answer was followed by a buzz that unlocked the door.

Joe, Destiny, and Northrup climbed the steel and concrete stairs to the second floor. The building had a faint odor of chemicals and dust. Wally met them in the hallway. He was a thin man in his early forties with hair pulled back into a ponytail.

"I take it you're the head I'm going to make," Wally said to Northrup as he looked him over.

"I guess so," replied Northrup.

"Come on."

Wally turned, and they followed him down the hall, where he opened the door to a room resembling a macabre setting for a horror classic. The place had realistic body parts hanging from the ceiling and grotesque heads, and gruesome torsos sitting on shelves. He led them to a room with a modified barber chair and a table off to one side.

"Have a seat," Wally said to Northrup.

Northrup looked at Joe with some reluctance but sat in the chair.

"What do you have planned, Wally?" asked Joe.

"I need to make a mold of his head." Then he turned to Northrup and asked, "What's your name, anyway?"

"Austin. Austin Northrup."

"Okay, Austin Northrup. This isn't going to hurt a bit. I might give you cancer, but it won't hurt." Then he picked up a 3D scanner from the table and said, "Just kidding. This won't give you cancer or make you sterile or any of that crap. Now hold still. Don't move."

Wally began scanning Northrup's face and head. After about five minutes, he put the scanner down and took a lot of photos from different angles with his phone.

After putting his phone in his pocket, Wally said, "I'm done. I'll have a mannequin ready for you in three days."

"What's all this going to cost?" asked Joe.

"Cost? You can't put a price on this shit! This is my gift to Chicago PD."

"You know this head may be destroyed by a sniper's bullet, right?"

"Right. Hey...I could make it bleed when it's shot. Blood and brains flyin' out and—"

"You don't have to go that far," interrupted Joe.

Wally looked at Destiny and said, "What do you think? Should I make it bleed when it's shot?"

"Up to you," said Destiny. "You're the artist."

Wally laughed and said to Joe, "I like her."

Joe chuckled. "All right. It's up to you. As long as we have the mannequin in three days."

"No problemo! Ready for pickup in three days. Guaranteed."

Out on the street, Northrup turned to Joe. "Can you trust that guy?"

"Oh, yeah. I worked with him before. He's eccentric, but he's good."

"He'll surprise you. Wait and see," said Destiny.

"If you say so," said Northrup. "We'll find out in three days, won't we?"

Northrup said goodbye and left. As Joe and Destiny were watching him walk down the street, Joe said, "I think Wally unnerved him a little."

"Well, at least he didn't tell him that crazy penis story he told us last year."

Back at Area 3, Joe called Greg Campbell, and his call went to voicemail. He left a message asking Greg to call him to set up a meeting to get a photo with Campbell and Northrup for the Facebook page. An hour later, Greg called back and said his schedule was open for an hour, starting from eleven o'clock until noon.

"That time should work," said Joe. "I'll text Northrup and confirm the time.

CHAPTER THIRTY-FIVE

Where should we shoot the photo?"

"Why don't we do it at my house. I have one of Andy and me in the backyard. We can get another one, kind of like it. I can give him one of Andy's shirts to wear. And we can shoot another one inside the house."

Joe confirmed his address and said he would text him once he heard from Northrup. The next three days would be busy as the elements of the trap would be coming together. Joe was making a list and checking it twice, but he didn't feel like Santa Claus. He had a knot in his stomach. There was a lot that could go wrong. He was determined to make everything go as planned.

Chapter Thirty-Six

In addition to planning and executing the sting, Joe and Sam had three open murders on their caseload, and they had to keep up with those investigations, too. Lieutenant Bell was making sure that no new cases came their way. This would not have happened if Yvonne Briggs was still their lieutenant.

In the past three days, the apartment was secured, and furniture moved in; Andrew Campbell's name was placed on the apartment's list of residents; photos were taken of Greg Campbell with Austin Northrup for their Facebook pages; the driver's license was created for Austin under Andrew Campbell's name; and both Greg Campbell and Andy Campbell had cleansed their social media of any photos and information that could link them to each other.

When Joe got a call from Wally Kozlov saying the mannequin was ready for pickup, Austin Northrup accompanied him to Wally's studio. They were buzzed in, and as they reached the top of the stairs, Wally met them in the hall.

"Greetings and salutations," he said, flinging his arms wide.

"Hello, Wally," said Joe.

Looking at Northrup, Wally said, "I did you proud, if I do say so myself. Come with me."

They followed Wally through a door into the room where he had scanned Northrup three days before. A sheet covered something in the barber chair.

"Voilà," said Wally, pointing at the sheet. Then he carefully removed it. There, in a chair, sat another Austin Northrup. The mannequin was unbelievably life-like. The face had glass eyes, eyelashes, eyebrows, and the skin of the face and hands had been airbrushed to simulate the color and texture of real skin. The wig was a perfect replication of Northrup's own hair.

Standing with his mouth open, Northrup took a step closer and said, "Oh…my…god. What…"

"Silicone, some airbrushing…Think it'll do?" asked Wally.

"You've outdone yourself, Wally," said Joe.

"This is…incredible," said Northrup, looking up at Wally. "It's another me."

"I call him 'Austin Two,'" said Wally. He's jointed, so you can stand him up or sit him down, and you can move his arms and legs if you want to position him. I dressed him a pair of jeans and a sweatshirt, so he'd look like a college kid."

"Perfect," said Joe. He put a stool next to the barber chair, had Northrup sit down next to his likeness, and took a photo with his phone. He sent it to Destiny with the message, "Which one is the real Austin Northrup?"

After thanking Wally for his work, Joe and Northrup covered "Austin Two" with a sheet, transported him over to the apartment, and placed him on the couch next to the window. They found that laying him down on the couch was the quickest, easiest way to move him in and out of position. Once set up, Northrup could crawl away out of sight. Around midnight, he could crawl over to Austin Two, lay him down, and then crawl back and turn off the lights.

When they got back to Area 3, Joe checked his phone and saw a message from Destiny. It read, "Are you kidding me?!!!" He chuckled and stepped to Sam to show him the photo.

"Wow. That guy is good," said Sam.

"Yeah. We've got everything in place. Let's go talk with Bell."

They walked down to Lieutenant Bell's office and stopped at Sergeant Pierce's desk to see if Bell was busy. They were told he wasn't. Joe knocked on Bell's door and opened it.

"You busy?"

"No. Come in."

Sitting in front of Bell's desk, Joe said, "We have everything set up for the sting, Lieutenant. The apartment is furnished, the mannequin is finished, and on site, Northrup has been instructed what to do, websites are doctored with new photos, and Northrup has a driver's license in the database under the witness's name. We're ready."

"Then the next step is arresting Byrne?" asked Bell.

"Yeah," said Sam.

"How are you going to drop the kid's name?"

"I'm going to do it," said Sam. "When we arrest him."

"Byrne will be able to figure it out," said Joe. "I'm sure he'll remember the kid. His father made him drop his sponsorship of the swim team."

"Okay. Bring him in and tell Northrup it's a go."

Joe and Sam left Area 3 and drove to Byrne's office. When she saw them, his receptionist picked up the phone, but before she could call, they barged past her into Byrne's office. He was visiting with a man they assumed to be a constituent.

Byrne stood up as his receptionist blurted out, "I tried to call you, but they—"

"This is outrageous!" exclaimed Byrne.

"Yes, it is," said Joe as he began cuffing him. His constituent looked on in horror as Joe said, "You're under arrest for predatory criminal sexual assault of a child."

"You tried this once before. I'm gonna sue you for this."

"We didn't have Andrew Campbell willing to testify against you before," said Sam. "Remember little Andy Campbell, the one you were seen raping on that videotape? You're toast, Byrne."

At that moment, Stan Zelenko and Cindy, Byrne's assistant, came through the door. Seeing her, Byrne said, "Call my attorney, Cindy."

"Mr. Byrne?" asked Zelenko, seeking instructions.

"Stay here," said Byrne. "Whittier will have me out soon." Looking at Joe, he said, "And he'll have your ass for this."

"Other people have tried. Let's go," said Joe, pushing Byrne forward and out through the door as he began reading him his rights.

Byrne was brought up on charges, and his attorney, Richard Whittier, had him out on bail one hour after he surrendered his passport. Joe called Austin Northrup.

"Hey, Joe," answered Northrup.

"Are you at the apartment?" asked Joe.

"Yeah. I'm here."

"We arrested Byrne, and he just made bail."

"Got it. So, this could possibly happen tonight?"

"Could, but probably not. They'll need some time to find your address and make plans. But we'll have eyes on the building across the street just in case."

"Okay. Thanks for the cable TV hook-up. It makes the time go faster."

"I didn't have anything to do with that. You're probably finishing out the month on the previous tenant's account."

"Whatever. I appreciate it."

"Talk to you later. Enjoy your frozen pizzas."

That night while Sam surveilled Zelenko, Joe kept his eye on Crouse. Nothing happened as both stayed at home. If they communicated with each other, it was done via Zoom or some other form of communication that Joe and Sam were unable to trace.

The same was true of the next night. Nothing other than the fact Crouse spent the night with Yvonne Briggs. He arrived by Uber or Lyft at seven o'clock and did not leave until the early hours of the next morning.

On the third evening, Joe followed Crouse to a storage unit, where he emerged carrying a rifle case which he placed in the trunk of his Cadillac. *Now, we're getting somewhere*, thought Joe. He called Sam.

"Hey, Sam. Are you watching Zelenko?"

"Yeah."

"Something might be happening tonight."

"Oh, yeah?"

"Get over to the apartment. I saw Crouse picking up a rifle case from a storage unit. I'm following him now. I'll keep you posted. I'll call Northrup and let him know."

"On my way."

Joe followed Crouse to Briggs' apartment and watched Crouse transfer the rifle case to the trunk of an older, black Toyota Camry parked in front of the apartment building. Then he drove away in his Caddy. *Whose car was that?* Joe wondered. But then he thought, if he was going to travel to the scene of an assassination, he would use a car he could ditch. About five minutes later, he saw Crouse walking back to Briggs' apartment building.

Joe kept surveilling Briggs' residence, and shortly after ten o'clock, both Briggs and Crouse came out of the apartment wearing black clothing. Crouse got behind the wheel of the Toyota, and they drove away. Joe followed at a discreet distance as they drove to the area where Northrup's apartment setup was located. When the Toyota stopped, Joe turned and went down another street and parked. He called Sam.

"Sam?"

"Yeah."

"You spotted the black Toyota?"

"Yeah. Two people in black got out wearing ski masks. They got a rifle case from the trunk, and they're heading for the construction site now. One has the rifle case, and one has a bolt cutter. For cutting the fence, I imagine."

"Okay. I'll take the shooter. You keep an eye on the car. I'll let you know when the shot's been taken. If they split up, you can take down the one in the car."

"Gotcha. I'm calling in backup as planned."

Joe called Northrup.

"Yeah, Joe."

"The shooter's heading for the construction site. Stay on with me and let me know as soon as the shot's been taken."

"Roger. Austin Two is in place and ready."

"Where are you?"

"In the kitchen. I have a clear view of the window and Austin Two."

"Great."

Joe carefully made his way to the construction site. It was dark, but he could make out one figure lift a section of the chain-link fence that encircled the site and let the other one inside. Then the one remaining left, walking back in the direction of the car. After a couple of minutes, Joe moved to place himself closer to the opening cut in the fence, choosing the side of a nearby dumpster out of sight of the fence.

Waiting was nerve-wracking. The shot was going to come, but when? He held the phone up to his ear.

"You still there?"

"Yeah," replied Northrup.

"Hang in there. Snipers take their time."

Five minutes went by. Joe looked at his watch. Ten minutes. Then...

"JESUS CHRIST," yelled Northrup.

"What?"

"His fuckin' head exploded. There's blood and brains all over!"

Wally! Joe called Sam. "The shot's been taken. Arrest the person in the car. I'll get the shooter."

"Got it."

Putting his phone in his pocket, Joe pulled his Glock and peered around the corner of the dumpster, waiting for the shooter to come through the fence. Finally, he saw the fence push up and the rifle case slide through. When he saw a black figure emerge through the opening, Joe sprang, clicking on his flashlight and holding his Glock on the black-clad offender.

"POLICE! FREEZE!"

The person did not move from a crouching position. Joe could see the suspect was carrying a sidearm, and he kept a close watch on the suspect's gloved hands.

"Now get on your knees and put your hands on your head. You go for that sidearm, and you're dead."

The suspect obeyed, and Joe moved behind him, disarming and then cuffing him. Moving around to the front, Joe reached down and pulled off the black ski mask, expecting to see Crouse's face. To his total surprise, it revealed the face of Yvonne Briggs.

"Briggs?" exclaimed Joe, his face slowly changing from surprise to anger.

She looked up at Joe with hate in her eyes. He never liked her, and he knew the feeling was mutual.

"You just can't leave anything alone, can you, Erickson?" she said with clenched teeth.

"No, I can't." Joe walked behind her and pushed her hard to the ground with his foot. Then he called Sam.

"Hey, Joe."

"What do you have, Sam?"

"I have former Captain Crouse in cuffs. What about you?"

"I have former Lieutenant Briggs in cuffs. And she was carrying a sniper rifle."

"Wow. So, she turned out to be the shooter?"

"Yeah. My guess, she took out Vincenzo, too. Crouse probably acted as her driver."

"I'm letting backup know to move in."

After ending the call, Joe dialed Margaret Kummeyer.

"Good evening, Joe."

"It is a good evening, Margaret. You might want to know that former Lieutenant Yvonne Briggs and former Captain Jerome Crouse were just arrested in a sting operation. Briggs was the sniper who tried to kill a witness in Carson Byrne's arrest. Crouse was her co-conspirator and driver."

"Was anyone hurt?"

"A mannequin, that we placed in the window received a fatal bullet wound in the head."

"Mannequin?"

Joe gave her the address and said he could explain if she was on site. He knew Margaret would be there post haste.

Following his call to Margaret Kummeyer, Joe made a call to Lieutenant Bell to let him know that the sting worked as planned. Bell was shocked to find out that Briggs was the sniper.

"What a cold-blooded piece of work," said Bell. "I'll be there in a few."

Northrup came down to the scene of the arrest to speak with Joe and Sam. Once Briggs and Crouse had been transported to lockup, Joe accompanied Northrup to the apartment.

"You're not gonna believe this," said Northrup. "The place looks like a crime scene."

"It is a crime scene," said Joe. "Let me check it out."

On the floor of the living room, next to the couch, lay Austin Two, a section of his forehead blown off from the bullet's exit. Red simulated blood and gray matter were spattered all over the floor and the lower part of the wall facing the window.

"See what I mean?"

"It's just Wally getting his rocks off."

"That guy's gotta have a screw loose. Who would do this?"

Joe simply smiled and said, "Wally Kozlov, that who." He pulled out his phone and began taking photos of Austin Two and the blood-spattered room.

"What are you doing?" asked Northrup.

"Wally and Destiny will want to see this."

"Out of curiosity, what will become of Austin Two?"

"Wally said he was a gift to Chicago PD. I don't know. Why? You want him?"

"Actually...I know this is going to sound weird...but I wouldn't mind having him for my apartment. You know, as a conversation piece."

"You're welcome to him. I doubt if Chicago PD would object."

* * *

The next morning, Joe made a call to Steve Vincenzo to let him know about the progress made in his father's case.

"Detective Erickson. Good to hear from you. Do you have an update?"

"I do, Steve. We set up a sting operation, and we made two arrests last evening in addition to one we'd made previously. I'm certain we have your father's killer, Steve. I'll keep you apprised as things go forward."

"Who was it?"

"There's a conspiracy involving city alderman Carson Byrne, former Police Captain Jerome Crouse, former Police Lieutenant Yvonne Briggs, and possibly Byrnes' bodyguard, Stan Zelenko. We believe Yvonne Briggs was the sniper who shot your father."

"A woman?"

"We're pretty sure."

"Wow. I didn't expect that."

"Yeah. Surprised the hell out of us, too. You'll let your brother know?"

"I will. Thank you, Detective. I'm most grateful for what you've done. I know my dad would be proud of you.

"Thanks, Steve."

Chapter Thirty-Seven

Yvonne Briggs and Jerome Crouse were both charged with attempted murder as a result of the sting operation. The sniper rifle retrieved during the arrest was tested by ballistics, and the round fired from it matched the round recovered from the body of Captain Vincenzo.

Joe and Sam arrested Stan Zelenko for conspiracy. DNA evidence taken from under Joe's fingernails following the scuffle in Merlin Fitzgerald's hospital room matched Zelenko's DNA, and Zelenko was charged with felonious assault and attempted murder. Later, DNA found at the scene of Patricia Thorpe's murder was found to be a match to Zelenko, and he was charged with first-degree murder in her death.

Former Captain Jerome Crouse agreed to turn state's evidence in exchange for immunity from prosecution for his testimony in the Byrne conspiracy. During the trials of Carson Byrne and Yvonne Briggs, Crouse testified that Carson Byrne had Robert Wallingford killed. Yvonne Briggs, acting under orders from Byrne, shot and killed Wallingford. He also testified that Briggs was the sniper who killed Captain Sal Vincenzo.

Exercising his ribald sense of humor, Sam mused, "I guess Crouse screwed Briggs in more ways than one, huh?"

In addition, during the trial of Stan Zelenko, Crouse testified that Zelenko attempted to kill Merlin Fitzgerald with an injection of succinylcholine and that he killed Patricia Thorpe in an attempt to locate the copy of the sex tape. They learned about it from Briggs hacking Joe Erickson's and Sam Renaldo's accounts at Area 3 and reading their case notes.

Based on Crouse's depositions, two counts of murder were added to charges against Carson Byrne, and two counts of murder were added to charges against Yvonne Briggs.

Joe was livid that Jerome Crouse escaped prosecution. But Crouse was immediately dismissed from his job as a consultant with the mayor's office, and he became persona non grata with most of his former police colleagues.

Carson Byrne, Yvonne Briggs, and Stan Zelenko were convicted on all counts, and each received life sentences for their crimes. They are presently serving out their sentences in Illinois' correctional system.

Immediately following the trials, during one of his days off, Joe paid a visit to St. Boniface Catholic Cemetery on North Clark Street. It is an old cemetery founded in 1863, and Vincenzo had been interred there in the Vincenzo family plot. A small, black granite stone marked his grave. It was simply inscribed with "Salvatore G. Vincenzo, Captain, Chicago Police Department", along with his birth and death dates. The base read "Father of Steven and Mark."

After reciting the prayer for the faithful departed, Joe crossed himself and kneeled next to the marker. Placing his hand on it, he said, "We got 'em, Captain. We solved your case, and we put away your killers. They won't see the light of day again. Except one. But if there's any justice in the world, he'll get his one day. Rest in peace, sir."

When Joe rose to his feet, something inexplicable happened. He didn't hear it with his ears. He heard it with his mind. But he heard it as clearly as if he was sitting in Vincenzo's office, and it raised the hair on the back of his neck.

"All right, get outta here." It was Vincenzo's voice, and Joe realized it was his former lieutenant telling him it was time to move on.

Six months after the trials concluded, Jerome Crouse was found shot to death while sitting in his Cadillac, the victim of what police deemed a random shooting. Some believe it was payback for his involvement in the killing of Captain Vincenzo. Others believe it was for turning state's evidence. No one knows for sure, and chances are, no one ever will. The case remains open.

Acknowledgements

Joyce Johanson; Susan Van Kirk; Richard Helms; Detective Timothy O'Brien, Chicago PD; Harriette Sackler; Shawn Reilly Simmons; and Verena Rose.

About the Author

Lynn-Steven Johanson is an award-winning playwright and novelist whose plays have been produced on four continents. Born and raised in Northwest Iowa, Lynn holds a Master of Fine Arts degree from the University of Nebraska-Lincoln. His previous Joe Erickson mysteries, *Rose's Thorn*, *Havana Brown*, and *Corrupted Souls* are published by Level Best Books. He lives in Illinois with his wife, and they have three adult children.

SOCIAL MEDIA HANDLES:
  Twitter: @JohansonLS
  Instagram: lsjohanson

AUTHOR WEBSITE:
  https://LSJohanson.com

Also by Lynn-Steven Johanson

Rose's Thorn

Havana Brown

Corrupted Souls

CPSIA information can be obtained
at www.ICGtesting.com
Printed in the USA
BVHW081025040423
661729BV00002BA/196